DATE DUE

THE WORKS OF
W. SOMERSET MAUGHAM

This is a volume in the Arno Press collection

THE WORKS OF
W. SOMERSET MAUGHAM

Introduction by Michael G. Wood

See last pages of this volume for a complete list of titles.

AH KING

By W. Somerset Maugham

ARNO PRESS

A New York Times Company

New York / 1977

Reprint Edition 1977 by Arno Press Inc.

THE WORKS OF W. SOMERSET MAUGHAM
ISBN for complete set: 0-405-07804-8
See last pages of this volume for titles.

Manufactured in the United States of America

———◆———

Library of Congress Cataloging in Publication Data

Maugham, William Somerset, 1874-1965.
  Ah king.

  (The works of W. Somerset Maugham)
  Reprint of the ed. published by Doubleday, Doran,
Garden City, N. Y.
  CONTENTS: Footprints in the jungle.--The door of
opportunity.--The vessel of wrath. [etc.]
  I. Title. II. Series: Maugham, William Somerset,
1874-1965. Works. 1976.
PZ3.M442Ah20 [PR6025.A86] 823'.9'12   75-26127
ISBN 0-405-07850-1

Introduction

"I have put the whole of my life into my books," Somerset Maugham wrote. The remark suggests a career of confession, and it is true that Maugham is the author of one long, intensely autobiographical novel: *Of Human Bondage*. He himself describes the writing of the book as an act of therapy and exorcism:

> My memories would not let me be. They became such a torment that I determined at last to have done with the theatre until I had released myself from them. My book took two years to write. I was disconcerted by its length, but I was not writing to please: I was writing to free myself from an intolerable obsession. I achieved the result I aimed at, for after I had corrected the proofs, I found all those ghosts were laid, and neither the people nor the incidents ever crossed my mind again.

The ghosts had their small revenge, however. When Maugham began to read *Of Human Bondage* for a recording company, some thirty years after the book was published, he broke down and cried, and the record was never made.

Maugham spoke often of the power of writing to allay a writer's sorrows:

> Whenever he has anything on his mind, whether it be a harassing reflection, grief at the death of a friend, unrequited love, wounded pride, anger at the treachery of someone to whom he has shown kindness, in short any emotion or any perplexing thought, he has only to put it down in black and white, using it as the theme of a story or the decoration of an essay, to forget all about it . . .

> . . . illness, privation, his hopes abandoned, his griefs, humiliations, everything is transformed by his power into material and by writing it he can overcome it . . . Nothing befalls him that he cannot transmute into a stanza, a song or a story, and having done this be rid of it. The artist is the only free man.

We may find the completeness and finality of some of those phrases — he has *only* to put it down to forget *all* about it, *nothing* befalls him that he cannot transmute into art — have a rather wishful ring, and of course we don't need Maugham's returning ghosts to remind us that the accounts of the heart are rarely so thoroughly and so easily settled. As Maugham himself says elsewhere, the imagination compensates us for all the things we have missed or lost in life. But if we hadn't missed or lost them we should not need the compensation: "To imagine is to fail; for it is the acknowledgement of defeat in the encounter with reality."

Still, there is nothing odd in Maugham's insistence on writing as exorcism, since the exorcism, at least once, worked well enough for him. It didn't defeat the ghosts for good, but it kept them quiet for a long spell. What is odd, in the light of Maugham's views, is that apart from *Of Human Bondage* there is scarcely an autobiographical work among all the novels, plays, stories, essays and travel books that Maugham wrote in a long and prolific life. Even his autobiography, he tells us in its opening words, is not an autobiography, and a phrase from the beginning of that book sheds some light on this curious puzzle. "In one way or another," Maugham says, "I have used in my writings whatever has happened to me in the course of my life." He means not that he has confessed all but that he hasn't wasted any of his material. It is in this sense that the whole of his life has gone into his books. His books have said as much about him as he is going to say. Before and after *Of Human Bondage* Maugham is not a writer who consoles himself in fiction for distresses suffered in reality. He is a writer who, in and out of fiction, cultivates a blend of irony and controlled curiosity which keeps reality's distresses at a comfortable distance. The ghosts are not exorcised. Where possible, they are headed off before they get a chance to do any haunting.

In spite of the considerable fame of *Of Human Bondage,* this second, more distant Maugham is undoubtedly the more famous one. This is the writer whose cherished themes, as Graham Greene once said, are usually thought to be adultery in China, murder in Malaya and suicide in the South Seas; whose chief subject is the ragged edge of the British Empire. He is Kipling turned inside out, as V. S. Pritchett suggested, discovering that the white man's burden is as often as not the white woman's infidelity, which is in turn a sort of infection by strange places and loneliness. Maugham writes of England too, of course, of country houses and upper-class London and the more respectable fringes of the literary life, but the constant feature of Maugham's stories and plays and novels, whether they are set in Batavia or in Belgrave Square, is Maugham's own wry, observing presence, the weary, witty, detached intelligence which directs the dialogue of the plays and frequently appears to comment on the goings-on in the novels and stories. It is a portrait of the artist as a man of the world, and it can produce a certain glibness. On the other hand, there is mostly an undercurrent of worry even in the glibness, a nervous streak in the man of the world, and it is the mixture that matters. Maugham speaks of ethics, for example. "It may be that in goodness we may see, not a reason for life nor an explanation, but an extenuation . . ." The idea is familiar enough, but the word *extenuation* gives a disconcerting twist to the tail of the sentence. Or again: "He was developing a sense of humor, and found he had a knack of saying bitter things, which caught people on the raw . . ." Is that what we usually mean by humor? Sometimes Maugham's irony is more carefully and consciously balanced: "I do not think a thought of self ever entered her untidy head. She was a miracle of unselfishness. It was really hardly human." Sometimes it is frankly comic: "Miss Jones was resolutely cheerful. She grimly looked on the bright side of things." Sometimes it conceals a subdued sense of outrage:

> When we went there (a missionary is speaking) they had no sense of sin at all. They broke the commandments one after the other and never knew they were doing wrong. And I think that was the most difficult part of my work, to instill into the natives the sense of sin.

And sometimes it brings off extraordinary, shifting combinations of denunciation and tribute, subtle praise and sharp blame:

> Hypocrisy is the most difficult and nerve-racking vice that any man can pursue; it needs an unceasing vigilance and a rare detachment of spirit. It cannot, like adultery or gluttony, be practised at spare moments; it is a whole-time job.

Maugham is not a difficult or complicated writer, and we can miss all the undercurrents in his prose and still enjoy him a great deal. But the undercurrents are likely to keep Maugham's writing alive when the simpler enjoyment has faded, and in any case I wonder whether anyone misses them entirely. They are like a nameless taste caught up in a taste we know well, a touch of bitterness in a sweet dish — or to be more precise, a touch of genuine bitterness in a bitter-seeming dish, a flavour of real, unnerving acrimony in the midst of a calm and worldly cynicism. Certainly a sense of these undercurrents is what separates Maugham's serious admirers from his serious detractors. Thus Edmund Wilson, seeing nothing of the sceptic within the popular writer, could say Maugham was "a half-trashy novelist, who writes badly, but is patronised by half-serious readers, who do not care much about writing", while Cyril Connolly, who could hardly be called a half-serious reader, saw mainly the scepticism, and insisted on Maugham's continuing dissatisfaction with the things that satisfy too many of us, on his discontent "with the banal routine of self-esteem and habit, with which most of us . . . fidget away our one-and-only lives." Both men are more or less right, because Maugham really had it both ways. He was one of the most successful writers of the century, and yet he seems to peer out at us from the heart of his success with a disappointed, dissenting face, seems to assure us in a whisper that money and fame are merely toys, ways of passing the time, better than most and certainly worth having, but not the secret of eternal life or even, when it comes down to it, of much temporal happiness.

Maugham's friends and family agree in finding him elusive. "I am indebted to him for nearly fifty years of kindness and hospitality," Noel Coward wrote, "but I cannot truthfully say that I really knew him intimately." "Looking back," Maugham's nephew Robin Maugham says, "I realize that though I sometimes feared him, I was fond of him; but I am afraid I never understood him." This is exactly the quality of Maugham's writing. He is present to the reader, an engaging, even a compelling story-teller — it is very hard to put down a Maugham story or novel once you have taken it up — but he is a man who is giving nothing away. Maugham's prose is lucid and musical, but above all it is remarkable for what it *doesn't* say. Consider this little story, one of Maugham's working notes:

> The peacock. We were driving through the jungle. It was not thick and presently we caught sight of a peacock among the trees with its beautiful tail outspread. It walked, a proud, magnificent object, treading the ground with a peculiar delicacy, with a sort of deliberation, and its walk was so elegant, so wonderfully graceful that it recalled to my memory Nijinsky stepping on to the stage at Covent Garden and walking with just such a delicacy, grace and elegance. I have seldom seen a sight more thrilling than that peacock threading its solitary way through the jungle. My companion told the driver to stop and seized his gun.
>
> "I'm going to have a shot at it."
>
> My heart stopped still. He fired, and I hoped he'd miss, but he didn't. The driver jumped out of the car and brought back the dead bird which a moment before had been so exultantly alive. It was a cruel sight.
>
> We ate the breast for dinner that night. The flesh was white, tender and succulent; it was a welcome change from the scraggy chickens which are brought to the table evening after evening in India.

Is there sarcasm there? A comment on the sudden switches of human feeling? A dark warning about the transience of beauty and the lure of food? No, there is just a vivid unsettling sequence: the bird is alive, the bird is dead, the bird is eaten. All interpretation, all attempts to say what such a sequence *means,* are left to us. Maugham merely records the sequence.

In his life and in his writing, Maugham appears to have found a tone which was a perfect disguise, which kept the world away. Even the malice which many often-told stories attribute to him can be seen as part of a role he is playing. "Tra-la-la-la," Maugham is supposed to have sung when he received the news of the death of his wife, divorced from him some twenty years earlier. "No more alimony. Tra-la-, tra-la." Perhaps Maugham's real feelings corresponded closely enough to the feelings he was expressing. But the expression itself still contains a large element of pose: there is a sense of the audience there. Somerset Maugham, seventy years old, is playing at being Somerset Maugham, the shocking, wicked old man. Behind that role, another Maugham, quite unknowable, entertaining who knows what complex configurations of guilt and joy and regret and relief and perfect indifference, lives **his** entirely private life. "I have put the whole of my life into my books." That innocent-seeming sentence turns into a sly joke. Both books and life for Maugham, apart from *Of Human Bondage* and the painful experiences that went into it, were a system of defences, high walls around a very secret self.

William Somerset Maugham was born in Paris in 1874, the youngest of six sons. His father was solicitor to the British Embassy, and his mother, generally acknowledged to have been a beautiful and charming woman, was well-known in Parisian high society. Maugham spoke only French until he was nine or ten years old. His mother died when he was eight, his father died two years later, and Maugham was sent to live with his uncle and aunt in Whitestable, on the coast of Kent, in England. He spent a number of miserable years there, interspersed in term-time with equally miserable periods at the King's School, Canterbury — all to be recorded with unforgiving anger in *Of Human Bondage.* The young Maugham had a stammer which he felt to be a severe handicap, and which never left him, although in later life he converted it into something of an asset in story-telling. Garson Kanin describes a speech made by Maugham, which began, "There are many . . . virtues in . . . growing old." A long pause followed, which lengthened into an uncomfortable silence. Finally Maugham continued, "I'm just . . . trying . . . to think what they are."

In 1890, Maugham contracted tuberculosis, and underwent a cure at Hyéres in the south of France. A year later he finished his secondary schooling and went to Heidelberg, in Germany, for a year, where he attended lectures at the university and began to take an interest in the theatre. In 1892, he entered St. Thomas' Medical School in London, and in 1897, having served as an intern and delivered some sixty-three babies, he qualified as a doctor, although he was never to practise. Maugham's first novel, *Liza of Lambeth,* based on his medical experiences in the slums and at the hospital, was published in 1897, and on the strength of its moderate success he decided to devote his life to writing. For the next few years he lived in Spain, Italy, London and Paris, published stories and novels, and wrote plays. These were the years of *The Making of a Saint* (1898), *The Hero* (1901), *Mrs. Craddock* (1902), *The Merry-Go-Round* (1904) and *The Magician* (1908) — all novels — and *Orientations* (1899), a collection of short stories. Maugham's first stage success was *Lady Frederick,* produced in London in 1907, and the following year saw two more hits — *Jack Straw* and *Mrs. Dot* — and one near-flop — *The Explorer* — so that four of Maugham's plays were then running in London at one time, and a cartoon published in *Punch* showed Shakespeare biting his nails and brooding in front of the boards which advertised Maugham's four productions. Not all his subsequent plays were to be resounding successes, but many of them were, with long runs both in England and America. Almost overnight, Maugham had become a playwright with a major reputation, and that he remained until *Sheppey,* his last play, was performed in 1933, and for some time afterwards, of course.

When war came to Europe in 1914, Maugham joined a Red Cross unit, and it was in Belgium that he corrected the proofs of *Of Human Bondage,* published the following year. Soon, however, he was transferred to the Intelligence Service, on the grounds that the writer's trade was a good cover for a secret agent. "The work appealed," Maugham wrote later, "both to my sense of romance and my sense of the ridiculous." His missions took him to Switzerland, the South Seas and Russia — this last excursion involving an attempt to halt the Revolution of 1917. Much of his experience at this time found its way into *Ashenden,* a collection of short stories published in 1928, the first (and still one of the best) of the works of anti-romantic spy fiction, a portrait of the grubby, heartless world of espionage which points away from John Buchan's *The Thirty-nine Steps,* for example, and towards John Le Carré's *The Spy Who Came In From The Cold.*

In the midst of his activities as writer and spy, Maugham somehow found time to carry on an affair with, and then to marry Syrie Wellcome in 1916. The marriage was not a happy one; it ended in divorce in 1927. There was one child, Liza.

Towards the end of the war, Maugham's tuberculosis flared up again, and he spent two years in a sanatorium in Scotland. "He enjoyed his illness," Maugham's biographer Richard A. Cordell writes. And Maugham himself later said, "I had a grand time. I discovered for the first time in my life how very delightful it is to lie in bed . . . I delighted in the privacy of my room with the immense window wide open to the starry winter night. It gave me a delicious sense of security, aloofness and freedom."

In 1919, Maugham published *The Moon and Sixpence,* a novel suggested by the life of the painter Gauguin, and in 1925 he published *The Painted Veil,* a novel with a contemporary Chinese setting, but based on an incident in Dante. Several of Maugham's best-known plays — *The Circle* (1921), *East of Suez* (1922), *The Constant Wife* (1926), *The Sacred Flame* (1928) — were produced in the twenties, and there were also three volumes of short stories: *The Trembling of a Leaf* (1921), *The Casuarina Tree* (1926), and as already mentioned, *Ashenden* (1928). Maugham travelled a great deal in these years — to the Far East, the Near East, to America, to North Africa — and wrote two remarkable travel books: *On a Chinese Screen* (1922) and *The Gentleman in the*

Parlour (1930). In 1928 he bought the Villa Mauresque, a house in the south of France, at St. Jean-Cap-Ferrat, between Monaco and Nice, and it was there that he lived for the rest of his life when he wasn't travelling or uprooted by war. He spent the years of the second world war in America, mainly in North Carolina at the house of his publisher, Nelson Doubleday, and returned to the Villa Mauresque in 1946.

In 1930, Maugham published *Cakes and Ale,* a bitter and witty novel about a famous writer and his two successive, contrasting wives, and a work which many people, myself included, regard as Maugham's finest achievement. It was followed by eight more novels, the last of which is *Catalina* (1948) and the most important of which is *The Razor's Edge* (1944). There were five more collections of short stories, some essays and criticism and the literary last will and testament which is called *The Summing Up* (1938). In 1949 Maugham brought out *A Writer's Notebook,* a selection from his working notes taken over nearly sixty years — the first entry is dated 1892 — and in 1952, in a preface to the second volume of his collected short stories, he took his leave as a writer of fiction. If a writer is "so impudent," he wrote, "as to live to a ripe age," then "the time comes at last when, having given what he has to give, his powers fail . . . It is well then if he can bring himself to cease writing stories which might just as well have remained unwritten . . . I have written my last story." Maugham was seventy-eight years old. He continued to write essays, but in 1959 he had most of his remaining papers burned, although some, apparently, did survive the raid. At the age of ninety-one, seriously ill, his memory failing, this man who had once thought of committing suicide at sixty-five, but who now clung to life with the tenacity he had himself described, with some distaste, some fifty years before — "He was set upon one thing indomitably," he wrote of his hero's moribund uncle in *Of Human Bondage,* "and that was living, just living" — had a stroke, lost consciousness and soon died. His ashes were buried in the grounds of the King's School, Canterbury, which was home, of a sort, after all.

"For many years I have been described as a cynic." Maugham's supposed cynicism is partly a matter of his aloofness, of the careful privacy he preserved in his life and his work. This aloofness, as I suggested earlier, is a complicated affair, a game of mischief and masquerade as well as a means of self-protection. But it is also, at times, simply aloofness, absence. Maugham often seems to move his fictional characters around with a chilly, clinical indifference to their feelings, and while the following statement is impressively honest, it doesn't exactly warm the heart:

> I have been interested in men in general not for their own sakes, but for the sake of my work. I have not, as Kant enjoined, regarded each man as an end in himself, but as material that might be useful to me as a writer.

Maugham tended to see people as elements in a pattern, and when he glimpsed, or could invent, a pattern in the lives he observed or encountered, he had a story. One of his notes, for example, describes a successful and much-admired woman who is unhappy until she falls in love with a man much younger than herself, who subsequently dies in an air crash. "Her friends were afraid she would commit suicide. Not at all. She became happy, fat and contented. She had had her tragedy." Obviously there is an interesting human truth in such a reversal of what we would all expect, but above all there is a pattern, a marked neatness of design. Maugham looked for the same thing in his own life, thought of writing a last novel about the London slums because his first novel had been set there, spoke of completing the edifice of his life's works by writing *The Summing Up:*

> If I live I shall write other books, for my amusement and I hope for the amusement of my readers, but I do not think they will add anything essential to my design. The house is built.

There is a striking fidelity here to the philosophy developed by Philip Carey, the young hero of *Of Human Bondage.* Life has no meaning, Philip decides, so the best we can do is to treat life as if it were a rich carpet, and trace out the designs of our doings on it:

> There was one pattern, the most obvious, perfect, and beautiful, in which a man was born, grew to manhood, married, produced children, toiled for his bread, and died; but there were others, intricate and wonderful, in which happiness did not enter and in which success was not attempted; and in them might be discovered a troubling grace. Some lives . . . the blind indifference of chance cut off while the design was still imperfect; and then the solace was comfortable that it did not matter; other lives . . . offered a pattern which was difficult to follow: the point of view had to be shifted and old standards had to be altered before one could understand that such a life was its own justification.

The troubling grace of a life without happiness and without success is a powerful notion, and troubling grace is perhaps the chief quality of Maugham's best work, which creates the sense of a fragile order being rescued from an encroaching confusion. But the rest of the passage has an awkward complacency — "in such a philosophy there is consolation aplenty even for the least consolable of lives," — since everything is bound to make a pattern of some sort and suggests an instinct for tidiness rather than any large depth of sensibility or intellect. Maugham recognized this tendency in himself when he spoke of the "tightness of effect" and the "sensation of airlessness" provoked by fiction that is too well-made, and of course it is present in the remarks I quoted near the beginning of this piece, where literature is seen as too neat a solution to the upsets of life. Interestingly enough, one of the best of all Maugham's stories, *The Lotus Eater,* portrays a man who shapes his life perfectly, only to discover that his nerve is not as good as he thought it was. At the age of thirty-five Thomas Wilson has left England and the bank he worked in, and settled in Capri, where he leads a modest but pleasant and carefree existence. He has just enough money to last him until he is sixty, and then he intends to take his own life. "Don't you think after twenty-five years of perfect happiness one ought to be satisfied to call it a day?" he asks. When he reaches sixty, though, Wilson keeps postponing his final act, subsists on credit as long as his credit lasts, botches an attempt at suicide, and lives out the rest of his life, sick and poor and humiliated, on the charity of his old landlord. The story bears a disturbing, prophetic relation to Maugham's own end, serene at sixty-four ("I look forward to old age without dismay"), prepared for death at seventy-five ("I am on the wing"), but hanging on in angry senility by the time he was eighty-six, quarrelling with his family, and publishing a rancourous memoir about his marriage. As Maugham must have known all along, there are many things more important than patterns.

What seems to be Maugham's cynicism, then, is often merely his aloofness or his tidiness. But a question remains, which is not a question of Maugham's manner but of what he has to *say,* explicitly and implicitly. "I have been accused of making men out worse than they are," he said. "I do not think I have done this. All I have done is to bring into prominence certain traits that many writers shut their eyes to." Perhaps. There is a great deal of cruelty and violence and revenge in Maugham's fiction. Mackintosh, a British administrator in Samoa, so hates his superior that he leaves his gun lying around for a hostile native to use on the hated man. When the native does use it, Mackintosh, in an excess of guilt, walks out into the lagoon and shoots himself. Another administrator, in Borneo, has a subordinate who arouses such anger in the natives that they kill him. The administrator feels a great, quiet exultation: he had disliked the man, and is delighted to be rid of him. A husband finds out about his wife's infidelity, but creates no fuss and causes no trouble. He simply makes sure that she knows he knows. Another husband in the same situation takes his wife off with him to a cholera-infected town. When she asks him, later, whether he meant to kill her that way, he says, after a long hesitation, "At first." He himself dies of cholera, and she survives, to return to England.

Obviously popular fiction feeds on melodrama, which in turn feeds on acts of violence, but there is in Maugham an insistence on retaliation which goes well beyond the needs of the kind of fiction he is writing. There is a recurring pleasure in the sight of an enmity or a rancour which is actively satisfied, which finds a thorough, practical expression. We should not forget, either, that Maugham can take an almost aesthetic delight in random acts of mischief and malice. In the story *A Friend in Need* a kindly, respectable, humorous man sends another, younger man off on a long and dangerous swim, with the promise that he will give him a job when he gets back. The young man drowns in the offshore currents, and when asked whether he knew the young man would drown, the older man says, "Well, I hadn't got a vacancy in my office at the moment." Maugham also tells the story of Elizabeth Russell, who is said to have read out to her sick husband those passages in a book of hers where he appeared in a damaging light. When she finished, he turned his face to the wall and died. Maugham, with obvious relish, asks Mrs. Russell whether this terrible tale is true, and she looks blandly at him and says, "He was very ill. He would have died in any case."

A moralist may frown at all this, and a sentimentalist will be distressed. Maugham himself is being slightly disingenuous when he says he simply tells the truth in such matters, since he is clearly selecting, with great skill, those truths which have an ugly, malevolent glitter to them. Nevertheless, I think there is a genuine, uncompromising vision here, as well as a lot of gratuitous cruelty. At his best Maugham forces us to see that hatred has its own authentic joys and rewards, and I think of a line in Emily Brontë's *Wuthering Heights,* where Heathcliff is admonished to leave his revenge to God, and replies, "No, God won't have the satisfaction that I shall." The real question, perhaps, is not so much whether we have all felt such hatred at any time in our lives as whether we would be able to admit it if we did. There is a kind of courage in Maugham's allowing those grim and terminal revenges to have their day in his fiction.

The ground for most of these revenges in Maugham is humiliation, and Maugham's sourest and most famous contribution to the moral life of our century is probaly his diagnosis of love itself as above all, humiliation. Love in Maugham is either a helpless, unconditional surrender to instinct, an undignified collapse of all our best intentions; or it is a quest for disgrace, an infatuation with a creature we cannot respect and who will bring us only confused and ignoble pain. There is a sequence in *Of Human Bondage* which at first sight appears mismanaged, a clumsy attempt at pathos and suspense, but which then emerges as a strong portrait of love as masochism. Philip Carey introduces Mildred, the girl he loves, to his handsome and lively best friend, and Mildred and the best friend, predictably enough, go off together. It is only when we understand that Philip has not made a mistake, that indeed he has got just what he wanted, that things fall into place. Masochism, Maugham wrote much later, "is a sexual desire in a man to be subjected to ill treatment, physical and mental, by the woman he loves." Philip doesn't seek or receive physical ill treatment from Mildred, but he suffers mental unkindnesses constantly, eagerly. Having brought his friend and his girl together for his own anguish, he is soon offering them money so that they can spend a weekend in Oxford without him. Again, with this view of love as with Maugham's cases of satisfied hatred and cruelty, the question is not whether it is true in any complete sense, whether it is the whole story about human affections. Plainly it is not. The question, as with Proust, for example, is how we are to defend ourselves against a view of love which is obviously true *enough* to shake our most cherished assumptions about our relations with the people we care about.

Maugham was clear, even harsh, about his own limitations. He had some power of invention, he said, but only "small power of imagination."

> I have taken living people and put them into the situations, tragic or comic, that their characters suggested. I might well say that they invented their own stories . . .

> I knew that I had no lyrical quality. I had a small vocabulary and no efforts that I could make to enlarge it much availed me. I had little gift of metaphor; the original and striking simile seldom occurred to me.

The lucidity and simplicity of Maugham's style have often been praised. It is a style which does its job, but it is also the style of a man who has an ear for the flow and fall of a sentence, and occasionally there *is* a metaphor or a simile which stays in the mind. In the cholera epidemic in *The Painted Veil,* death is said to stand round the corner, "taking lives like a gardener digging up potatoes," and the casual, domestic image is perfect, just what is needed. Above all, of course, Maugham is a *readable* writer, a man who knows the art of keeping his audience with him, and the best test of his readability is to read him. A simple illustration of the way he makes himself readable, though, is his knack of suggesting exotic locations without brandishing foreign names or going in for that rather flashy familiarity with strange customs which is characteristic of Lawrence and Hemingway and Durrell and Lowry. A mention of the Pacific, of a Chinese cook, of hot weather, a reef and a lagoon, and we are in Samoa. Sunshine, coolies, rickshaws, a Chinese clerk, an electric fan, and we are in Singapore. These scenes are set with an immaculate discretion. And of course there is always a story being told.

This is true even of Maugham's non-fiction. His travel books are the notes of a man looking for stories. *On a Chinese Screen,* for example, is a set of jottings which Maugham decided to leave as jottings, but some of them were so close to fiction that he could include them, much later, among his *Complete Short Stories.* Similarly, Maugham's essays and criticism are composed mainly of anecdotes. Maugham looks at his favourite writers much as he looks at the people around him, and *The Art of Fiction,* an introduction to ten great novelists and their novels, spends most of its time telling the "stories," as it were, of Fielding and Jane Austen and Stendhal and Balzac and Melville and others. Maugham's criticism is limited by a rather depressing common sense — it may be true that obscurities arise in *Othello* because Shakespeare couldn't think of a better way of doing things, but I think a critic has to do better than that by way of interpretation all the same — and by the taste for tidiness I have already mentioned. I doubt whether many people would agree, for example, that *Wuthering Heights* is "clumsily constructed." Still, he has excellent taste and a gift for making fine and useful distinctions. He is a good companion rather than a provocative critic, and this is perhaps as it should be. Essays, travel books, over a hundred short stories: such works are the natural, continuing expression of the life of a writer who reads a lot and travels a great deal.

The plays and the novels are a slightly different matter, if only because they involve larger and more sustained excursions away from the pose of the casual story-teller. Maugham's plays are skillful and intelligent, but even the best of them — *Our Betters, The Circle, The Constant Wife* — seem rather brittle now, caught in a rather strange zone between nature and artifice. There is an air of elegant clockwork about them, which oddly enough tends to make them seem insufficiently artificial, makes them seem as if they were not quite acting on the strength of their own conventions, so that they have neither the force of naturalism nor the pace and folly of the plays of Congreve, say, or Wilde. Nevertheless, they are consistently playable and entertaining, and full of good lines:

— You have no heart, and you can't imagine that anyone else should have.

— I have plenty of heart, but it beats for people of my own class . . .

— If a man's unfaithful to his wife she's an object of sympathy, whereas if a woman's unfaithful to her husband he's merely an object of ridicule.

— That is one of those conventional prejudices that sensible people must strive to ignore . . .

Among the novels, *Of Human Bondage* is taken by many people to be Maugham's masterpiece, his "one great novel," according to Malcolm Cowley, who speculated on what he called the Somerset Maugham enigma: "Why has he never written another book that was half so good as *Of Human Bondage?*" The short answer, I would say, is that he has, and several of them at that. *Of Human Bondage* is a patient and precise account of a boy's growing up, and the story of Philip Carey's tortured, grovelling love for Mildred is intense and compelling. But otherwise there is a certain blandness about the novel which makes it easy to read but also easy to forget. It is not to be compared with its close contemporaries, Joyce's *Portrait of the Artist as a Young Man* or Lawrence's *Sons and Lovers. Cakes and Ale,* on the other hand, Maugham's own favourite among his novels, escapes blandness because it is so fiercely and unfailingly witty, and because Maugham is on his true home ground, talking not about his personal past but about the business of writing, which is the consuming interest of his present life. The book opens with a cruel portrait of Maugham's friends Hugh Walpole, but the portrait is also a mocking version of Maugham himself as the successful writer who has made a little talent go a very long way. People have been shocked by the book's disrespectful depiction of a figure much resembling Thomas Hardy, who had died only two years before the book appeared. But at this distance in time Maugham's view of Hardy seems extremely affectionate. Hardy is not the lofty and magisterial man of letters he is supposed to be, but he is something better. He is perky and alive and irreverent, the model of a man who has managed to survive his own greatness. Of Maugham's other novels, *The Moon and Sixpence, The Painted Veil* and *The Razor's Edge* are the most successful, although all three of them tend to alternate between masterly scenes and moments of glibness. But then even *Catalina* and *Then and Now,* which Maugham's admirers usually concede to the opposition, seem to me genuinely enjoyable, and that, perhaps, is the truest measure of Maugham's achievement. He never wrote an uninteresting book, and no doubt that is the right reward for knowing your own limitations so well.

Some critics rate Maugham's stories above his novels, but I think that only serves to displace the central question. It is true that the best of Maugham's stories are as good as the best of his novels, but the question is, How good is that? Maugham himself thought he had only "slender baggage" for his journey into posterity, and saw himself as standing "in the very front row of the second-raters." But then that judgement implies a view of who the other second-raters are. Richard A. Cordell puts Maugham alongside Thackeray, Gide, Hardy, Conrad, Bennett and Galsworthy in that category, which I think both subtly inflates Maugham's standing and confuses the issue. On the one hand at least three of those writers are first-rate by any standard, and on the other Maugham is almost certainly more important than Galsworthy, for example. His true peers, perhaps, to take an instance from each of three succeeding generations, are Arnold Bennett, Aldous Huxley and Graham Greene: honourable company, it seems to me. But such games are better not played too long. The names serve only as bearings, means of finding Maugham's domain on the map of modern literature.

Maugham's legacy to other writers is an ideal of perfect craftsmanship, and a reassurance that an author can be extremely popular without sacrificing either his intelligence or his culture. His larger, more general legacy to literature, I think, is the record of a lifelong exploration of a crippling respectability, of a sense of the pressure of opinion which is all the more painful because you know the pressure would vanish if you were brave enough to ignore it. "The Maughams had the intense respectability of the upper middle class," Maugham's nephew Robin writes. Maugham appears never to have felt that being a writer was a respectable profession, and of course his own homosexuality can't have helped much. He told Robin that his greatest mistake was to have persuaded himself that he was "three quarters normal and . . . only a quarter . . . queer — whereas really it was the other way round." Some of Maugham's heroes defeat respectability, flout convention and manage to live a life of their own. But his work contains far more victims than heroes, and most of his characters either succumb to propriety and regret their cowardice for the rest of their days, or they throw over the traces, and then sink further and further into disgrace and degradation, ending all too often in suicide. Maugham plays both roles in these stories, for all his aloofness and cynicism. He is the person who fails and the society which rules on the failure, he is respectability's enemy and the agent of respectability itself. V. S. Pritchett suggested that Maugham's fiction catered to our wish to be worldly and wise in the manner of Maugham's much-travelled, never-ruffled narrators, and that this accounted largely for his huge success. I think the fiction speaks to something more serious than that. It speaks to our profoundly divided social loyalties, to our mixed satisfaction and resentment at the lives we live, to our longing to drop out of it all like Paul Gauguin and to our knowledge that we are really not going to do it. It doesn't ask us to leave the world or change the world, and it doesn't invite us to indulge in regret. It does confront us with the long disappointment which is one of the costs of life in human society, and it reminds us how much of our time, even when we are quite alone, is spent in the confining stare of other people's eyes.

Michael Wood
Columbia University

AH KING

By W. Somerset Maugham

MCMXXXIII

———————————————

DOUBLEDAY, DORAN & COMPANY, INC.

GARDEN CITY, NEW YORK

PRINTED AT THE *Country Life Press*, GARDEN CITY, N. Y., U. S. A.

CONTENTS

AH KING

AH KING

I was in Singapore, about to start on a journey through Borneo, Indo-China and Siam, and I wanted a servant who could turn his hand to anything. I asked my friends if they knew a Chinese who was looking for a job, and they all knew the very man who would have suited me, but unfortunately he had just taken a place or had gone back to Canton for a holiday. Then someone gave me the address of a registry office. I went there, finding it with some difficulty; it was a trim little bungalow, standing in its own small garden, and somehow or other it gave me a sinister impression. I was received by a Eurasian, with flashing eyes, a flat muddy face and glittering teeth. He was ingratiating; he smiled a great deal and knew, almost before I began to speak, so exactly what I wanted that I despaired of explaining myself. He told me that he would have no difficulty at all in finding me what I wanted and impressively opened a huge ledger in which were the names of the servants on his list. He was very much annoyed when he discovered that every likely man had either just got a place or had gone for a holiday to Canton. At last he besought me, with tears in his eyes, to come back in three or four days, or a week, or maybe a month and he was quite sure that he would have the perfect servant for me. I explained that I was leaving Singapore next

day and must have a boy to take with me. He vowed it
was impossible and in his distress wrung his hands,
and then said that if I would wait half an hour he would
see what he could do. I lit a cigarette and prepared to
wait. He left me.

He returned in an hour bringing with him a youth of
twenty, with a smooth yellow face, a shy look in his
black eyes, smallish, but very neat in his white clothes
and self-possessed. His name was Ah King and he was
prepared to travel. He spoke English. He showed me
his references, written on grubby half-sheets of paper,
and they were very satisfactory. He was said to be
clean and willing, industrious and well up in his duties.
I liked his look and at once engaged him.

Next day we set out. I soon found that though he
could speak English tolerably he could not understand
it, so that our conversation was one-sided. He was with
me for six months. He was a perfect servant. He could
cook, he could valet, he could pack, he could wait at
table. He was quick, neat and silent. He was imperturb-
able. Nothing surprised him, no catastrophe dismayed
him, no hardship ruffled him, no novelty took him
unawares. It was impossible to tire him. He smiled all
day long. I have never met anyone so good-humoured.
He had his idiosyncrasies. He was very fond of having
a bath and at first when I discovered that the moment
my back was turned he went into my bathroom and
washed himself with my soap and dried himself with
my towel I felt a little uncomfortable. But I told myself
that I must not be pernickety. His only fault was that
when I was just starting to catch a train or get on to
a boat he was nowhere to be found. I would send people

hunting for him. He had vanished. No one knew where
he was. In the end I had to set off without him, but
always, just as the train was steaming out or the last
tender about to leave the quay, he would stroll along,
unhurried and smiling; and when, fuming with rage,
I asked him what the devil he meant by going off like
that he continued to smile.

"I no miss train," he said. "Plenty time. Train always wait."

And when I asked him where he had been he looked
at me with his calm, untroubled eyes and answered:

"Nowhere. I go for a walk."

My journey came to an end and I returned to Singapore, intending from there to sail for Europe. I told
Ah King that I should not want him any more. He
asked me for a testimonial. I gave him this and his
wages and a present.

"Good-bye, Ah King," I said. "I hope you'll find
another job soon."

Then I saw that he was crying. I stared at him with
amazement. An excellent servant, he had attended to
all my wants for six months, but he had always seemed
to me strangely detached; he had been as indifferent
to my praise as he was unconcerned at my reproofs.
It had never occurred to me for an instant that he
looked upon me as anything but an odd, rather silly
person who paid his wages and gave him board and
lodging. That he had any feeling for me had never
entered my head. I was embarrassed. I felt a little
uncomfortable. I knew that I had often been impatient
with him, tiresome and exacting. I had never thought
of him as a human being. He wept because he was

leaving me. It is for these tears that I now give his name to this collection of stories that I invented while he was travelling with me. To the best of my belief the characters that play their part in them are creatures of my own fancy.

FOOTPRINTS IN THE JUNGLE

THERE is no place in Malaya that has more charm than Tanah Merah. It lies on the sea and the sandy shore is fringed with casuarinas. The government offices are still in the old Raad Huis that the Dutch built when they owned the land, and on the hill stand the grey ruins of the fort by aid of which the Portuguese maintained their hold over the unruly natives. Tanah Merah has a history and in the vast labyrinthine houses of the Chinese merchants, backing on the sea so that in the cool of the evening they may sit in their loggias and enjoy the salt breeze, families dwell that have been settled in the country for three centuries. Many have forgotten their native language and hold intercourse with one another in Malay and pidgin English. The imagination lingers here gratefully, for in the Federated Malay States the only past is within the memory for the most part of the fathers of living men.

Tanah Merah was for long the busiest mart of the Middle East and its harbour was crowded with shipping when the clipper and the junk still sailed the China seas. But now it is dead. It has the sad and romantic air of all places that have once been of importance and live now on the recollection of a vanished grandeur. It is a sleepy little town and strangers that come to it, losing their native energy, insensibly drop into its easy and lethargic ways. Successive rubber booms bring it no prosperity and the ensuing slumps hasten its decay.

The European quarter is very silent. It is trim and neat and clean. The houses of the white men—Government servants and agents of companies—stand round an immense padang, agreeable and roomy bungalows shaded by great cassias, and the padang is vast and green and well cared for, like the lawn of a cathedral close, and indeed there is in the aspect of this corner of Tanah Merah something quiet and delicately secluded that reminds you of the precincts of Canterbury.

The Club faces the sea; it is a spacious but shabby building; it has an air of neglect and when you enter you feel that you intrude. It gives you the impression that it is closed really, for alterations and repairs, and that you have taken indiscreet advantage of an open door to go where you are not wanted. In the morning you may find there a couple of planters who have come in from their estates on business and are drinking a gin-sling before starting back again; and latish in the after-noon a lady or two may perhaps be seen looking with a furtive air through old numbers of the Illustrated London News. At nightfall a few men saunter in and sit about the billiard-room watching the play and drinking sukus. But on Wednesdays there is a little more animation. On that day the gramophone is set going in the large room upstairs and people come in from the surrounding country to dance. There are sometimes no less than a dozen couples and it is even possible to make up two tables of bridge.

It was on one of these occasions that I met the Cart-wrights. I was staying with a man called Gaze who was head of the police and he came into the billiard-room, where I was sitting, and asked me if I would make up a four. The Cartwrights were planters and they came in to Tanah Merah on Wednesdays because it gave their girl a chance of a little fun. They were very nice people, said Gaze, quiet and unobtrusive, and played a very pleasant game of bridge. I followed Gaze into the card-room and was introduced to them. They were already seated at a table and Mrs. Cartwright was shuffling the cards. It inspired me with confidence to see the competent way in which she did it. She took half the pack in each hand, and her hands were large and strong, deftly inserted the corners of one half under the corners of the others, and with a click and a neat bold gesture cascaded the cards together.

It had all the effect of a conjuring trick. The card-player knows that it can be done perfectly only after incessant practice. He can be fairly sure that anyone who can so shuffle a pack of cards loves cards for their own sake.

"Do you mind if my husband and I play together?" asked Mrs. Cartwright. "It's no fun for us to win one another's money."

"Of course not."

We cut for deal and Gaze and I sat down.

Mrs. Cartwright drew an ace and while she dealt, quickly and neatly, chatted with Gaze of local affairs. But I was aware that she took stock of me. She looked shrewd but good-natured.

She was a woman somewhere in the fifties (though in the East, where people age quickly, it is difficult to tell their ages), with white hair very untidily arranged, and a constant gesture with her was an impatient movement of the hand to push back a long wisp of hair that kept falling over her forehead. You wondered why she did not, by the use of a hairpin or two, save herself so much trouble. Her blue eyes were large, but pale and a little tired; her face was lined and sallow; I think it was her mouth that gave it the expression which I felt was characteristic of caustic but tolerant irony. You saw that here was a woman who knew her mind and was never afraid to speak it. She was a chatty player (which some people object to strongly, but which does not disconcert me, for I do not see why you should behave at the card-table as though you were at a memorial service) and it was soon apparent that she had an effective knack of badinage. It was pleasantly acid, but it was amusing enough to be offensive only to a fool. If now and then she uttered a remark so sarcastic that you wanted all your sense of humour to see the fun in it, you could not but quickly see that she was willing to take as much as she gave. Her large, thin mouth broke into a dry smile and her eyes shone brightly when by a lucky chance you brought off a repartee that turned the laugh against her.

I thought her a very agreeable person. I liked her frankness. I liked her quick wit. I liked her plain face. I never met a woman who obviously cared so little how she looked. It was not only her head that was untidy, everything about her was slovenly; she wore a high-necked silk blouse, but for coolness had unbuttoned the top buttons and showed a gaunt and withered neck; the blouse was crumpled and none too clean, for she smoked innumerable cigarettes and covered herself with ash. When she got up for a moment to speak to somebody I saw that her blue skirt was rather ragged at the hem and badly needed a brush, and she wore heavy, low-heeled boots. But none of this mattered. Everything she wore was perfectly in character.

And it was a pleasure to play bridge with her. She played very quickly, without hesitation, and she had not only knowledge but flair. Of course she knew Gaze's game, but I was a stranger and she soon took my measure. The team-work between her husband and herself was admirable; he was sound and cautious, but knowing him, she was able to be bold with assurance and brilliant with safety. Gaze was a player who founded a foolish optimism on the hope that his opponents would not have the sense to take advantage of his errors, and the pair of us were no match for the Cartwrights. We lost one rubber after another, and there was nothing to do but smile and look as if we liked it.

"I don't know what's the matter with the cards," said Gaze at last, plaintively. "Even when we have every card in the pack we go down."

"It can't be anything to do with your play," answered Mrs. Cartwright, looking him full in the face with those pale blue eyes of hers, "it must be bad luck pure and simple. Now if you hadn't had your hearts mixed up with your diamonds in that last hand you'd have saved the game."

Gaze began to explain at length how the misfortune, which had cost us dear, occurred, but Mrs. Cartwright, with a deft flick of the hand, spread out the cards in a great circle so that we should cut for deal. Cartwright looked at the time.

"This will have to be the last, my dear," he said.

"Oh, will it?" She glanced at her watch and then called to a young man who was passing through the room. "Oh, Mr. Bullen, if you're going upstairs tell Olive that we shall be going in a few minutes." She turned to me. "It takes us the best part of an hour to get back to the estate and poor Theo has to be up at the crack of dawn."

"Oh, well, we only come in once a week," said Cartwright, "and it's the one chance Olive gets of being gay and abandoned."

I thought Cartwright looked tired and old. He was a man of middle height, with a bald, shiny head, a stubbly grey moustache, and gold-rimmed spectacles. He wore white ducks and a black-and-white tie. He was rather neat and you could see he took much more pains with his clothes than his untidy wife. He talked little, but it was plain that he enjoyed his wife's caustic humour and sometimes he made quite a neat retort. They were evidently very good friends. It was pleasing to see so solid and tolerant an affection between two people who were almost elderly and must have lived together for so many years.

It took but two hands to finish the rubber and we had just ordered a final gin and bitters when Olive came down.

"Do you really want to go already, Mumsey?" she asked.

Mrs. Cartwright looked at her daughter with fond eyes.

"Yes, darling. It's nearly half-past eight. It'll be ten before we get our dinner."

"Damn our dinner," said Olive, gaily.

"Let her have one more dance before we go," suggested Cartwright.

"Not one. You must have a good night's rest."

Cartwright looked at Olive with a smile.

"If your mother has made up her mind, my dear, we may just as well give in without any fuss."

"She's a determined woman," said Olive, lovingly stroking her mother's wrinkled cheek.

Mrs. Cartwright patted her daughter's hand, and kissed it.

Olive was not very pretty, but she looked extremely nice. She was nineteen or twenty, I suppose, and she had still the plumpness of her age; she would be more attractive when she had fined down a little. She had none of the determination that gave her mother's face so much character, but resembled her father; she had his dark eyes and slightly aquiline nose, and his look of rather weak good nature. It was plain that she was strong and healthy. Her cheeks were red and her eyes bright. She had a vitality that he had long since lost. She seemed to be the perfectly normal English girl, with high spirits, a great desire to enjoy herself, and an excellent temper.

When we separated, Gaze and I set out to walk to his house.

"What did you think of the Cartwrights?" he asked me.

"I liked them. They must be a great asset in a place like this."

"I wish they came oftener. They live a very quiet life."

"It must be dull for the girl. The father and mother seem very well satisfied with one another's company."

"Yes, it's been a great success."

"Olive is the image of her father, isn't she?"

Gaze gave me a sidelong glance.

"Cartwright isn't her father. Mrs. Cartwright was a widow when he married her. Olive was born four months after her father's death."

"Oh!"

I drew out the sound in order to put in it all I could of surprise, interest and curiosity. But Gaze said nothing and we walked the rest of the way in silence. The boy was waiting at the door as we entered the house and after a last gin pahit we sat down to dinner.

At first Gaze was inclined to be talkative. Owing to the restriction of the output of rubber there had sprung up a considerable activity among the smugglers and it was part of his duty to circumvent their knavishness. Two junks had been captured that day and he was rubbing his hands over his success. The go-downs were full of confiscated rubber and in a little while it was going to be solemnly burnt. But presently he fell into silence and we finished without a word. The boys brought in coffee and brandy and we lit our cheroots. Gaze leaned back in his chair. He looked at me reflectively and then looked at his brandy. The boys had left the room and we were alone.

"I've known Mrs. Cartwright for over twenty years," he said slowly. "She wasn't a bad-looking woman in those days. Always untidy, but when she was young it didn't seem to matter so much. It was rather attractive. She was married to a man called Bronson. Reggie Bronson. He was a planter. He was manager of an estate up in Selantan and I was stationed at Alor Lipis. It was a much smaller place than it is now; I don't suppose there were more than twenty people in the whole community, but they had a jolly little club, and we used to have a very good time. I remember the first time I met Mrs. Bronson as though it was yesterday. There were no cars in those days and she and Bronson had ridden in on their bicycles. Of course then she didn't look so determined as she looks now. She was much thinner, she had a nice colour, and her eyes were very pretty—blue, you know—and she had a lot of dark hair. If she'd only taken more trouble with herself she'd have been rather stunning. As it was she was the best-looking woman there."

I tried to construct in my mind a picture of what Mrs. Cartwright—Mrs. Bronson as she was then—looked like from what she was now and from Gaze's not very graphic description. In the solid woman, with her well-covered bones, who sat rather heavily at the bridge-table, I tried to see a slight young thing with buoyant movements and graceful, easy gestures. Her chin now was square and her nose decided, but the roundness of youth must have masked this: she must have been charming with a pink and white skin and her hair carelessly dressed, brown and abundant. At that period she wore a long skirt, a tight waist and a picture hat. Or did women in Malaya still wear the topis that you see in old numbers of the illustrated papers?

"I hadn't seen her for—oh, nearly twenty years,"

Gaze went on. "I knew she was living somewhere in the F.M.S., but it was a surprise when I took this job and came here to run across her in the club just as I had up in Selantan so many years before. Of course she's an elderly woman now and she's changed out of all recognition. It was rather a shock to see her with a grown-up daughter, it made me realise how the time had passed; I was a young fellow when I met her last and now, by Jingo, I'm due to retire on the age limit in two or three years. Bit thick, isn't it?"

Gaze, a rueful grin on his ugly face, looked at me with faint indignation, as though I could help the hurrying march of the years as they trod upon one another's heels.

"I'm no chicken myself," I replied.

"You haven't lived out East all your life. It ages one before one's time. One's an elderly man at fifty and at fifty-five one's good for nothing but the scrap heap."

But I did not want Gaze to wander off into a disquisition on old age.

"Did you recognise Mrs. Cartwright when you saw her again?" I asked.

"Well, I did and I didn't. At the first glance I thought I knew her, but couldn't quite place her. I thought perhaps she was someone I'd met on board ship when I was going on leave and had known only by sight. But the moment she spoke I remembered at once. I remembered the dry twinkle in her eyes and the crisp sound of her voice. There was something in her voice that seemed to mean: you're a bit of a damned fool, my lad, but you're not a bad sort and upon my soul I rather like you."

"That's a good deal to read into the sound of a voice," I smiled.

"She came up to me in the club and shook hands with me. 'How do you do, Major Gaze? Do you remember me?' she said.

"'Of course I do.'

"'A lot of water has passed under the bridge since we met last. We're none of us as young as we were. Have you seen Theo?'

"For a moment I couldn't think whom she meant. I suppose I looked rather stupid, because she gave a little smile, that chaffing smile that I knew so well, and explained.

"'I married Theo, you know. It seemed the best thing to do. I was lonely and he wanted it.'

"'I heard you married him,' I said. 'I hope you've been very happy.'

"'Oh, very. Theo's a perfect duck. He'll be here in a minute. He'll be so glad to see you.'

"I wondered. I should have thought I was the last man Theo would wish to see. I shouldn't have thought she would wish it very much either. But women are funny."

"Why shouldn't she wish to see you?" I asked.

"I'm coming to that later," said Gaze. "Then Theo turned up. I don't know why I call him Theo; I never called him anything but Cartwright, I never thought of him as anything but Cartwright. Theo was a shock. You know what he looks like now; I remembered him as a curly-headed youngster, very fresh and clean looking; he was always neat and dapper, he had a good figure and he held himself well, like a man who's used to taking a lot of exercise. Now I come to think of it he wasn't bad looking, not in a big, massive way, but graceful, you know, and lithe. When I saw this bowed, cadaverous, bald-headed old buffer with spectacles I could hardly believe my eyes. I shouldn't have known him from Adam. He seemed pleased to see me, at least, interested; he wasn't effusive, but he'd always been on the quiet side and I didn't expect him to be.

"'Are you surprised to find us here?' he asked me.

"'Well, I hadn't the faintest notion where you were.'

"'We've kept track of your movements more or less. We've seen your name in the paper every now and then. You must come out one day and have a look at our place. We've been settled there a good many years, and I suppose we shall stay there till we go home for good. Have you ever been back to Alor Lipis?'

"'No, I haven't,' I said.

"'It was a nice little place. I'm told it's grown. I've never been back.'

"'It hasn't got the pleasantest recollections for us,' said Mrs. Cartwright.

"I asked them if they'd have a drink and we called the boy. I daresay you noticed that Mrs. Cartwright likes her liquor; I don't mean that she gets tight or anything like that, but she drinks her stengah like a man. I couldn't help looking at them with a certain amount of curiosity. They seemed perfectly happy; I gathered that they hadn't done at all badly, and I found out later that they were quite well off. They had a very nice car, and when they went on leave they denied themselves nothing. They were on the best of terms with one another. You know how jolly it is to see two people who've been married a great many years obviously better pleased with their own company than anyone else's. Their marriage had evidently been a great success. And they were both of them devoted to Olive and very proud of her, Theo especially."

"Although she was only his step-daughter?" I said.

"Although she was only his step-daughter," answered Gaze. "You'd think that she would have taken his name. But she hadn't. She called him Daddy, of course, he was the only father she'd ever known, but she signed her letters, Olive Bronson."

"What was Bronson like, by the way?"

"Bronson? He was a great big fellow, very hearty, with a loud voice and a bellowing laugh, beefy, you know, and a fine athlete. There was not very much to him but he was as straight as a die. He had a red face and red hair. Now I come to think of it I remember that I never saw a man sweat as much as he did. Water just poured off him, and when he played tennis he always used to bring a towel on the court with him."

"It doesn't sound very attractive."

"He was a handsome chap. He was always fit. He was keen on that. He hadn't much to talk about but rubber and games, tennis, you know, and golf and shooting; and I don't suppose he read a book from year's end to year's end. He was the typical public-school boy. He was about thirty-five when I first knew him, but he had the mind of a boy of eighteen. You know how many fellows when they come out East seem to stop growing."

I did indeed. One of the most disconcerting things to the traveller is to see stout, middle-aged gentlemen, with bald heads, speaking and acting like schoolboys. You might almost think that no idea has entered their heads since they first passed through the Suez Canal. Though married and the fathers of children, and perhaps in control of a large business, they continue to look upon life from the standpoint of the sixth form.

"But he was no fool," Gaze went on. "He knew his work from A to Z. His estate was one of the best managed in the country and he knew how to handle his labour. He was a damned good sort, and if he did get on your nerves a little you couldn't help liking him. He was generous with his money, and always ready to do anybody a good turn. That's how Cartwright happened to turn up in the first instance."

"Did the Bronsons get on well together?"

"Oh, yes, I think so. I'm sure they did. He was good natured and she was very jolly and gay. She was very outspoken, you know. She can be very amusing when she likes even now, but there's generally a sting lurking in the joke; when she was a young woman and married to Bronson it was just pure fun. She had high spirits and liked having a good time. She never cared a hang what she said, but it went with her type, if you understand what I mean; there was something so open and frank and careless about her that you didn't care what she said to you. They seemed very happy.

"Their estate was about five miles from Alor Lipis. They had a trap and they used to drive in most evenings about five. Of course it was a very small community and men were in the majority. There were only about six women. The Bronsons were a god-send. They bucked things up the moment they arrived. We used to have very jolly times in that little club. I've often thought of them since and I don't know that on the whole I've ever enjoyed myself more than I did when I was stationed there. Between six and eight-thirty the club at Alor Lipis twenty years ago was about as lively a place as you could find between Aden and Yokohama.

"One day Mrs. Bronson told us that they were expecting a friend to stay with them and a few days later they brought Cartwright along. It appeared that he was an old friend of Bronson's, they'd been at school together, Marlborough, or some place like that, and they'd first come out East on the same ship. Rubber had taken a toss and a lot of fellows had lost their jobs. Cartwright was one of them. He'd been out of work for the greater part of a year and he hadn't anything to fall back on. In those days planters were even worse paid than they are now and a man had to be very lucky to put by something for a rainy day. Cartwright had gone to Singapore. They all go there when there's a slump, you know. It's awful then, I've seen it; I've known of planters sleeping in the street because they hadn't the price of a night's lodging. I've known them stop strangers outside the Europe and ask for a dollar to get a meal, and I think Cartwright had had a pretty rotten time.

"At last he wrote to Bronson and asked him if he couldn't do something for him. Bronson asked him to come and stay till things got better, at least it would be free board and lodging, and Cartwright jumped at the chance, but Bronson had to send him the money to pay his railway fare. When Cartwright arrived at Alor Lipis he hadn't ten cents in his pocket. Bronson had a little money of his own, two or three hundred a year, I think, and though his salary had been cut, he'd kept his job, so that he was better off than most planters. When Cartwright came Mrs. Bronson told him that he was to look upon the place as his home and stay as long as he liked."

"It was very nice of her, wasn't it?" I remarked.

"Very."

Gaze lit himself another cheroot and filled his glass. It was very still and but for the occasional croak of the chik-chak the silence was intense. We seemed to be alone in the tropical night and heaven only knows how far from the habitations of men. Gaze did not speak for so long that at last I was forced to say something.

"What sort of a man was Cartwright at that time?" I asked. "Younger, of course, and you told me rather nice looking; but in himself?"

"Well, to tell you the truth, I never paid much attention to him. He was pleasant and unassuming. He's very quiet now, as I daresay you noticed; well, he wasn't exactly lively then. But he was perfectly in-offensive. He was fond of reading and he played the piano rather nicely. You never minded having him about, he was never in the way, but you never bothered very much about him. He danced well and the women rather liked that, but he also played billiards quite decently and he wasn't bad at tennis. He fell into our little groove very naturally. I wouldn't say that he ever became wildly popular, but everybody liked him. Of course we were sorry for him, as one is for a man who's down and out, but there was nothing we could do, and, well, we just accepted him and then forgot that he hadn't always been there. He used to come in with the Bronsons every evening and pay for his drinks like everyone else, I suppose Bronson had lent a bit of money for current expenses, and he was always very civil. I'm rather vague about him, because really he didn't make any particular impression on me; in the East one meets such a lot of people, and he seemed very much like anybody else. He did everything he could to get something to do, but he had no luck; the fact is, there were no jobs going, and sometimes he seemed rather depressed about it. He was with the Bronsons for over a year. I remember his saying to me once:

"'After all I can't live with them for ever. They've been most awfully good to me, but there are limits.'

"'I should think the Bronsons would be very glad to have you,' I said. 'It's not particularly gay on a rubber estate, and as far as your food and drink go, it must make precious little difference if you're there or not.'"

Gaze stopped once more and looked at me with a sort of hesitation.

"What's the matter?" I asked.

"I'm afraid I'm telling you this story very badly," he said. "I seem to be just rambling on. I'm not a damned novelist, I'm a policeman, and I'm just telling you the facts as I saw them at the time; and from my point of view all the circumstances are important; it's important, I mean, to realise what sort of people they were."

"Of course. Fire away."

"I remember someone, a woman, I think it was, the doctor's wife, asking Mrs. Bronson if she didn't get tired sometimes of having a stranger in the house.

You know, in places like Alor Lipis there isn't very much to talk about, and if you didn't talk about your neighbours there'd be nothing to talk about at all.

"'Oh, no,' she said, 'Theo's no trouble.' She turned to her husband who was sitting there mopping his face. 'We like having him, don't we?'

"'He's all right,' said Bronson.

"'What does he do with himself all day long?'

"'Oh, I don't know,' said Mrs. Bronson. 'He walks round the estate with Reggie sometimes, and he shoots a bit. He talks to me.'

"'He's always glad to make himself useful,' said Bronson. 'The other day when I had a go of fever, he took over my work and I just lay in bed and had a good time.'"

"Hadn't the Bronsons any children?" I asked.

"No," Gaze answered. "I don't know why, they could well have afforded it."

Gaze leant back in his chair. He took off his glasses and wiped them. They were very strong and hideously distorted his eyes. Without them he wasn't so homely. The chik-chak on the ceiling gave its strangely human cry. It was like the cackle of an idiot child.

"Bronson was killed," said Gaze suddenly.

"Killed?"

"Yes, murdered. I shall never forget that night. We'd been playing tennis, Mrs. Bronson and the doctor's wife, Theo Cartwright and I; and then we played bridge. Cartwright had been off his game and when we sat down at the bridge-table Mrs. Bronson said to him: 'Well, Theo, if you play bridge as rottenly as you played tennis we shall lose our shirts.'

"We'd just had a drink, but she called the boy and ordered another round.

"'Put that down your throat,' she said to him, 'and don't call without top honours and an outside trick.'

"Bronson hadn't turned up, he'd cycled in to Kabulong to get the money to pay his coolies their wages and was to come along to the club when he got back. The Bronsons' estate was nearer Alor Lipis than it was to Kabulong, but Kabulong was a more important place commercially, and Bronson banked there.

"'Reggie can cut in when he turns up,' said Mrs. Bronson.

"'He's late, isn't he?' said the doctor's wife.

"'Very. He said he wouldn't get back in time for tennis, but would be here for a rubber. I have a suspicion that he went to the club at Kabulong instead of coming straight home and is having drinks, the ruffian.'

"'Oh, well, he can put away a good many without their having much effect on him,' I laughed.

"'He's getting fat, you know. He'll have to be careful.'

"We sat by ourselves in the card-room and we could hear the crowd in the billiard-room talking and laughing. They were all on the merry side. It was getting on to Christmas Day and we were all letting ourselves go a little. There was going to be a dance on Christmas Eve.

"I remembered afterwards that when we sat down the doctor's wife asked Mrs. Bronson if she wasn't tired.

"'Not a bit,' she said. 'Why should I be?'

"I didn't know why she flushed.

"'I was afraid the tennis might have been too much for you,' said the doctor's wife.

"'Oh, no,' answered Mrs. Bronson, a trifle abruptly, I thought, as though she didn't want to discuss the matter.

"I didn't know what they meant, and indeed it wasn't till later that I remembered the incident.

"We played three or four rubbers and still Bronson didn't turn up.

"'I wonder what's happened to him,' said his wife. 'I can't think why he should be so late.'

"Cartwright was always silent, but this evening he had hardly opened his mouth. I thought he was tired and asked him what he'd been doing.

"'Nothing very much,' he said. 'I went out after tiffin to shoot pigeon.'

"'Did you have any luck?' I asked.

"'Oh, I got half a dozen. They were very shy.'

"But now he said: 'If Reggie got back late, I daresay he thought it wasn't worth while to come here. I expect he's had a bath and when we get in we shall find him asleep in his chair.'

"'It's a good long ride from Kabulong,' said the doctor's wife.

"'He doesn't take the road, you know,' Mrs. Bronson explained. 'He takes the short cut through the jungle.'

"'Can he get along on his bicycle?' I asked.

"'Oh, yes, it's a very good track. It saves about a couple of miles.'

"We had just started another rubber when the bar-boy came in and said there was a police-sergeant outside who wanted to speak to me.

"'What does he want?' I asked.

"The boy said he didn't know, but he had two coolies with him.

"'Curse him,' I said. 'I'll give him hell if I find he's disturbed me for nothing.'

"I told the boy I'd come and I finished playing the hand. Then I got up.

"'I won't be a minute,' I said. 'Deal for me, will you?' I added to Cartwright.

"I went out and found the sergeant with two Malays waiting for me on the steps. I asked him what the devil he wanted. You can imagine my consternation when he told me that the Malays had come to the police-station and said there was a white man lying dead on the path that led through the jungle to Kabulong. I immediately thought of Bronson.

"'Dead?' I cried.

"'Yes, shot. Shot through the head. A white man with red hair.'

"Then I knew it was Reggie Bronson, and indeed, one of them naming his estate said he'd recognised him as the tuan. It was an awful shock. And there was Mrs. Bronson in the card-room waiting impatiently for me to sort my cards and make a bid. For a moment I really didn't know what to do. I was frightfully upset. It was dreadful to give her such a terrible and unexpected blow without a word of preparation, but I found myself quite unable to think of any way to soften it. I told the sergeant and the coolies to wait and went back into the club. I tried to pull myself together. As I entered the card-room Mrs. Bronson said: 'You've been an awful long time.' Then she caught sight of my face.

'Is anything the matter?' I saw her clench her fists and go white. You'd have thought she had a presentiment of evil.

"'Something dreadful has happened,' I said, and my throat was all closed up so that my voice sounded even to myself hoarse and uncanny. 'There's been an accident. Your husband's been wounded.'

"She gave a long gasp, it was not exactly a scream, it reminded me oddly of a piece of silk torn in two.

"'Wounded?'

"She leapt to her feet and with her eyes starting from her head stared at Cartwright. The effect on him was ghastly, he fell back in his chair and went as white as death.

"'Very, very badly, I'm afraid,' I added.

"I knew that I must tell her the truth, and tell it then, but I couldn't bring myself to tell it all at once.

"'Is he,' her lips trembled so that she could hardly form the words, 'is he—conscious?'

"I looked at her for a moment without answering. I'd have given a thousand pounds not to have to.

"'No, I'm afraid he isn't.'

"Mrs. Bronson stared at me as though she were trying to see right into my brain.

"'Is he dead?'

"I thought the only thing was to get it out and have done with it.

"'Yes, he was dead when they found him.'

"Mrs. Bronson collapsed into her chair and burst into tears.

"'Oh, my God,' she muttered. 'Oh, my God.'

"The doctor's wife went to her and put her arms

round her. Mrs. Bronson with her face in her hands swayed to and fro weeping hysterically. Cartwright, with that livid face, sat quite still, his mouth open, and stared at her. You might have thought he was turned to stone.

"'Oh, my dear, my dear,' said the doctor's wife, 'you must try and pull yourself together.' Then, turning to me. 'Get her a glass of water and fetch Harry.'

"Harry was her husband and he was playing billiards. I went in and told him what had happened.

"'A glass of water be damned,' he said. 'What she wants is a good long peg of brandy.'

"We took it in to her and forced her to drink it and gradually the violence of her emotion exhausted itself. In a few minutes the doctor's wife was able to take her into the ladies' lavatory to wash her face. I'd made up my mind now what had better be done. I could see that Cartwright wasn't good for much; he was all to pieces. I could understand that it was a fearful shock to him, for after all Bronson was his greatest friend and had done everything in the world for him.

"'You look as though you'd be all the better for a drop of brandy yourself old man,' I said to him.

"He made an effort.

"'It's shaken me, you know,' he said. 'I . . . I didn't . . .' He stopped as though his mind was wandering; he was still fearfully pale; he took out a packet of cigarettes and struck a match, but his hand was shaking so that he could hardly manage it.

"'Yes, I'll have a brandy.'

"'Boy,' I shouted, and then to Cartwright: 'Now, are you fit to take Mrs. Bronson home?'

"'Oh, yes,' he answered.

"'That's good. The doctor and I will go along with the coolies and some police to where the body is.'

"'Will you bring him back to the bungalow?' asked Cartwright.

"'I think he'd better be taken straight to the mortuary,' said the doctor before I could answer. 'I shall have to do a P.M.'

"When Mrs. Bronson, now so much calmer that I was amazed, came back, I told her what I suggested. The doctor's wife, kind woman, offered to go with her and spend the night at the bungalow, but Mrs. Bronson wouldn't hear of it. She said she would be perfectly all right, and when the doctor's wife insisted—you know how bent some people are on forcing their kindness on those in trouble—she turned on her almost fiercely.

"'No, no, I must be alone,' she said. 'I really must. And Theo will be there.'

"They got into the trap. Theo took the reins and they drove off. We started after them, the doctor and I, while the sergeant and the coolies followed. I had sent my seis to the police station with instructions to send two men to the place where the body was lying. We soon passed Mrs. Bronson and Cartwright.

"'All right?' I called.

"'Yes,' he answered.

"For some time the doctor and I drove without saying a word; we were both of us deeply shocked. I was worried as well. Somehow or other I'd got to find the murderers and I foresaw that it would be no easy matter.

"'Do you suppose it was gang robbery?' said the doctor at last.

"He might have been reading my thoughts.

"'I don't think there's a doubt of it,' I answered. 'They knew he'd gone into Kabulong to get the wages and lay in wait for him on the way back. Of course he should never have come alone through the jungle when everyone knew he had a packet of money with him.'

"'He'd done it for years,' said the doctor. 'And he's not the only one.'

"'I know. The question is, how we're going to get hold of the fellows that did it.'

"'You don't think the two coolies who say they found him could have had anything to do with it?'

"'No. They wouldn't have the nerve. I think a pair of Chinks might think out a trick like that, but I don't believe Malays would. They'd be much too frightened. Of course we'll keep an eye on them. We shall soon see if they seem to have any money to fling about.'

"'It's awful for Mrs. Bronson,' said the doctor. 'It would have been bad enough at any time, but now she's going to have a baby . . .'

"'I didn't know that,' I said, interrupting him.

"'No, for some reason she wanted to keep it dark. She was rather funny about it, I thought.'

"I recollected then that little passage between Mrs. Bronson and the doctor's wife. I understood why that good woman had been so anxious that Mrs. Bronson should not overtire herself.

"'It's strange her having a baby after being married so many years.'

"'It happens, you know. But it was a surprise to her. When first she came to see me and I told her what was the matter she fainted, and then she began to cry. I should have thought she'd be as pleased as Punch. She told me that Bronson didn't like children and he'd be awfully bored at the idea, and she made me promise to say nothing about it till she had had a chance of breaking it to him gradually.'

"I reflected for a moment.

"'He was the kind of breezy, hearty cove whom you'd expect to be as keen as mustard on having kids.'

"'You never can tell. Some people are very selfish and just don't want the bother.'

"'Well, how did he take it when she did tell him? Wasn't he rather bucked?'

"'I don't know that she ever told him. Though she couldn't have waited much longer; unless I'm very much mistaken she ought to be confined in about five months.'

"'Poor devil,' I said. 'You know, I've got a notion that he'd have been most awfully pleased to know.'

"We drove in silence for the rest of the way and at last came to the point at which the short cut to Kabulong branched off from the road. Here we stopped and in a minute or two my trap, in which were the police-sergeant and the two Malays, came up. We took the head-lamps to light us on our way. I left the doctor's seis to look after the ponies and told him that when the policemen came they were to follow the path till they found us. The two coolies, carrying the lamps, walked ahead and we followed them. It was a fairly broad track, wide enough for a small cart to pass, and before the road was built it had been the highway between Kabulong and Alor Lipis. It was firm to the foot and good walking. The surface here and there was sandy and in places you could see quite plainly the mark of a bicycle wheel. It was the track Bronson had left on his way to Kabulong.

"We walked twenty minutes, I should think, in single file, and on a sudden the coolies, with a cry, stopped sharply. The sight had come upon them so abruptly that notwithstanding they were expecting it they were startled. There, in the middle of the pathway lit dimly by the lamps the coolies carried, lay Bronson; he'd fallen over his bicycle and lay across it in an ungainly heap. I was too shocked to speak, and I think the doctor was, too. But in our silence the din of the jungle was deafening; those damned cicadas and the bull-frogs were making enough row to wake the dead. Even under ordinary circumstances the noise of the jungle at nights always seems to me uncanny; because you feel that at that hour there should be an utter silence it has an odd effect on you, that ceaseless and invisible uproar that beats upon your nerves. It surrounds you and hems you in. But just then, believe me, it was terrifying. That poor fellow lay dead and all round him the restless life of the jungle pursued its indifferent and ferocious course.

"He was lying face downwards. The sergeant and the coolies looked at me as though awaiting an order. I was a young fellow then and I'm afraid I felt a little frightened. Though I couldn't see the face I had no doubt that it was Bronson, but I felt that I ought to turn the body over to make sure. I suppose we all have our little squeamishnesses; you know, I've always had a horrible distaste for touching dead bodies. I've had to do it fairly often now, but it still makes me feel slightly sick.

"'It's Bronson, all right,' I said.

"The doctor—by George, it was lucky for me he was there—the doctor bent down and turned the head. The sergeant directed the lamp on the dead face.

"'My God, half his head's been shot away,' I cried.

"'Yes.'

"The doctor stood up straight and wiped his hands on the leaves of a tree that grew beside the path.

"'Is he quite dead?' I asked.

"'Oh, yes. Death must have been instantaneous. Whoever shot him must have fired at pretty close range.'

"'How long has he been dead, d'you think?'

"'Oh, I don't know, several hours.'

"'He would have passed here about five o'clock, I suppose, if he was expecting to get to the club for a rubber at six.'

"'There's no sign of any struggle,' said the doctor.

"'No, there wouldn't be. He was shot as he was riding along.'

"I looked at the body for a little while. I couldn't help thinking how short a time ago it was since Bronson, noisy and loud-voiced, had been so full of hearty life.

"'You haven't forgotten that he had the coolies' wages on him,' said the doctor.

"'No, we'd better search him.'

"'Shall we turn him over?'

"'Wait a minute. Let us just have a look at the ground first.'

"I took the lamp and as carefully as I could looked all about me. Just where he had fallen the sandy pathway was trodden and confused; there were our foot-

prints and the footprints of the coolies who had found
him. I walked two or three paces and then saw quite
clearly the mark of his bicycle wheels; he had been
riding straight and steadily. I followed it to the spot
where he had fallen, to just before that rather, and there
saw very distinctly the prints on each side of the wheels
of his heavy boots. He had evidently stopped there and
put his feet to the ground, then he'd started off again,
there was a great wobble of the wheel, and he'd crashed.

"'Now let's search him,' I said.

"The doctor and the sergeant turned the body over
and one of the coolies dragged the bicycle away. They
laid Bronson on his back. I supposed he would have
had the money partly in notes and partly in silver.
The silver would have been in a bag attached to the
bicycle and a glance told me that it was not there.
The notes he would have put in a wallet. It would
have been a good thick bundle. I felt him all over, but
there was nothing; then I turned out the pockets, they
were all empty except the right trouser pocket, in
which there was a little small change.

"'Didn't he always wear a watch?' asked the doctor.

"'Yes, of course he did.'

"I remembered that he wore the chain through the
buttonhole in the lapel of his coat and the watch and
some seals and things in his handkerchief pocket.
But watch and chain were gone.

"'Well, there's not much doubt now, is there?' I
said.

"It was clear that he had been attacked by gang
robbers who knew he had money on him. After killing
him they had stripped him of everything. I suddenly

remembered the footprints that proved that for a moment he had stood still. I saw exactly how it had been done. One of them had stopped him on some pretext and then, just as he started off again, another, slipping out of the jungle behind him, had emptied the two barrels of a gun into his head.

"'Well,' I said to the doctor, 'it's up to me to catch them, and I'll tell you what, it'll be a real pleasure to me to see them hanged.'

"Of course there was an inquest. Mrs. Bronson gave evidence, but she had nothing to say that we didn't know already. Bronson had left the bungalow about eleven, he was to have tiffin at Kabulong and was to be back between five and six. He asked her not to wait for him, he said he would just put the money in the safe and come straight to the club. Cartwright confirmed this. He had lunched alone with Mrs. Bronson and after a smoke had gone out with a gun to shoot pigeon. He had got in about five, a little before perhaps, had a bath and changed to play tennis. He was shooting not far from the place where Bronson was killed, but never heard a shot. That, of course, meant nothing; what with the cicadas and the frogs, and the other sounds of the jungle he would have had to be very near to hear any-thing; and besides, Cartwright was probably back in the bungalow before Bronson was killed. We traced Bronson's movements. He had lunched at the club, he had got money at the bank just before it closed, had gone back to the club and had one more drink, and then started off on his bicycle. He had crossed the river by the ferry, the ferryman remembered distinctly seeing him, but was positive that no one else with a bicycle had crossed. That looked as though the murderers were not following, but lying in wait for him. He rode along the main road for a couple of miles and then took the path which was a short cut to his bungalow.

"It looked as though he had been killed by men who knew his habits, and suspicion, of course, fell immediately on the coolies of his estate. We examined them all—pretty carefully—but there was not a scrap of evidence to connect any of them with the crime. In fact, most of them were able satisfactorily to account for their actions and those who couldn't seemed to me for one reason and another out of the running. There were a few bad characters among the Chinese at Alor Lipis and I had them looked up. But somehow I didn't think it was the work of the Chinese; I had a feeling that Chinese would have used revolvers and not a shot gun. Anyhow, I could find out nothing there. So then we offered a reward of a thousand dollars to anyone who could put us in the way of discovering the murderers. I thought there were a good many people to whom it would appeal to do a public service and at the same time earn a tidy sum. But I knew that an informer would take no risks, he wouldn't want to tell what he knew till he knew he could tell it safely, and I armed myself with patience. The reward had brightened the interest of my police and I knew they would use every means they had to bring the criminals to trial. In a case like this they could do more than I.

"But it was strange, nothing happened; the reward seemed to tempt no one. I cast my net a little wider. There were two or three kampongs along the road and I wondered if the murderers were there; I saw the head-

men, but got no help from them. It was not that they
would tell me nothing, I was sure they had nothing to
tell. I talked to the bad hats, but there was absolutely
nothing to connect them with the murder. There was
not the shadow of a clue.

"'Very well, my lads,' I said to myself, as I drove
back to Alor Lipis, 'there's no hurry; the rope won't
spoil by keeping.'

"The scoundrels had got away with a considerable
sum, but money is no good unless you spend it. I felt
I knew the native temperament enough to be sure that
the possession of it was a constant temptation. The
Malays are an extravagant race, and a race of gamblers,
and the Chinese are gamblers, too; sooner or later
someone would start flinging his money about, and then
I should want to know where it came from. With a few
well-directed questions I thought I could put the fear
of God into the fellow and then, if I knew my business,
it shouldn't be hard to get a full confession.

"The only thing now was to sit down and wait till
the hue and cry had died down and the murderers
thought the affair was forgotten. The itch to spend
those ill-gotten dollars would grow more and more
intolerable till at last it could be resisted no longer. I
would go about my business, but I meant never to
relax my watch, and one day, sooner or later, my time
must come.

"Cartwright took Mrs. Bronson down to Singapore.
The company Bronson had worked for asked him if
he would care to take Bronson's place, but he said,
very naturally, that he didn't like the idea of it; so they
put another man in and told Cartwright that he could

have the job that Bronson's successor had vacated. It was the management of the estate that Cartwright lives on now. He moved in at once. Four months after this Olive was born at Singapore, and a few months later, when Bronson had been dead just over a year, Cartwright and Mrs. Bronson were married. I was surprised; but on thinking it over I couldn't help confessing that it was very natural. After the trouble Mrs. Bronson had leant much on Cartwright and he had arranged everything for her; she must have been lonely, and rather lost, and I daresay she was grateful for his kindness, he did behave like a brick; and so far as he was concerned I imagined he was sorry for her, it was a dreadful position for a woman, she had nowhere to go, and all they'd gone through must have been a tie between them. There was every reason for them to marry and it was probably the best thing for them both.

"It looked as though Bronson's murderers would never be caught, for that plan of mine didn't work; there was no one in the district who spent more money than he could account for, and if anyone had that hoard buried away under his floor he was showing a self-control that was super-human. A year had passed and to all intents and purposes the thing was forgotten. Could anyone be so prudent as after so long not to let a little money dribble out? It was incredible. I began to think that Bronson had been killed by a couple of wandering Chinese who had got away, to Singapore perhaps, where there would be small chance of catching them. At last I gave it up. If you come to think of it, as a rule, it's just those crimes, crimes of robbery, in which there is least chance of getting the culprit; for there's nothing to attach suspicion to him, and if he's caught it can only be by his own carelessness. It's different with crimes of passion or vengeance, then you can find out who had a motive to put the victim out of the way.

"It's no use grizzling over one's failures, and bringing my common sense to bear I did my best to put the matter out of my mind. No one likes to be beaten, but beaten I was and I had to put as good a face on it as I could. And then a Chinaman was caught trying to pawn poor Bronson's watch.

"I told you that Bronson's watch and chain had been taken, and of course Mrs. Bronson was able to give us a fairly accurate description of it. It was a half-hunter, by Benson, there was a gold chain, three or four seals and a sovereign purse. The pawnbroker was a smart fellow and when the Chinaman brought the watch he recognised it at once. On some pretext he kept the man waiting and sent for a policeman. The man was arrested and immediately brought to me. I greeted him like a long-lost brother. I was never so pleased to see anyone in my life. I have no feeling about criminals, you know; I'm rather sorry for them, because they're playing a game in which their opponents hold all the aces and kings; but when I catch one it gives me a little thrill of satisfaction, like bringing off a neat finesse at bridge. At last the mystery was going to be cleared up, for if the Chinaman hadn't done the thing himself we were pretty sure through him to trace the murderers. I beamed on him.

"I asked him to account for his possession of the watch. He said he had bought it from a man he didn't know. That was very thin. I explained the circumstances briefly and told him he would be charged with murder. I meant to frighten him and I did. He said then that he'd found the watch.

"'Found it?' I said. 'Fancy that. Where?'

"His answer staggered me; he said he'd found it in the jungle; I laughed at him; I asked him if he thought watches were likely to be left lying about in the jungle; then he said he'd been coming along the pathway that led from Kabulong to Alor Lipis, and had gone into the jungle and caught sight of something gleaming and there was the watch. That was odd. Why should he have said he found the watch just there? It was either true or excessively astute. I asked him where the chain and the seals were, and he produced them immediately. I'd got him scared, and he was pale and shaking; he was a knock-kneed little fellow and I should have been a fool not to see that I hadn't got hold of the murderer there. But his terror suggested that he knew something.

"I asked him when he'd found the watch.

"'Yesterday,' he said.

"I asked him what he was doing on the short-cut from Kabulong to Alor Lipis. He said that he'd been working in Singapore and had gone to Kabulong because his father was ill, and that he himself had come to Alor Lipis to work. A friend of his father, a carpenter by trade, had given him a job. He gave me the name of the man with whom he had worked in Singapore and the name of the man who had engaged him at Alor Lipis. All he said seemed plausible and could so easily be verified that it was hardly likely to be false. Of course it occurred to me that if he had found the watch as he said it must have been lying in the jungle for more

than a year. It could hardly be in very good condition;
I tried to open it, but couldn't. The pawnbroker had
come to the police-station and was waiting in the next
room. Luckily he was also something of a watch-
maker. I sent for him and asked him to look at the
watch; when he opened it he gave a little whistle, the
works were thick with rust.

"'This watch no good,' he said, shaking his head.
'Him never go now.'

"I asked him what had put it in such a state, and
without a word from me he said that it had been long
exposed to wet. For the moral effect I had the prisoner
put in a cell and I sent for his employer. I sent a wire
to Kabulong and another to Singapore. While I waited
I did my best to put two and two together. I was inclined to believe the man's story true; his fear might be
ascribed to no more guilt than consisted in his having
found something and tried to sell it. Even quite innocent persons are apt to be nervous when they're in
the hands of the police; I don't know what there is
about a policeman, people are never very much at their
ease in his company. But if he really had found the
watch where he said, someone had thrown it there.
Now that was funny. Even if the murderers had thought
the watch a dangerous thing to possess, one would have
expected them to melt down the gold case; that would
be a very simple thing for any native to do; and the
chain was of so ordinary a pattern they could hardly
have thought it possible to trace that. There were
chains like it in every jeweller's shop in the country.
Of course there was the possibility that they had
plunged into the jungle and having dropped the watch

in their hurry had been afraid to go back and look for it. I didn't think that very likely: the Malays are used to keeping things tucked away in their sarongs, and the Chinese have pockets in their coats. Besides, the moment they got into the jungle they knew there was no hurry; they probably waited and divided the swag then and there.

"In a few minutes the man I had sent for came to the police-station and confirmed what the prisoner had said, and in an hour I got an answer from Kabulong. The police had seen his father who told them that the boy had gone to Alor Lipis to get a job with a carpenter. So far everything he had said seemed true. I had him brought in again, and told him I was going to take him to the place where he said he had found the watch and he must show me the exact spot. I handcuffed him to a policeman, though it was hardly necessary, for the poor devil was shaking with fright, and took a couple of men besides. We drove out to where the track joined the road and walked along it; within five yards of the place where Bronson was killed the Chinaman stopped.

"'Here,' he said.

"He pointed to the jungle and we followed him in. We went in about ten yards and he pointed to a chink between two large boulders and said that he found the watch there. It could only have been by the merest chance that he noticed it, and if he really had found it there it looked very much as though someone had put it there to hide it."

Gaze stopped and gave me a reflective look.

"What would you have thought then?" he asked.

"I don't know," I answered.

"Well, I'll tell you what I thought. I thought that if the watch was there the money might be there, too. It seemed worth while having a look. Of course, to look for something in the jungle makes looking for a needle in a bundle of hay a drawing-room pastime. I couldn't help that. I released the Chinaman, I wanted all the help I could get, and set him to work. I set my three men to work, and I started in myself. We made a line —there were five of us—and we searched from the road; for fifty yards on each side of the place at which Bronson was murdered and for a hundred yards in we went over the ground foot by foot. We routed among dead leaves and peered in bushes, we looked under boulders and in the hollows of trees. I knew it was a foolish thing to do, for the chances against us were a thousand to one; my only hope was that anyone who had just committed a murder would be rattled and if he wanted to hide anything would hide it quickly; he would choose the first obvious hiding-place that offered itself. That is what he had done when he hid the watch.   My only reason for looking in so circumscribed an area was that as the watch had been found so near the road, the person who wanted to get rid of the things must have wanted to get rid of them quickly.

"We worked on. I began to grow tired and cross. We were sweating like pigs. I had a maddening thirst and nothing in the world to drink. At last I came to the conclusion that we must give it up as a bad job, for that day at least, when suddenly the Chinaman—he must have had sharp eyes, that young man—uttered a guttural cry. He stooped down and from under the winding root of a tree drew out a messy, mouldering, stinking thing. It was a pocket-book that had been out in the rain for a year, that had been eaten by ants and beetles and God knows what, that was sodden and foul, but it was a pocket-book all right, Bronson's, and inside were the shapeless, mushed-up, fetid remains of the Singapore notes he had got from the bank at Kabulong. There was still the silver and I was convinced that it was hidden somewhere about, but I wasn't going to bother about that. I had found out something very important; whoever had murdered Bronson had made no money out of it.

"Do you remember my telling you that I'd noticed the print of Bronson's feet on each side of the broad line of the pneumatic tyre, where he had stopped, and presumably spoken to someone? He was a heavy man and the prints were well marked. He hadn't just put his feet on the soft sand and taken them off, but must have stopped at least for a minute or two. My explanation was that he had stopped to chat with a Malay or a Chinaman, but the more I thought of it the less I liked it. Why the devil should he? Bronson wanted to get home, and though a jovial chap, he certainly was not hail-fellow-well-met with the natives. His relations towards them were those of master and servants. Those footprints had always puzzled me. And now the truth flashed across me. Whoever had murdered Bronson hadn't murdered him to rob and if he'd stopped to talk with someone it could only be with a friend. I knew at last who the murderer was."

I have always thought the detective story a most diverting and ingenious variety of fiction, and have regretted that I never had the skill to write one, but I have read a good many, and I flatter myself it is rarely that I have not solved the mystery before it was disclosed to me; and now for some time I had foreseen what Gaze was going to say, but when at last he said it I confess that it gave me, notwithstanding, somewhat of a shock.

"The man he met was Cartwright. Cartwright was pigeon-shooting. He stopped and asked him what sport he had had, and as he rode on Cartwright raised his gun and discharged both barrels into his head. Cartwright took the money and the watch in order to make it look like the work of gang robbers and hurriedly hid them in the jungle, then made his way along the edge till he got to the road, went back to the bungalow, changed into his tennis things and drove with Mrs. Bronson to the club.

"I remembered how badly he'd played tennis, and how he'd collapsed when, in order to break the news more gently to Mrs. Bronson, I said Bronson was wounded and not dead. If he was only wounded he might have been able to speak. By George, I bet that was a bad moment. The child was Cartwright's. Look at Olive: why, you saw the likeness yourself. The doctor had said that Mrs. Bronson was upset when he told her she was going to have a baby and made him promise not to tell Bronson. Why? Because Bronson knew that he couldn't be the father of the child."

"Do you think that Mrs. Bronson knew what Cartwright had done?" I asked.

"I'm sure of it. When I look back on her behaviour that evening at the club I am convinced of it. She was upset, but not because Bronson was killed; she was upset because I said he was wounded; on my telling her that he was dead when they found him she burst out crying, but from relief. I know that woman. Look at that square chin of hers and tell me that she hasn't got the courage of the devil. She has a will of iron. She made Cartwright do it. She planned every detail and every move. He was completely under her influence; he is now."

"But do you mean to tell me that neither you nor anyone else ever suspected that there was anything between them?"

"Never. Never."

"If they were in love with one another and knew that she was going to have a baby, why didn't they just bolt?"

"How could they? It was Bronson who had the money; she hadn't a bean and neither had Cartwright. He was out of a job. Do you think he would have got another with that story round his neck? Bronson had taken him in when he was starving and he'd stolen his wife from him. They wouldn't have had a dog's chance. They couldn't afford to let the truth come out, their only chance was to get Bronson out of the way, and they got him out of the way."

"They might have thrown themselves on his mercy."

"Yes, but I think they were ashamed. He'd been so good to them, he was such a decent chap, I don't think they had the heart to tell him the truth. They preferred to kill him."

There was a moment's silence while I reflected over what Gaze said.

"Well, what did you do about it?" I asked.

"Nothing. What was there to do? What was the evidence? That the watch and notes had been found? They might easily have been hidden by someone who was afterwards afraid to come and get them. The murderer might have been quite content to get away with the silver. The footprints? Bronson might have stopped to light a cigarette or there might have been a tree trunk across the path and he waited while the coolies he met there by chance moved it away. Who could prove that the child that a perfectly decent, respectable woman had had four months after her husband's death was not his child? No jury would have convicted Cartwright. I held my tongue and the Bronson murder was forgotten."

"I don't suppose the Cartwrights have forgotten," I suggested.

"I shouldn't be surprised. Human memory is astonishingly short and if you want my professional opinion I don't mind telling you that I don't believe remorse for a crime ever sits very heavily on a man when he's absolutely sure he'll never be found out."

I thought once more of the pair I had met that afternoon, the thin, elderly, bald man with gold-rimmed spectacles, and that white-haired untidy woman with her frank speech and kindly, caustic smile. It was almost impossible to imagine that in the distant past they had been swayed by so turbulent a passion, for that alone made their behaviour explicable, that it had brought them in the end to such a pass that they could see no other issue than a cruel and cold-blooded murder.

"Doesn't it make you feel a little uncomfortable to be with them?" I asked Gaze. "For, without wishing to be censorious, I'm bound to say that I don't think they can be very nice people."

"That's where you're wrong. They are very nice people; they're about the pleasantest people here. Mrs. Cartwright is a thoroughly good sort and a very amusing woman. It's my business to prevent crime and to catch the culprit when crime is committed, but I've known far too many criminals to think that on the whole they're worse than anybody else. A perfectly decent fellow may be driven by circumstances to commit a crime and if he's found out he's punished; but he may very well remain a perfectly decent fellow. Of course society punishes him if he breaks its laws, and it's quite right, but it's not always his actions that indicate the essential man. If you'd been a policeman as long as I have, you'd know it's not what people do that really matters, it's what they are. Luckily a policeman has nothing to do with their thoughts, only with their deeds; if he had, it would be a very different, a much more difficult matter."

Gaze flicked the ash from his cheroot and gave me his wry, sardonic, but agreeable smile.

"I'll tell you what, there's one job I *shouldn't* like," he said.

"What is that?" I asked.

"God's, at the Judgment Day," said Gaze. "No, sir."

THE DOOR OF OPPORTUNITY

THEY got a first-class carriage to themselves. It was lucky, because they were taking a good deal in with them, Alban's suit-case and a hold-all, Anne's dressing-case and her hat-box. They had two trunks in the van, containing what they wanted immediately, but all the rest of their luggage Alban had put in the care of an agent who was to take it up to London and store it till they had made up their minds what to do. They had a lot, pictures and books, curios that Alban had collected in the East, his guns and saddles. They had left Sondurah for ever. Alban, as was his way, tipped the porter generously and then went to the book-stall and bought papers. He bought The New Statesman and The Nation, and The Tatler and The Sketch, and the last number of The London Mercury. He came back to the carriage and threw them on the seat.

"It's only an hour's journey," said Anne.

"I know, but I wanted to buy them. I've been starved so long. Isn't it grand to think that to-morrow morning we shall have to-morrow's Times, and The Express and The Mail?"

She did not answer and he turned away, for he saw coming towards them two persons, a man and his wife, who had been fellow-passengers from Singapore.

"Get through the customs all right?" he cried to them cheerily.

The man seemed not to hear, for he walked straight on, but the woman answered.

"Yes, they never found the cigarettes."

She saw Anne, gave her a friendly little smile, and passed on. Anne flushed.

"I was afraid they'd want to come in here," said Alban. "Let's have the carriage to ourselves if we can."

She looked at him curiously.

"I don't think you need worry," she answered. "I don't think anyone will come in."

He lit a cigarette and lingered at the carriage door. On his face was a happy smile. When they had passed through the Red Sea and found a sharp wind in the Canal, Anne had been surprised to see how much the men who had looked presentable enough in the white ducks in which she had been accustomed to see them, were changed when they left them off for warmer clothes. They looked like nothing on earth then. Their ties were awful and their shirts all wrong. They wore grubby flannel trousers and shabby old golf-coats that had too obviously been bought off the nail, or blue serge suits that betrayed the provincial tailor. Most of the passengers had got off at Marseilles, but a dozen or so, either because after a long period in the East they thought the trip through the Bay would do them good, or, like themselves, for economy's sake, had gone all the way to Tilbury, and now several of them walked along the platform. They wore solar topis or double-brimmed terais, and heavy greatcoats, or else shapeless soft hats or bowlers, not too well brushed, that looked too small for them. It was a shock to see them. They looked suburban and a trifle second-rate. But Alban had already a London look. There was not a speck of dust on his smart greatcoat, and his black Homburg hat looked brand-new. You would never have guessed that he had not been home for three years. His collar fitted closely round his neck and his foulard tie was neatly tied. As Anne looked at him she could not but think how good-looking he was. He was just under six feet tall, and slim, and he wore his clothes well, and his clothes were well cut. He had fair hair, still thick, and blue eyes and the faintly yellow skin common to men of that complexion after they have lost the pink and white freshness of early youth. There was no colour in his cheeks. It was a fine head, well-set on rather a long neck, with a somewhat prominent Adam's apple; but you were more impressed with the distinction than with the beauty of his face. It was because his features were so regular, his nose so straight, his brow so broad that he photographed so well. Indeed, from his photographs you would have thought him extremely handsome. He was not that, perhaps because his eyebrows and his eyelashes were pale, and his lips thin, but he looked very intellectual. There was refinement in his face and a spirituality that was oddly moving. That was how you thought a poet should look; and when Anne became engaged to him she told her girl friends who asked her about him that he looked like Shelley. He turned to her now with a little smile in his blue eyes. His smile was very attractive.

"What a perfect day to land in England!"

It was October. They had steamed up the Channel on a grey sea under a grey sky. There was not a breath of wind. The fishing boats seemed to rest on the placid water as though the elements had forever forgotten their old hostility. The coast was incredibly green, but with a bright cosy greenness quite unlike the luxuriant, vehement verdure of Eastern jungles. The red towns they passed here and there were comfortable and homelike. They seemed to welcome the exiles with a smiling friendliness. And when they drew into the estuary of the Thames they saw the rich levels of Essex and in a little while Chalk Church on the Kentish shore, lonely in the midst of weather-beaten trees, and beyond it the woods of Cobham. The sun, red in a faint mist, set on the marshes, and night fell. In the station the arc-lamps shed a light that spotted the darkness with cold hard patches. It was good to see the porters lumbering about in their grubby uniforms and the station-master fat and important in his bowler hat. The stationmaster blew a whistle and waved his arm. Alban stepped into the carriage and seated himself in the corner opposite to Anne. The train started.

"We're due in London at six-ten," said Alban. "We ought to get to Jermyn Street by seven. That'll give us an hour to bath and change and we can get to the Savoy for dinner by eight-thirty. A bottle of pop to-night, my pet, and a slap-up dinner." He gave a chuckle. "I heard the Strouds and the Maundys arranging to meet at the Trocadero Grill-Room."

He took up the papers and asked if she wanted any of them. Anne shook her head.

"Tired?" he smiled.

"No."

"Excited?"

In order not to answer she gave a little laugh. He

began to look at the papers, starting with the publish-
ers' advertisements, and she was conscious of the intense
satisfaction it was to him to feel himself through them
once more in the middle of things. They had taken in
those same papers in Sondurah, but they arrived six
weeks old, and though they kept them abreast of what
was going on in the world that interested them both,
they emphasised their exile. But these were fresh from
the press. They smelt different. They had a crispness
that was almost voluptuous. He wanted to read them
all at once. Anne looked out of the window. The country was dark, and she could see little but the lights of
their carriage reflected on the glass, but very soon the
town encroached upon it, and then she saw little sordid
houses, mile upon mile of them, with a light in a window here and there, and the chimneys made a dreary
pattern against the sky. They passed through Barking
and East Ham and Bromley—it was silly that the name
on the platform as they went through the station should
give her such a tremor—and then Stepney. Alban put
down his papers.

"We shall be there in five minutes now."

He put on his hat and took down from the racks the
things the porter had put in them. He looked at her
with shining eyes and his lips twitched. She saw that
he was only just able to control his emotion. He looked
out of the window, too, and they passed over brightly
lighted thoroughfares, close packed with tram-cars,
buses and motor-vans, and they saw the streets thick
with people. What a mob! The shops were all lit up.
They saw the hawkers with their barrows at the curb.

"London," he said.

He took her hand and gently pressed it. His smile was so sweet that she had to say something. She tried to be facetious.

"Does it make you feel all funny inside?"

"I don't know if I want to cry or if I want to be sick."

Fenchurch Street. He lowered the window and waved his arm for a porter. With a grinding of brakes the train came to a standstill. A porter opened the door and Alban handed him out one package after another. Then in his polite way, having jumped out, he gave his hand to Anne to help her down to the platform. The porter went to fetch a barrow and they stood by the pile of their luggage. Alban waved to two passengers from the ship who passed them. The man nodded stiffly.

"What a comfort it is that we shall never have to be civil to those awful people any more," said Alban lightly.

Anne gave him a quick glance. He was really incomprehensible. The porter came back with his barrow, the luggage was put on and they followed him to collect their trunks. Alban took his wife's arm and pressed it.

"The smell of London. By God, it's grand."

He rejoiced in the noise and the bustle, and the crowd of people who jostled them; the radiance of the arc-lamps and the black shadows they cast, sharp but full-toned, gave him a sense of elation. They got out into the street and the porter went off to get them a taxi. Alban's eyes glittered as he looked at the buses and the policemen trying to direct the confusion. His distinguished face bore a look of something like inspiration. The taxi came. Their luggage was stowed away and piled up beside the driver, Alban gave the porter half-

a-crown, and they drove off. They turned down **Grace-**
church Street and in Cannon Street were held up by
a block in the traffic. Alban laughed out loud.

"What's the matter?" said Anne.

"I'm so excited."

They went along the Embankment. It was relatively
quiet there. Taxis and cars passed them. The bells of
the trams were music in his ears. At Westminster Bridge
they cut across Parliament Square and drove through
the green silence of St. James's Park. They had engaged
a room at a hotel just off Jermyn Street. The reception
clerk took them upstairs and a porter brought up their
luggage. It was a room with twin beds and a bathroom.

"This looks all right," said Alban. "It'll do us till we
can find a flat or something."

He looked at his watch.

"Look here, darling, we shall only fall over one another if we try to unpack together. We've got oodles of
time and it'll take you longer to get straight and dress
than me. I'll clear out. I want to go to the club and see
if there's any mail for me. I've got my dinner-jacket
in my suit-case and it'll only take me twenty minutes
to have a bath and dress. Does that suit you?"

"Yes. That's all right."

"I'll be back in an hour."

"Very well."

He took out of his pocket the little comb he always
carried and passed it through his long fair hair. Then
he put on his hat. He gave himself a glance in the mirror.

"Shall I turn on the bath for you?"

"No, don't bother."

"All right. So long."

He went out.

When he was gone Anne took her dressing-case and her hat-box and put them on the top of her trunk. Then she rang the bell. She did not take off her hat. She sat down and lit a cigarette. When a servant answered the bell she asked for the porter. He came. She pointed to the luggage.

"Will you take those things and leave them in the hall for the present. I'll tell you what to do with them presently."

"Very good, ma'am."

She gave him a florin. He took the trunk out and the other packages and closed the door behind him. A few tears slid down Anne's cheeks, but she shook herself; she dried her eyes and powdered her face. She needed all her calm. She was glad that Alban had conceived the idea of going to his club. It made things easier and gave her a little time to think them out.

Now that the moment had come to do what she had for weeks determined, now that she must say the terrible things she had to say, she quailed. Her heart sank. She knew exactly what she meant to say to Alban, she had made up her mind about that long ago, and had said the very words to herself a hundred times, three or four times a day every day of the long journey from Singapore, but she was afraid that she would grow confused. She dreaded an argument. The thought of a scene made her feel slightly sick. It was something at all events to have an hour in which to collect herself. He would say she was heartless and cruel and unreasonable. She could not help it.

"No, no, no," she cried aloud.

She shuddered with horror. And all at once she saw herself again in the bungalow, sitting as she had been sitting when the whole thing started. It was getting on towards tiffin time and in a few minutes Alban would be back from the office. It gave her pleasure to reflect that it was an attractive room for him to come back to, the large verandah which was their parlour, and she knew that though they had been there eighteen months he was still alive to the success she had made of it. The jalousies were drawn now against the midday sun and the mellowed light filtering through them gave an impression of cool silence. Anne was house-proud, and though they were moved from district to district according to the exigencies of the Service and seldom stayed anywhere very long, at each new post she started with new enthusiasm to make their house cosy and charming. It amused her to devise fresh schemes of decoration. She was very modern. People were surprised because there were no knick-knacks. They were taken aback by the bold colour of her curtains and they could not at all make out the tinted reproductions of pictures by Marie Laurencin and Gauguin in silvered frames which were placed on the walls with such cunning skill. She was conscious that few of them quite approved and the good ladies of Port Wallace and Pemberton thought such arrangements odd, affected and out of place; but this left her calm. They would learn. It did them good to get a bit of a jolt. And now she looked round the long, spacious verandah with the complacent sigh of the artist satisfied with his work. It was gay. It was bare. It was restful. It refreshed the spirit and gently excited the fancy. Three immense bowls of yellow cannas completed the colour scheme. Her eyes lingered for a moment on the bookshelves filled with books; that was another thing that disconcerted the colony, all the books they had, and strange books too, heavy they thought them for the most part; and she gave them a little affectionate look as though they were living things. Then she gave the piano a glance. A piece of music was still open on the rack, it was something of Debussy, and Alban had been playing it before he went to the office.

Her friends in the colony had condoled with her when Alban was appointed D.O. at Daktar, for it was the most isolated district in Sondurah. It was connected with the town which was the headquarters of the government neither by telegraph nor telephone. But she liked it. They had been there for some time and she hoped they would remain till Alban went home on leave in another twelve months. It was as large as an English county, with a long coast line, and the sea was dotted with little islands. A broad, winding river ran through it and on each side of this stretched hills densely covered with virgin forest. The station, a good way up the river, consisted of a row of Chinese shops and a little native village nestling amid coconut trees, the District Office, the D.O.'s bungalow, the Clerk's quarters and the barracks. Their only neighbours were the manager of a rubber estate a few miles up the river and the manager and his assistant, Dutchmen both, of a timber camp on one of the river's tributaries. The rubber estate's launch went up and down twice a month and was their only means of regular communication with the outside world. But though they were lonely they were not dull. Their days were full. Their ponies waited for them at dawn and they rode while the day was still fresh and in the bridle-paths through the jungle lingered the mystery of the tropical night. They came back, bathed, changed and had breakfast, and Alban went to the office. Anne spent the morning writing letters and working. She had fallen in love with the country from the first day she arrived in it and had taken pains to master the common language spoken. Her imagination was inflamed by the stories she heard of love and jealousy and death. She was told romantic tales of a time that was only just past. She sought to steep herself in the lore of those strange people. Both she and Alban read a great deal. They had for the country a considerable library and new books came from London by nearly every mail. Little that was noteworthy escaped them. Alban was fond of playing the piano. For an amateur he played very well. He had studied rather seriously, and he had an agreeable touch and a good ear; he could read music with ease, and it was always a pleasure to Anne to sit by him and follow the score when he tried something new. But their great delight was to tour the district. Sometimes they would be away for a fortnight at a time. They would go down the river in a prahu and then sail from one little island to another, bathe in the sea, and fish, or else row upstream till it grew shallow and the trees on either bank were so close to one another that you only saw a slim strip of sky between. Here the boatmen had to pole and they would spend the night in a native house. They bathed in a river pool so clear that you could see the sand shining silver at the bottom and the spot was so lovely, so peaceful and remote, that you felt you could stay there for ever. Sometimes, on the other hand, they would tramp for days along the jungle paths, sleeping under canvas, and notwithstanding the mosquitoes that tormented them and the leeches that sucked their blood, enjoy every moment. Who ever slept so well as on a camp bed? And then there was the gladness of getting back, the delight in the comfort of the well-ordered establishment, the mail that had arrived with letters from home and all the papers, and the piano.

Alban would sit down to it then, his fingers itching to feel the keys, and in what he played, Stravinsky, Ravel, Darius Miehaud, she seemed to feel that he put in something of his own, the sounds of the jungle at night, dawn over the estuary, the starry nights, and the crystal clearness of the forest pools.

Sometimes the rain fell in sheets for days at a time. Then Alban worked at Chinese. He was learning it so that he could communicate with the Chinese of the country in their own language, and Anne did the thousand and one things for which she had not had time before. Those days brought them even more closely together; they always had plenty to talk about, and when they were occupied with their separate affairs they were pleased to feel in their bones that they were near to one another. They were wonderfully united. The rainy days that shut them up within the walls of the bungalow made them feel as if they were one body in face of the world.

On occasion they went to Port Wallace. It was a change, but Anne was always glad to get home. She was never quite at her ease there. She was conscious that none of the people they met liked Alban. They were very ordinary people, middle-class and suburban and dull, without any of the intellectual interests that made life so full and varied to Alban and her, and many of them were narrow-minded and ill-natured; but since they had to pass the better part of their lives in contact with them, it was tiresome that they should feel so unkindly towards Alban. They said he was conceited. He was always very pleasant with them, but she was aware that they resented his cordiality. When he tried to be jovial they said he was putting on airs, and when he chaffed them they thought he was being funny at their expense.

Once they stayed at Government House, and Mrs. Hannay, the Governor's wife, who liked her, talked to her about it. Perhaps the Governor had suggested that she should give Anne a hint.

"You know, my dear, it's a pity your husband doesn't try to be more come-hither with people. He's very intelligent; don't you think it would be better if he didn't let others see he knows it quite so clearly? My husband said to me only yesterday: of course I know that Alban Torel is the cleverest young man in the Service, but he does manage to put my back up more than anyone I know. I am the Governor, but when he talks to me he always gives me the impression that he looks upon me as a damned fool."

The worst of it was that Anne knew how low an opinion Alban had of the Governor's parts.

"He doesn't mean to be superior," Anne answered, smiling. "And he really isn't in the least conceited. I think it's only because he has a straight nose and high cheek-bones."

"You know, they don't like him at the club. They call him Powder-Puff Percy."

Anne flushed. She had heard that before and it made her very angry. Her eyes filled with tears.

"I think it's frightfully unfair."

Mrs. Hannay took her hand and gave it an affectionate little squeeze.

"My dear, you know I don't want to hurt your feelings. Your husband can't help rising very high in the Service. He'd make things so much easier for himself if he were a little more human. Why doesn't he play football?"

"It's not his game. He's always only too glad to play tennis."

"He doesn't give that impression. He gives the impression that there's no one here who's worth his while to play with."

"Well, there isn't," said Anne, stung.

Alban happened to be an extremely good tennis player. He had played a lot of tournaments in England and Anne knew that it gave him a grim satisfaction to knock those beefy, hearty men all over the court. He could make the best of them look foolish. He could be maddening on the tennis court and Anne was aware that sometimes he could not resist the temptation.

"He does play to the gallery, doesn't he?" said Mrs. Hannay.

"I don't think so. Believe me, Alban has no idea he isn't popular. As far as I can see he's always pleasant and friendly with everybody."

"It's then he's most offensive," said Mrs. Hannay dryly.

"I know people don't like us very much," said Anne, smiling a little. "I'm very sorry, but really I don't know what we can do about it."

"Not you, my dear," cried Mrs. Hannay. "Everybody adores you. That's why they put up with your husband. My dear, who could help liking you?"

"I don't know why they should adore me," said Anne. But she did not say it quite sincerely. She was deliberately playing the part of the dear little woman and within her she bubbled with amusement. They disliked Alban because he had such an air of distinction, and because he was interested in art and literature; they did not understand these things and so thought them unmanly; and they disliked him because his capacity was greater than theirs. They disliked him because he was better bred than they. They thought him superior; well, he was superior, but not in the sense they meant. They forgave her because she was an ugly little thing. That was what she called herself, but she wasn't that, or if she was it was with an ugliness that was most attractive. She was like a little monkey, but a very sweet little monkey and very human. She had a neat figure. That was her best point. That and her eyes. They were very large, of a deep brown, liquid and shining; they were full of fun, but they could be tender on occasion with a charming sympathy. She was dark, her frizzy hair was almost black, and her skin was swarthy; she had a small fleshy nose, with large nostrils, and much too big a mouth. But she was alert and vivacious. She could talk with a show of real interest to the ladies of the colony about their husbands and their servants and their children in England, and she could listen appreciatively to the men who told her stories that she had often heard before. They thought her a jolly good sort. They did not know what clever fun she made of them in private. It never occurred to them that she thought them narrow, gross and pretentious. They found no glamour in the East because they looked at it vulgarly with material eyes. Romance lingered at their threshold and they drove it away like an importunate beggar. She was aloof. She repeated to herself Landor's line:

"Nature I loved, and next to nature, art."

She reflected on her conversation with Mrs. Hannay, but on the whole it left her unconcerned. She wondered whether she should say anything about it to Alban; it had always seemed a little odd to her that he should be so little aware of his unpopularity; but she was afraid that if she told him of it he would become self-conscious.

He never noticed the coldness of the men at the club. He made them feel shy and therefore uncomfortable. His appearance there caused a sort of awkwardness, but he, happily insensible, was breezily cordial to all and sundry. The fact was that he was strangely unconscious of other people. She was in a class by herself, she and a little group of friends they had in London, but he could never quite realise that the people of the colony, the government officials and the planters and their wives, were human beings. They were to him like pawns in a game. He laughed with them, chaffed them, and was amiably tolerant of them; with a chuckle Anne told herself that he was rather like a master of a preparatory school taking little boys out on a picnic and anxious to give them a good time.

She was afraid it wasn't much good telling Alban. He

was incapable of the dissimulation which, she happily realised, came so easily to her. What was one to do with these people? The men had come out to the colony as lads from second-rate schools, and life had taught them nothing. At fifty they had the outlook of hobble-dehoys. Most of them drank a great deal too much. They read nothing worth reading. Their ambition was to be like everybody else. Their highest praise was to say that a man was a damned good sort. If you were interested in the things of the spirit you were a prig. They were eaten up with envy of one another and devoured by petty jealousies. And the women, poor things, were obsessed by petty rivalries. They made a circle that was more provincial than any in the smallest town in England. They were prudish and spiteful. What did it matter if they did not like Alban? They would have to put up with him because his ability was so great. He was clever and energetic. They could not say that he did not do his work well. He had been successful in every post he had occupied. With his sensitiveness and his imagination he understood the native mind and he was able to get the natives to do things that no one in his position could. He had a gift for languages, and he spoke all the local dialects. He knew not only the common tongue that most of the government officials spoke, but was acquainted with the niceties of the language and on occasion could make use of a ceremonial speech that flattered and impressed the chiefs. He had a gift for organisation. He was not afraid of responsibility. In due course he was bound to be made a Resident. Alban had some interest in England; his father was a brigadier-general killed in the war, and though he had no private means he had influential friends. He spoke of them with pleasant irony.

"The great advantage of democratic government," he said, "is that merit, with influence to back it, can be pretty sure of receiving its due reward."

Alban was so obviously the ablest man in the Service that there seemed no reason why he should not eventually be made Governor. Then, thought Anne, his air of superiority, of which they complained, would be in place. They would accept him as their master and he would know how to make himself respected and obeyed. The position she foresaw did not dazzle her. She accepted it as their right. It would be fun for Alban to be Governor and for her to be the Governor's wife. And what an opportunity! They were sheep, the government servants and the planters; when Government House was the seat of culture they would soon fall into line. When the best way to the Governor's favour was to be intelligent, intelligence would become the fashion. She and Alban would cherish the native arts and collect carefully the memorials of a vanished past. The country would make an advance it had never dreamed of. They would develop it, but along lines of order and beauty. They would instil into their subordinates a passion for that beautiful land and a loving interest in these romantic races. They would make them realise what music meant. They would cultivate literature. They would create beauty. It would be the golden age.

Suddenly she heard Alban's footstep. Anne awoke from her day-dream. All that was far away in the future. Alban was only a District Officer yet and what was important was the life they were living now. She heard

Alban go into the bath-house and splash water over himself. In a minute he came in. He had changed into a shirt and shorts. His fair hair was still wet.

"Tiffin ready?" he asked.

"Yes."

He sat down at the piano and played the piece that he had played in the morning. The silvery notes cascaded coolly down the sultry air. You had an impression of a formal garden with great trees and elegant pieces of artificial water and of leisurely walks bordered with pseudo-classical statues. Alban played with an exquisite delicacy. Lunch was announced by the head boy. He rose from the piano and gave her his hand. They walked into the dining-room hand in hand. A punkah lazily fanned the air. Anne gave the table a glance. With its bright-coloured tablecloth and the amusing plates it looked very gay.

"Anything exciting at the office this morning?" she asked.

"No, nothing much. A buffalo case. Oh, and Prynne has sent along to ask me to go up to the estate. Some coolies have been damaging the trees and he wants me to come along and look into it."

Prynne was manager of the rubber estate up the river and now and then they spent a night with him. Sometimes when he wanted a change he came down to dinner and slept at the D.O.'s bungalow. They both liked him. He was a man of five and thirty, with a red face, with deep furrows in it, and very black hair. He was quite uneducated, but cheerful and easy, and being the only Englishman within two days' journey they could not but be friendly with him. He had been a little shy of them at first. News spreads quickly in the East and long before they arrived in the district he heard that they were highbrows. He did not know what he would make of them. He probably did not know that he had charm, which makes up for many more commendable qualities, and Alban with his almost feminine sensibilities was peculiarly susceptible to this. He found Alban much more human than he expected, and of course Anne was stunning. Alban played ragtime for him, which he would not have done for the Governor, and played dominoes with him. When Alban was making his first tour of the district with Anne, and suggested that they would like to spend a couple of nights on the estate, he had thought it as well to warn him that he lived with a native woman and had two children by her. He would do his best to keep them out of Anne's sight, but he could not send them away, there was nowhere to send them. Alban laughed.

"Anne isn't that sort of woman at all. Don't dream of hiding them. She loves children."

Anne quickly made friends with the shy, pretty little native woman and soon was playing happily with the children. She and the girl had long confidential chats. The children took a fancy to her. She brought them lovely toys from Port Wallace. Prynne, comparing her smiling tolerance with the disapproving acidity of the other white women in the colony, described himself as knocked all of a heap. He could not do enough to show his delight and gratitude.

"If all highbrows are like you," he said, "give me highbrows every time."

He hated to think that in another year they would

leave the district for good and the chances were that, if the next D.O. was married, his wife would think it dreadful that, rather than live alone, he had a native woman to live with him and, what was more, was much attached to her.

But there had been a good deal of discontent on the estate of late. The coolies were Chinese and infected with communist ideas. They were disorderly. Alban had been obliged to sentence several of them for various crimes to terms of imprisonment.

"Prynne tells me that as soon as their term is up he's going to send them all back to China and get Javanese instead," said Alban. "I'm sure he's right. They're much more amenable."

"You don't think there's going to be any serious trouble?"

"Oh, no. Prynne knows his job and he's a pretty determined fellow. He wouldn't put up with any nonsense and with me and our policemen to back him up I don't imagine they'll try any monkey tricks." He smiled. "The iron hand in the velvet glove."

The words were barely out of his mouth when a sudden shouting arose. There was a commotion and the sound of steps. Loud voices and cries.

"Tuan, Tuan."

"What the devil's the matter?"

Alban sprang from his chair and went swiftly on to the verandah. Anne followed him. At the bottom of the steps was a group of natives. There was the sergeant, and three or four policemen, boatmen and several men from the kampong.

"What is it?" called Alban.

Two or three shouted back in answer. The sergeant pushed others aside and Alban saw lying on the ground a man in a shirt and khaki shorts. He ran down the steps. He recognised the man as the assistant manager of Prynne's estate. He was a half-caste. His shorts were covered with blood and there was clotted blood all over one side of his face and head. He was unconscious.

"Bring him up here," called Anne.

Alban gave an order. The man was lifted up and carried on to the verandah. They laid him on the floor and Anne put a pillow under his head. She sent for water and for the medicine-chest in which they kept things for emergency.

"Is he dead?" asked Alban.

"No."

"Better try to give him some brandy."

The boatmen brought ghastly news. The Chinese coolies had arisen suddenly and attacked the manager's office. Prynne was killed and the assistant manager, Oakley by name, had escaped only by the skin of his teeth. He had come upon the rioters when they were looting the office, he had seen Prynne's body thrown out of the window, and had taken to his heels. Some of the Chinese saw him and gave chase. He ran for the river and was wounded as he jumped into the launch. The launch managed to put off before the Chinese could get on board and they had come down stream for help as fast as they could go. As they went they saw flames rising from the office buildings. There was no doubt that the coolies had burned down everything that would burn.

Oakley gave a groan and opened his eyes. He was a

little, dark-skinned man, with flattened features and thick coarse hair. His great native eyes were filled with terror.

"You're all right," said Anne. "You're quite safe."

He gave a sigh and smiled. Anne washed his face and swobbed it with antiseptics. The wound on his head was not serious.

"Can you speak yet?" said Alban.

"Wait a bit," she said. "We must look at his leg."

Alban ordered the sergeant to get the crowd out of the verandah. Anne ripped up one leg of the shorts. The material was clinging to the coagulated wound.

"I've been bleeding like a pig," said Oakley.

It was only a flesh wound. Alban was clever with his fingers, and though the blood began to flow again they stanched it. Alban put on a dressing and a bandage. The sergeant and a policeman lifted Oakley on to a long chair. Alban gave him a brandy and soda, and soon he felt strong enough to speak. He knew no more than the boatmen had already told. Prynne was dead and the estate was in flames.

"And the girl and the children?" asked Anne.

"I don't know."

"Oh, Alban."

"I must turn out the police. Are you sure Prynne is dead?"

"Yes, sir. I saw him."

"Have the rioters got fire-arms?"

"I don't know, sir."

"How d'you mean, you don't know?" Alban cried irritably. "Prynne had a gun, hadn't he?"

"Yes, sir."

"There must have been more on the estate. You had one, didn't you? The head overseer had one."

The half-caste was silent. Alban looked at him sternly.

"How many of those damned Chinese are there?"

"A hundred and fifty."

Anne wondered that he asked so many questions. It seemed waste of time. The important thing was to collect coolies for the transport up river, prepare the boats and issue ammunition to the police.

"How many policemen have you got, sir?" asked Oakley.

"Eight and the sergeant."

"Could I come too? That would make ten of us. I'm sure I shall be all right now I'm bandaged."

"I'm not going," said Alban.

"Alban, you must," cried Anne. She could not believe her ears.

"Nonsense. It would be madness. Oakley's obviously useless. He's sure to have a temperature in a few hours. He'd only be in the way. That leaves nine guns. There are a hundred and fifty Chinese and they've got firearms and all the ammunition in the world."

"How d'you know?"

"It stands to reason they wouldn't have started a show like this unless they had. It would be idiotic to go."

Anne stared at him with open mouth. Oakley's eyes were puzzled.

"What are you going to do?"

"Well, fortunately we've got the launch. I'll send it to Port Wallace with a request for reinforcements."

"But they won't be here for two days at least."

"Well, what of it? Prynne's dead and the estate

burned to the ground. We couldn't do any good by going up now. I shall send a native to reconnoitre so that we can find out exactly what the rioters are doing." He gave Anne his charming smile. "Believe me, my pet, the rascals won't lose anything by waiting a day or two for what's coming to them."

Oakley opened his mouth to speak, but perhaps he hadn't the nerve. He was a half-caste assistant manager and Alban, the D.O., represented the power of the Government. But the man's eyes sought Anne's and she thought she read in them an earnest and personal appeal.

"But in two days they're capable of committing the most frightful atrocities," she cried. "It's quite unspeakable what they may do."

"Whatever damage they do they'll pay for. I promise you that."

"Oh, Alban, you can't sit still and do nothing. I beseech you to go yourself at once."

"Don't be so silly. I can't quell a riot with eight policemen and a sergeant. I haven't got the right to take a risk of that sort. We'd have to go in boats. You don't think we could get up unobserved. The lalang along the banks is perfect cover and they could just take pot shots at us as we came along. We shouldn't have a chance."

"I'm afraid they'll only think it weakness if nothing is done for two days, sir," said Oakley.

"When I want your opinion I'll ask for it," said Alban acidly. "So far as I can see when there was danger the only thing you did was to cut and run. I can't persuade myself that your assistance in a crisis would be very valuable."

The half-caste reddened. He said nothing more. He looked straight in front of him with troubled eyes.

"I'm going down to the office," said Alban. "I'll just write a short report and send it down the river by launch at once."

He gave an order to the sergeant who had been standing all this time stiffly at the top of the steps. He saluted and ran off. Alban went into a little hall they had to get his topi. Anne swiftly followed him.

"Alban, for God's sake listen to me a minute," she whispered.

"I don't want to be rude to you, darling, but I am pressed for time. I think you'd much better mind your own business."

"You can't do nothing, Alban. You must go. Whatever the risk."

"Don't be such a fool," he said angrily.

He had never been angry with her before. She seized his hand to hold him back.

"I tell you I can do no good by going."

"You don't know. There's the woman and Prynne's children. We must do something to save them. Let me come with you. They'll kill them."

"They've probably killed them already."

"Oh, how can you be so callous! If there's a chance of saving them it's your duty to try."

"It's my duty to act like a reasonable human being. I'm not going to risk my life and my policemen's for the sake of a native woman and her half-caste brats. What sort of a damned fool do you take me for?"

"They'll say you were afraid."

"Who?"

"Everyone in the colony."

He smiled disdainfully.

"If you only knew what a complete contempt I have for the opinion of everyone in the colony."

She gave him a long searching look. She had been married to him for eight years and she knew every expression of his face and every thought in his mind. She stared into his blue eyes as if they were open windows. She suddenly went quite pale. She dropped his hand and turned away. Without another word she went back on to the verandah. Her ugly little monkey face was a mask of horror.

Alban went to his office, wrote a brief account of the facts, and in a few minutes the motor launch was pounding down the river.

The next two days were endless. Escaped nahois brought them news of happenings on the estate. But from their excited and terrified stories it was impossible to get an exact impression of the truth. There had been a good deal of bloodshed. The head overseer had been killed. They brought wild tales of cruelty and outrage. Anne could hear nothing of Prynne's woman and the two children. She shuddered when she thought of what might have been their fate. Alban collected as many natives as he could. They were armed with spears and swords. He commandeered boats. The situation was serious, but he kept his head. He felt that he had done all that was possible and nothing remained but for him to carry on normally. He did his official work. He played the piano a great deal. He rode with Anne in the early morning. He appeared to have forgotten that they had had the first serious difference of opinion in the whole of their married life. He took it that Anne had accepted the wisdom of his decision. He was as amusing, cordial and gay with her as he had always been. When he spoke of the rioters it was with grim irony: when the time came to settle matters a good many of them would wish they had never been born.

"What'll happen to them?" asked Anne.

"Oh, they'll hang." He gave a shrug of distaste. "I hate having to be present at executions. It always makes me feel rather sick."

He was very sympathetic to Oakley, whom they had put to bed and whom Anne was nursing. Perhaps he was sorry that in the exasperation of the moment he had spoken to him offensively, and he went out of his way to be nice to him.

Then on the afternoon of the third day, when they were drinking their coffee after luncheon, Alban's quick ears caught the sound of a motor boat approaching. At the same moment a policeman ran up to say that the government launch was sighted.

"At last," cried Alban.

He bolted out of the house. Anne raised one of the jalousies and looked out at the river. Now the sound was quite loud and in a moment she saw the boat come round the bend. She saw Alban on the landing-stage. He got into a prahu and as the launch dropped her anchor he went on board. She told Oakley that the reinforcements had come.

"Will the D.O. go up with them when they attack?" he asked her.

"Naturally," said Anne coldly.

"I wondered."

Anne felt a strange feeling in her heart. For the last two days she had had to exercise all her self-control not to cry. She did not answer. She went out of the room.

A quarter of an hour later Alban returned to the bungalow with the captain of constabulary who had been sent with twenty Sikhs to deal with the rioters. Captain Stratton was a little red-faced man with a red moustache and bow legs, very hearty and dashing, whom she had met often at Port Wallace.

"Well, Mrs. Torel, this is a pretty kettle of fish," he cried, as he shook hands with her, in a loud jolly voice. "Here I am, with my army all full of pep and ready for a scrap. Up, boys, and at 'em. Have you got anything to drink in this benighted place?"

"Boy," she cried, smiling.

"Something long and cool and faintly alcoholic, and then I'm ready to discuss the plan of campaign."

His breeziness was very comforting. It blew away the sullen apprehension that had seemed ever since the disaster to brood over the lost peace of the bungalow. The boy came in with a tray and Stratton mixed himself a stengah. Alban put him in possession of the facts. He told them clearly, briefly and with precision.

"I must say I admire you," said Stratton. "In your place I should never have been able to resist the temptation to take my eight cops and have a whack at the blighters myself."

"I thought it was a perfectly unjustifiable risk to take."

"Safety first, old boy, eh, what?" said Stratton jovially. "I'm jolly glad you didn't. It's not often we get the chance of a scrap. It would have been a dirty trick to keep the whole show to yourself."

Captain Stratton was all for steaming straight up the river and attacking at once, but Alban pointed out to him the inadvisability of such a course. The sound of the approaching launch would warn the rioters. The long grass at the river's edge offered them cover and they had enough guns to make a landing difficult. It seemed useless to expose the attacking force to their fire. It was silly to forget that they had to face a hundred and fifty desperate men and it would be easy to fall into an ambush. Alban expounded his own plan. Stratton listened to it. He nodded now and then. The plan was evidently a good one. It would enable them to take the rioters on the rear, surprise them, and in all probability finish the job without a single casualty. He would have been a fool not to accept it.

"But why didn't you do that yourself?" asked Stratton.

"With eight men and a sergeant?"

Stratton did not answer.

"Anyhow it's not a bad idea and we'll settle on it. It gives us plenty of time, so with your permission, Mrs. Torel, I'll have a bath."

They set out at sunset, Captain Stratton and his twenty Sikhs, Alban with his policemen and the natives he had collected. The night was dark and moonless. Trailing behind them were the dug-outs that Alban had gathered together and into which after a certain distance they proposed to transfer their force. It was important that no sound should give warning of their approach. After they had gone for about three hours by launch they took to the dug-outs and in them silently paddled up stream. They reached the border of the vast estate and landed. Guides led them along a path so narrow that they had to march in single file. It had been long unused and the going was heavy. They had twice to ford a stream. The path led them circuitously to the rear of the coolie lines, but they did not wish to reach them till nearly dawn and presently Stratton gave the order to halt. It was a long cold wait. At last the night seemed to be less dark; you did not see the trunks of the trees, but were vaguely sensible of them against its darkness. Stratton had been sitting with his back to a tree. He gave a whispered order to a sergeant and in a few minutes the column was once more on the march. Suddenly they found themselves on a road. They formed fours. The dawn broke and in the ghostly light the surrounding objects were wanly visible. The column stopped on a whispered order. They had come in sight of the coolie lines. Silence reigned in them. The column crept on again and again halted. Stratton, his eyes shining, gave Alban a smile.

"We've caught the blighters asleep."

He lined up his men. They inserted cartridges in their guns. He stepped forward and raised his hand. The carbines were pointed at the coolie lines.

"Fire."

There was a rattle as the volley of shots rang out. Then suddenly there was a tremendous din and the Chinese poured out, shouting and waving their arms, but in front of them, to Alban's utter bewilderment, bellowing at the top of his voice and shaking his fist at them, was a white man.

"Who the hell's that?" cried Stratton.

A very big, very fat man, in khaki trousers and a singlet, was running towards them as fast as his fat legs would carry him and as he ran shaking both fists at them and yelling:

"*Smerige flikkers! Verlockte ploerten!*"

"My God, it's Van Hasseldt," said Alban.

This was the Dutch manager of the timber camp which was situated on a considerable tributary of the river about twenty miles away.

"What the hell do you think you're doing?" he puffed as he came up to them.

"How the hell did you get here?" asked Stratton in turn.

He saw that the Chinese were scattering in all directions and gave his men instructions to round them up. Then he turned again to Van Hasseldt.

"What's it mean?"

"Mean? Mean?" shouted the Dutchman furiously. "That's what I want to know. You and your damned policemen. What do you mean by coming here at this hour in the morning and firing a damned volley? Target practice? You might have killed me. Idiots!"

"Have a cigarette," said Stratton.

"How did you get here, Van Hasseldt?" asked Alban again, very much at sea. "This is the force they've sent from Port Wallace to quell the riot."

"How did I get here? I walked. How did you think I got here? Riot be damned. I quelled the riot. If that's what you came for you can take your damned policemen home again. A bullet came within a foot of my head."

"I don't understand," said Alban.

"There's nothing to understand," spluttered Van Hasseldt, still fuming. "Some coolies came to my estate and said the chinks had killed Prynne and burned the bally place down, so I took my assistant and my head overseer and a Dutch friend I had staying with me and came over to see what the trouble was."

Captain Stratton opened his eyes wide.

"Did you just stroll in as if it was a picnic?" he asked.

"Well, you don't think after all the years I've been in this country I'm going to let a couple of hundred chinks put the fear of God into me? I found them all scared out of their lives. One of them had the nerve to pull a gun on me and I blew his bloody brains out. And the rest surrendered. I've got the leaders tied up. I was going to send a boat down to you this morning to come up and get them."

Stratton stared at him for a minute and then burst into a shout of laughter. He laughed till the tears ran down his face. The Dutchman looked at him angrily, then began to laugh too; he laughed with the big belly laugh of a very fat man and his coils of fat heaved and shook. Alban watched them sullenly. He was very angry.

"What about Prynne's girl and the kids?" he asked.

"Oh, they got away all right."

It just showed how wise he had been not to let himself be influenced by Anne's hysteria. Of course the children had come to no harm. He never thought they would.

Van Hasseldt and his little party started back for the timber camp, and as soon after as possible Stratton embarked his twenty Sikhs and leaving Alban with his sergeant and his policemen to deal with the situation

departed for Port Wallace. Alban gave him a brief report for the Governor. There was much for him to do.
It looked as though he would have to stay for a considerable time; but since every house on the estate had
been burned to the ground and he was obliged to install
himself in the coolie lines he thought it better that Anne
should not join him. He sent her a note to that effect.
He was glad to be able to reassure her of the safety of
poor Prynne's girl. He set to work at once to make his
preliminary enquiry. He examined a host of witnesses.
But a week later he received an order to go to Port
Wallace at once. The launch that brought it was to take
him and he was able to see Anne on the way down for
no more than an hour. Alban was a trifle vexed.

"I don't know why the Governor can't leave me to
get things straight without dragging me off like this.
It's extremely inconvenient."

"Oh, well, the Government never bothers very much
about the convenience of its subordinates, does it?"
smiled Anne.

"It's just red tape. I would offer to take you along,
darling, only I shan't stay a minute longer than I need.
I want to get my evidence together for the Sessions
Court as soon as possible. I think in a country like this
it's very important that justice should be prompt."

When the launch came in to Port Wallace one of the
harbour police told him that the harbour-master had a
chit for him. It was from the Governor's secretary and
informed him that His Excellency desired to see him
as soon as convenient after his arrival. It was ten in the
morning. Alban went to the club, had a bath and shaved,
and then in clean ducks, his hair neatly brushed, he

called a rickshaw and told the boy to take him to the Governor's office. He was at once shown in to the secretary's room. The secretary shook hands with him.

"I'll tell H.E. you're here," he said. "Won't you sit down?"

The secretary left the room and in a little while came back.

"H.E. will see you in a minute. Do you mind if I get on with my letters?"

Alban smiled. The secretary was not exactly come-hither. He waited, smoking a cigarette, and amused himself with his own thoughts. He was making a good job of the preliminary enquiry. It interested him. Then an orderly came in and told Alban that the Governor was ready for him. He rose from his seat and followed him into the Governor's room.

"Good-morning, Torel."

"Good-morning, sir."

The Governor was sitting at a large desk. He nodded to Alban and motioned to him to take a seat. The Governor was all grey. His hair was grey, his face, his eyes; he looked as though the tropical suns had washed the colour out of him; he had been in the country for thirty years and had risen one by one through all the ranks of the Service; he looked tired and depressed. Even his voice was grey. Alban liked him because he was quiet; he did not think him clever, but he had an unrivalled knowledge of the country, and his great experience was a very good substitute for intelligence. He looked at Alban for a full moment without speaking and the odd idea came to Alban that he was embarrassed. He very nearly gave him a lead.

"I saw Van Hasseldt yesterday," said the Governor suddenly.

"Yes, sir?'

"Will you give me your account of the occurrences at the Alud Estate and of the steps you took to deal with them."

Alban had an orderly mind. He was self-possessed. He marshalled his facts well and was able to state them with precision. He chose his words with care and spoke them fluently.

"You had a sergeant and eight policemen. Why did you not immediately go to the scene of the disturbance?"

"I thought the risk was unjustifiable."

A thin smile was outlined on the Governor's grey face.

"If the officers of this government had hesitated to take unjustifiable risks it would never have become a province of the British Empire."

Alban was silent. It was difficult to talk to a man who spoke obvious nonsense.

"I am anxious to hear your reasons for the decision you took."

Alban gave them coolly. He was quite convinced of the rightness of his action. He repeated, but more fully, what he had said in the first place to Anne. The Governor listened attentively.

"Van Hasseldt, with his manager, a Dutch friend of his, and a native overseer, seems to have coped with the situation very efficiently," said the Governor.

"He had a lucky break. That doesn't prevent him from being a damned fool. It was madness to do what he did."

"Do you realise that by leaving a Dutch planter to do what you should have done yourself, you have covered the Government with ridicule?"

"No, sir."

"You've made yourself a laughing-stock in the whole colony."

Alban smiled.

"My back is broad enough to bear the ridicule of persons to whose opinion I am entirely indifferent."

"The utility of a government official depends very largely on his prestige, and I'm afraid his prestige is likely to be inconsiderable when he lies under the stigma of cowardice."

Alban flushed a little

"I don't quite know what you mean by that, sir."

"I've gone into the matter very carefully. I've seen Captain Stratton, and Oakley, poor Prynne's assistant, and I've seen Van Hasseldt. I've listened to your defence."

"I didn't know that I was defending myself, sir."

"Be so good as not to interrupt me. I think you committed a grave error of judgment. As it turns out the risk was very small, but whatever it was, I think you should have taken it. In such matters promptness and firmness are essential. It is not for me to conjecture what motive led you to send for a force of constabulary and do nothing till they came. I am afraid, however, that I consider that your usefulness in the Service is no longer very great."

Alban looked at him with astonishment.

"But would you have gone under the circumstances?" he asked him.

"I should."

Alban shrugged his shoulders.

"Don't you believe me?" rapped out the Governor.

"Of course I believe you, sir. But perhaps you will allow me to say that if you had been killed the colony would have suffered an irreparable loss."

The Governor drummed on the table with his fingers. He looked out of the window and then looked again at Alban. When he spoke it was not unkindly.

"I think you are unfitted by temperament for this rather rough and tumble life, Torel. If you'll take my advice you'll go home. With your abilities I feel sure that you'll soon find an occupation much better suited to you."

"I'm afraid I don't understand what you mean, sir."

"Oh, come, Torel, you're not stupid. I'm trying to make things easy for you. For your wife's sake as well as for your own I do not wish you to leave the colony with the stigma of being dismissed from the Service for cowardice. I'm giving you the opportunity of resigning."

"Thank you very much, sir. I'm not prepared to avail myself of the opportunity. If I resign I admit that I committed an error and that the charge you make against me is justified. I don't admit it."

"You can please yourself. I have considered the matter very carefully and I have no doubt about it in my mind. I am forced to discharge you from the Service. The necessary papers will reach you in due course. Meanwhile you will return to your post and hand over to the officer appointed to succeed you on his arrival."

"Very good, sir," replied Alban, a twinkle of amusement in his eyes. "When do you desire me to return to my post?"

"At once."

"Have you any objection to my going to the club and having tiffin before I go?"

The Governor looked at him with surprise. His exasperation was mingled with an unwilling admiration.

"Not at all. I'm sorry, Torel, that this unhappy incident should have deprived the Government of a servant whose zeal has always been so apparent and whose tact, intelligence and industry seemed to point him out in the future for very high office."

"Your Excellency does not read Schiller, I suppose. You are probably not acquainted with his celebrated line: *mit der dummheit kämpfen die Götter selbst vergebens.*"

"What does it mean?"

"Roughly, against stupidity the gods themselves battle in vain."

"Good-morning."

With his head in the air, a smile on his lips, Alban left the Governor's office. The Governor was human, and he had the curiosity to ask his secretary later in the day if Alban Torel had really gone to the club.

"Yes, sir. He had tiffin there."

"It must have wanted some nerve."

Alban entered the club jauntily and joined the group of men standing at the bar. He talked to them in the breezy, cordial tone he always used with them. It was designed to put them at their ease. They had been discussing him ever since Stratton had come back to Port Wallace with his story, sneering at him and laughing at him, and all that had resented his superciliousness, and they were the majority, were triumphant because his pride had had a fall. But they were so taken aback at seeing him now, so confused to find him as confident as ever, that it was they who were embarrassed.

One man, though he knew perfectly, asked him what he was doing in Port Wallace.

"Oh, I came about the riot on the Alud Estate. H.E. wanted to see me. He does not see eye to eye with me about it. The silly old ass has fired me. I'm going home as soon as he appoints a D.O. to take over."

There was a moment of awkwardness. One, more kindly disposed than the others, said:

"I'm awfully sorry."

Alban shrugged his shoulders. "My dear fellow, what can you do with a perfect damned fool? The only thing is to let him stew in his own juice."

When the Governor's secretary had told his chief as much of this as he thought discreet, the Governor smiled.

"Courage is a queer thing. I would rather have shot myself than go to the club just then and face all those fellows."

A fortnight later, having sold to the incoming D.O. all the decorations that Anne had taken so much trouble about, with the rest of their things in packing-cases and trunks, they arrived at Port Wallace to await the local steamer that was to take them to Singapore. The padre's wife invited them to stay with her, but Anne refused; she insisted that they should go to the hotel. An hour after their arrival she received a very kind little letter from the Governor's wife asking her to go and have tea with her. She went. She found Mrs. Hannay alone, but in a minute the Governor joined them. He expressed his regret that she was leaving and told her how sorry he was for the cause.

"It's very kind of you to say that," said Anne, smiling gaily, "but you mustn't think I take it to heart. I'm entirely on Alban's side. I think what he did was absolutely right and if you don't mind my saying so I think you've treated him most unjustly."

"Believe me, I hated having to take the step I took."

"Don't let's talk about it," said Anne.

"What are your plans when you get home?" asked Mrs. Hannay.

Anne began to chat brightly. You would have thought she had not a care in the world. She seemed in great spirits at going home. She was jolly and amusing and made little jokes. When she took leave of the Governor and his wife she thanked them for all their kindness. The Governor escorted her to the door.

The next day but one, after dinner, they went on board the clean and comfortable little ship. The padre and his wife saw them off. When they went into their cabin they found a large parcel on Anne's bunk. It was addressed to Alban. He opened it and saw that it was an immense powder-puff.

"Hullo, I wonder who sent us this," he said, with a laugh. "It must be for you, darling."

Anne gave him a quick look. She went pale. The brutes! How could they be so cruel? She forced herself to smile.

"It's enormous, isn't it? I've never seen such a large powder-puff in my life."

But when he had left the cabin and they were out at sea, she threw it passionately overboard.

And now, now that they were back in London and Sondurah was nine thousand miles away, she clenched her hands as she thought of it. Somehow, it seemed the worst thing of all. It was so wantonly unkind to send that absurd object to Alban, Powder-puff Percy; it showed such a petty spite. Was that their idea of humour? Nothing had hurt her more and even now she felt that it was only by holding on to herself that she could prevent herself from crying. Suddenly she started, for the door opened and Alban came in. She was still sitting in the chair in which he had left her.

"Hullo, why haven't you dressed?" He looked about the room. "You haven't unpacked."

"No."

"Why on earth not?"

"I'm not going to unpack. I'm not going to stay here. I'm leaving you."

"What are you talking about?"

"I've stuck it out till now. I made up my mind I would till we got home. I set my teeth, I've borne more than I thought it possible to bear, but now it's finished. I've done all that could be expected of me. We're back in London now and I can go."

He looked at her in utter bewilderment.

"Are you mad, Anne?"

"Oh, my God, what I've endured! The journey to Singapore, with all the officers knowing, and even the Chinese stewards. And at Singapore, the way people looked at us at the hotel, and the sympathy I had to put **up with**, the bricks they dropped and their embarrassment when they realised what they'd done. My God, I could have killed them. That interminable journey home. There wasn't a single passenger on the ship who didn't know. The contempt they had for you and the kindness they went out of their way to show me. And you so self-complacent and so pleased with yourself, seeing nothing, feeling nothing. You must have the hide of a rhinoceros. The misery of seeing you so chatty and agreeable. Pariahs, that's what we were. You seemed to ask them to snub you. How can anyone be so shameless?"

She was flaming with passion. Now that at last she need not wear the mask of indifference and pride that she had forced herself to assume she cast aside all reserve and all self-control. The words poured from her trembling lips in a virulent stream.

"My dear, how can you be so absurd?" he said good-naturedly, smiling. "You must be very nervous and high-strung to have got such ideas in your head. Why didn't you tell me? You're like a country bumpkin who comes to London and thinks everyone is staring at him. Nobody bothered about us and if they did what on earth did it matter? You ought to have more sense than to bother about what a lot of fools say. And what do you imagine they were saying?"

"They were saying you'd been fired."

"Well, that was true," he laughed.

"They said you were a coward."

"What of it?"

"Well, you see, that was true too."

He looked at her for a moment reflectively. His lips tightened a little.

"And what makes you think so?" he asked acidly.

"I saw it in your eyes, that day the news came, when you refused to go to the estate and I followed you into the hall when you went to fetch your topi. I begged you to go, I felt that whatever the danger you must take it, and suddenly I saw the fear in your eyes. I nearly fainted with the horror."

"I should have been a fool to risk my life to no purpose. Why should I? Nothing that concerned me was at stake. Courage is the obvious virtue of the stupid. I don't attach any particular importance to it."

"How do you mean that nothing that concerned you was at stake? If that's true then your whole life is a sham. You've given away everything you stood for, everything we both stand for. You've let all of us down. We did set ourselves up on a pinnacle, we did think ourselves better than the rest of them because we loved literature and art and music, we weren't content to live a life of ignoble jealousies and vulgar tittle-tattle, we did cherish the things of the spirit, and we loved beauty. It was our food and drink. They laughed at us and sneered at us. That was inevitable. The ignorant and the common naturally hate and fear those who are interested in things they don't understand. We didn't care. We called them Philistines. We despised them and we had a right to despise them. Our justification was that we were better and nobler and wiser and braver than they were. And you weren't better, you weren't nobler, you weren't braver. When the crisis came you slunk away like a whipped cur with his tail between his legs. You of all people hadn't the right to be a coward. They despise *us* now and they have the right to despise

us. Us and all we stood for. Now they can say that art
and beauty are all rot; when it comes to a pinch people
like us always let you down. They never stopped looking
for a chance to turn and rend us and you gave it to them.
They can say that they always expected it. It's a triumph for them. I used to be furious because they called
you Powder-Puff Percy. Did you know they did?"

"Of course. I thought it very vulgar, but it left me
entirely indifferent."

"It's funny that their instinct should have been so
right."

"Do you mean to say you've been harbouring this
against me all these weeks? I should never have thought
you capable of it."

"I couldn't let you down when everyone was against
you. I was too proud for that. Whatever happened I
swore to myself that I'd stick to you till we got home.
It's been torture."

"Don't you love me any more?"

"Love you? I loathe the very sight of you."

"Anne."

"God knows I loved you. For eight years I worshipped the ground you trod on. You were everything
to me. I believed in you as some people believe in God.
When I saw the fear in your eyes that day, when you
told me that you weren't going to risk your life for a
kept woman and her half-caste brats, I was shattered.
It was as though someone had wrenched my heart out
of my body and trampled on it. You killed my love
there and then, Alban. You killed it stone dead. Since
then when you've kissed me I've had to clench my hands
so as not to turn my face away. The mere thought of

anything else makes me feel physically sick. I loathe your complacence and your frightful insensitiveness. Perhaps I could have forgiven it if it had been just a moment's weakness and if afterwards you'd been ashamed. I should have been miserable, but I think my love was so great that I should only have felt pity for you. But you're incapable of shame. And now I believe in nothing. You're only a silly, pretentious, vulgar poseur. I would rather be the wife of a second-rate planter so long as he had the common human virtues of a man than the wife of a fake like you."

He did not answer. Gradually his face began to discompose. Those handsome, regular features of his horribly distorted and suddenly he broke out into loud sobs. She gave a little cry.

"Don't, Alban, don't."

"Oh, darling, how can you be so cruel to me? I adore you. I'd give my whole life to please you. I can't live without you."

She put out her arms as though to ward off a blow.

"No, no, Alban, don't try to move me. I can't. I must go. I can't live with you any more. It would be frightful. I can never forget. I must tell you the truth, I have only contempt for you and repulsion."

He sank down at her feet and tried to cling to her knees. With a gasp she sprang up and he buried his head in the empty chair. He cried painfully with sobs that tore his chest. The sound was horrible. The tears streamed from Anne's eyes and, putting her hands to her ears to shut out that dreadful, hysterical sobbing, blindly stumbling she rushed to the door and ran out.

THE VESSEL OF WRATH

THERE are few books in the world that contain more meat than the Sailing Directions published by the Hydrographic Department by order of the Lords Commissioners of the Admiralty. They are handsome volumes, bound (very flimsily) in cloth of different colours, and the most expensive of them is cheap. For four shillings you can buy the Yangste Kiang Pilot, "containing a description of, and sailing directions for, the Yangste Kiang from the Wusung River to the highest navigable point, including the Han Kiang, the Kialing Kiang, and the Min Kiang"; and for three shillings you can get Part III of the Eastern Archipelago Pilot, "comprising the N.E. end of Celebes, Molucca and Gilolo passages, Banda and Arafura Seas, and North, West, and South-West coasts of New Guinea." But it is not very safe to do so if you are a creature of settled habits that you have no wish to disturb or if you have an occupation that holds you fast to one place. These business-like books take you upon enchanted journeys of the spirit; and their matter-of-fact style, the admirable order, the concision with which the material is set before you, the stern sense of the practical that informs every line, cannot dim the poetry that, like the spice-laden breeze that assails your senses with a more than material languor when you approach some of those magic islands of the Eastern seas, blows, with so sweet a fragrance through the printed pages. They tell you the anchorages and the landing places, what supplies you can get at each spot, and where you can get water; they tell you the lights and buoys, tides, winds and weather that you will find there. They give you brief information about the population and the trade. And it is strange when you think how sedately it is all set down, with no words wasted, that so much else is given you besides. What? Well, mystery and beauty, romance and the glamour of the unknown. It is no common book that offers you casually turning its pages such a paragraph as this: "Supplies. A few jungle fowl are preserved, the island is also the resort of vast numbers of sea birds. Turtle are found in the lagoon, as well as quantities of various fish, including grey mullet, shark, and dog-fish; the seine cannot be used with any effect; but there is a fish which may be taken on a rod. A small store of tinned provisions and spirits is kept in a hut for the relief of shipwrecked persons. Good water may be obtained from a well near the landing place." Can the imagination want more material than this to go on a journey through time and space?

In the volume from which I have copied this passage, the compilers with the same restraint have described the Alas Islands. They are composed of a group or chain of islands, "for the most part low and wooded, extending about 75 miles east and west, and 40 miles north and south." The information about them, you are told, is very slight; there are channels between the different groups, and several vessels have passed through them, but the passages have not been thoroughly explored, and the positions of many of the dangers not yet determined; it is therefore advisable to avoid them. The population of the group is estimated at about 8000, of whom 200 are Chinese and 400 Mohammedans. The rest are heathen. The principal island is called Baru, it is surrounded by a reef, and here lives a Dutch Controleur. His white house with its red roof on the top of a little hill is the most prominent object that the vessels of the Royal Netherlands Steam Packet Company see when every other month on their way up to Macassar and every four weeks on their way down to Merauke in Dutch New Guinea they touch at the island.

At a certain moment of the world's history the Controleur was Mynheer Evert Gruyter and he ruled the people who inhabited the Alas Islands with firmness tempered by a keen sense of the ridiculous. He had thought it a very good joke to be placed at the age of twenty-seven in a position of such consequence and at thirty he was still amused by it. There was no cable communication between his islands and Batavia, and the mail arrived after so long a delay that even if he asked advice, by the time he received it, it was useless, and so he equably did what he thought best and trusted to his good fortune to keep out of trouble with the authorities. He was very short, not more than five feet four in height, and extremely fat; he was of a florid complexion. For coolness' sake he kept his head shaved and his face was hairless. It was round and red. His eyebrows were so fair that you hardly saw them; and he had little twinkling blue eyes. He knew that he had no dignity, but for the sake of his position made up for it by dressing very dapperly. He never went to his office, nor sat in court, nor walked abroad but in spotless white. His stengah-shifter, with its bright brass buttons, fitted him very tightly and displayed the shocking fact that, young though he was, he had a round and protruding belly. His good-humoured face shone with sweat and he constantly fanned himself with a palm-leaf fan.

But in his house Mr. Gruyter preferred to wear nothing but a sarong and then with his white podgy little body he looked like a fat funny boy of sixteen. He was an early riser and his breakfast was always ready for him at six. It never varied. It consisted of a slice of papaia, three cold fried eggs, Edam cheese, sliced thin, and a cup of black coffee. When he had eaten it, he smoked a large Dutch cigar, read the papers if he had not read them through and through already, and then dressed to go down to his office.

One morning while he was thus occupied his head boy came into his bedroom and told him that Tuan Jones wanted to know if he could see him. Mr. Gruyter was standing in front of a looking-glass. He had his trousers on and was admiring his smooth chest. He arched his back in order to throw it out and throw in his belly and with a good deal of satisfaction gave his breast three or four resounding slaps. It was a manly chest. When the boy brought the message he looked at his own eyes in the mirror and exchanged a slightly ironic smile with them. He asked himself what the devil his visitor could want. Evert Gruyter spoke English, Dutch and Malay with equal facility, but he thought in Dutch. He liked to do this. It seemed to him a pleasantly ribald language.

"Ask the Tuan to wait and say I shall come directly."

He put on his tunic, over his naked body, buttoned it up, and strutted into the sitting-room. The Rev. Owen Jones got up.

"Good-morning, Mr. Jones," said the Controleur. "Have you come in to have a peg with me before I start my day's work?"

Mr. Jones did not smile.

"I've come to see you upon a very distressing matter, Mr. Gruyter," he answered.

The Controleur was not disconcerted by his visitor's gravity nor depressed by his words. His little blue eyes beamed amiably.

"Sit down, my dear fellow, and have a cigar."

Mr. Gruyter knew quite well that the Rev. Owen Jones neither drank nor smoked, but it tickled something prankish in his nature to offer him a drink and a smoke whenever they met. Mr. Jones shook his head.

Mr. Jones was in charge of the Baptist Mission on the Alas Islands. His headquarters were at Baru, the largest of them, with the greatest population, but he had meeting-houses under the care of native helpers in several other islands of the group. He was a tall, thin melancholy man, with a long face, sallow and drawn, of about forty. His brown hair was already white on the temples and it receded from the forehead. This gave him a look of somewhat vacuous intellectuality. Mr. Gruyter both disliked and respected him. He disliked him because he was narrow-minded and dogmatic. Himself a cheerful pagan who liked the good things of the flesh and was determined to get as many of them as his circumstances permitted, he had no patience with a man who disapproved of them all. He thought the customs of the country suited its inhabitants and had no patience with the missionary's energetic efforts to destroy a way of life that for centuries had worked very well. He respected him because he was honest, zealous and good. Mr. Jones, an Australian of Welsh descent, was the only qualified doctor in the group and it was a comfort to know that if you fell ill you need not rely only on a Chinese practitioner, and none knew better than the Controleur how useful to all Mr. Jones's skill had been and with what charity he had given it. On the occasion of an epidemic of influenza the missionary had done the work of ten men and no storm short of a typhoon could prevent him from crossing to one island or another if his help was needed.

He lived with his sister in a little white house about half a mile from the village and when the Controleur had arrived, came on board to meet him and begged him to stay till he could get his own house in order. The Controleur had accepted and soon saw for himself with what simplicity the couple lived. It was more than he could stand. Tea at three sparse meals a day and when he lit his cigar Mr. Jones politely but firmly asked him to be good enough not to smoke since both his sister and he strongly disapproved of it. In twenty-four hours Mr. Gruyter moved into his own house. He fled, with panic in his heart, as though from a plague-stricken city. The Controleur was fond of a joke and he liked to laugh; to be with a man who took your nonsense in deadly earnest and never even smiled at your best story was more than flesh and blood could stand. The Rev. Owen Jones was a worthy man, but as a companion he was impossible. His sister was worse. Neither had a sense of humour, but whereas the missionary was of a melancholy turn, doing his duty so conscientiously, with the obvious conviction that everything in the world was hopeless, Miss Jones was resolutely cheerful. She grimly looked on the bright side of things. With the ferocity of an avenging angel she sought out the good in her fellow men. Miss Jones taught in the mission school and helped her brother in his medical work. When he did operations she gave the anæsthetic and was matron, dresser and nurse of the tiny hospital which on his own initiative Mr. Jones had added to the mission. But the Controleur was an obstinate little fellow and he never lost his capacity of extracting amusement from the Rev. Owen's dour struggle with the infirmities of human nature, and Miss Jones's ruthless optimism. He had to get his fun where he could. The Dutch boats came in three times in two months for a few hours and then he could have a good old crack with the captain and chief engineer, and once in a blue moon a pearling lugger came in from Thursday Island or Port Darwin and for two or three days he had a grand time. They were rough fellows, the pearlers, for the most part, but they were full of guts, and they had plenty of liquor on board, and good stories to tell, and the Controleur had them up to his house and gave them a fine dinner and the party was only counted a success if they were all too drunk to get back on the lugger again that night. But besides the missionary the only white man who lived on Baru was Ginger Ted, and he, of course, was a disgrace to civilisation. There was not a single thing to be said in his favour. He cast discredit on the white race. All the same, but for Ginger Ted the Controleur some-

times thought he would find life on the island of Baru
almost more than he could bear.

Oddly enough it was on account of this scamp that
Mr. Jones, when he should have been instructing the
pagan young in the mysteries of the Baptist faith, was
paying Mr. Gruyter this early visit.

"Sit down, Mr. Jones," said the Controleur. "What
can I do for you?"

"Well, I've come to see you about the man they call
Ginger Ted. What are you going to do now?"

"Why, what's happened?"

"Haven't you heard? I thought the sergeant would
have told you."

"I don't encourage the members of my staff to come
to my private house unless the matter is urgent," said
the Controleur rather grandly. "I am unlike you, Mr.
Jones, I only work in order to have leisure and I like to
enjoy my leisure without disturbance."

But Mr. Jones did not care much for small talk and he
was not interested in general reflections.

"There was a disgraceful row in one of the Chinese
shops last night. Ginger Ted wrecked the place and
half killed a Chinaman."

"Drunk again, I suppose," said the Controleur
placidly.

"Naturally. When is he anything else? They sent for
the police and he assaulted the sergeant. They had to
have six men to get him to the gaol."

"He's a hefty fellow," said the Controleur.

"I suppose you'll send him to Macassar."

Evert Gruyter returned the missionary's outraged
look with a merry twinkle. He was no fool and he knew

already what Mr. Jones was up to. It gave him considerable amusement to tease him a little.

"Fortunately my powers are wide enough to enable me to deal with the situation myself," he answered.

"You have power to deport anyone you like, Mr. Gruyter, and I'm sure it would save a lot of trouble if you got rid of the man altogether."

"I have the power of course, but I am sure you would be the last person to wish me to use it arbitrarily."

"Mr. Gruyter, the man's presence here is a public scandal. He's never sober from morning till night; it's notorious that he has relations with one native woman after another."

"That is an interesting point, Mr. Jones. I had always heard that alcoholic excess, though it stimulated sexual desire, prevented its gratification. What you tell me about Ginger Ted does not seem to bear out this theory."

The missionary flushed a dull red.

"These are physiological matters which at the moment I have no wish to go into," he said, frigidly. "The behaviour of this man does incalculable damage to the prestige of the white race, and his example seriously hampers the efforts that are made in other quarters to induce the people of these islands to lead a less vicious life. He's an out and out bad lot."

"Pardon my asking, but have you made any attempts to reform him?"

"When he first drifted here I did my best to get in touch with him. He repelled all my advances. When there was that first trouble I went to him and talked to him straight from the shoulder. He swore at me."

"No one has a greater appreciation than I of the excellent work that you and other missionaries do on these islands, but are you sure that you always exercise your calling with all the tact possible?"

The Controleur was rather pleased with this phrase. It was extremely courteous and yet contained a reproof that he thought worth administering. The missionary looked at him gravely. His sad brown eyes were full of sincerity.

"Did Jesus exercise tact when he took a whip and drove the money-changers from the Temple? No, Mr. Gruyter. Tact is the subterfuge the lax avail themselves of to avoid doing their duty."

Mr. Jones's remark made the Controleur feel suddenly that he wanted a bottle of beer. The missionary leaned forward earnestly.

"Mr. Gruyter, you know this man's transgressions just as well as I do. It's unnecessary for me to remind you of them. There are no excuses for him. Now he really has overstepped the limit. You'll never have a better chance than this. I beg you to use the power you have and turn him out once for all."

The Controleur's eyes twinkled more brightly than ever. He was having a lot of fun. He reflected that human beings were much more amusing when you did not feel called upon in dealing with them to allot praise or blame.

"But Mr. Jones, do I understand you right? Are you asking me to give you an assurance to deport this man before I've heard the evidence against him and listened to his defence?"

"I don't know what his defence can be."

The Controleur rose from his chair and really he managed to get quite a little dignity into his five feet four inches.

"I am here to administer justice according to the laws of the Dutch Government. Permit me to tell you that I am exceedingly surprised that you should attempt to influence me in my judicial functions."

The missionary was a trifle flustered. It had never occurred to him that this little whipper-snapper of a boy, ten years younger than himself, would dream of adopting such an attitude. He opened his mouth to explain and apologise, but the Controleur raised a podgy little hand.

"It is time for me to go to my office, Mr. Jones. I wish you good-morning."

The missionary, taken aback, bowed and without another word walked out of the room. He would have been surprised to see what the Controleur did when his back was turned. A broad grin broke on his lips and he put his thumb to his nose and cocked a snook at the Rev. Owen Jones.

A few minutes later he went down to his office. His head clerk, who was a Dutch half-caste, gave him his version of the previous night's row. It agreed pretty well with Mr. Jones's. The Court was sitting that day.

"Will you take Ginger Ted first, sir?" asked the clerk.

"I see no reason to do that. There are two or three cases held over from the last sitting. I will take him in his proper order."

"I thought perhaps as he was a white man you would like to see him privately, sir."

"The majesty of the law knows no difference between

white and coloured, my friend," said Mr. Gruyter, somewhat pompously.

The Court was a big square room with wooden benches on which, crowded together, sat natives of all kinds, Polynesians, Bugis, Chinese, Malays, and they all rose when a door was opened and a sergeant announced the arrival of the Controleur. He entered with his clerk and took his place on a little dais at a table of varnished pitch pine. Behind him was a large engraving of Queen Wilhelmina. He despatched half a dozen cases and then Ginger Ted was brought in. He stood in the dock, handcuffed, with a warder on either side of him. The Controleur looked at him with a grave face, but he could not keep the amusement out of his eyes.

Ginger Ted was suffering from a hangover. He swayed a little as he stood and his eyes were vacant. He was a man still young, thirty perhaps, of somewhat over the middle height, rather fat, with a bloated red face and a shock of curly red hair. He had not come out of the tussle unscathed. He had a black eye and his mouth was cut and swollen. He wore khaki shorts, very dirty and ragged, and his singlet had been almost torn off his back. A great rent showed the thick mat of red hair with which his chest was covered, but showed also the astonishing whiteness of his skin. The Controleur looked at the charge sheet. He called the evidence. When he had heard it, when he had seen the Chinaman whose head Ginger Ted had broken with a bottle, when he had heard the agitated story of the sergeant who had been knocked flat when he tried to arrest him, when he had listened to the tale of the havoc wrought by Ginger Ted who in his drunken fury had smashed everything he could lay hands on, he turned and addressed the accused in English.

"Well, Ginger, what have you got to say for yourself?"

"I was blind. I don't remember a thing about it. If they say I half killed 'im I suppose I did. I'll pay the damage if they'll give me time."

"You will, Ginger," said the Controleur, "but it's me who'll give you time."

He looked at Ginger Ted for a minute in silence. He was an unappetising object. A man who had gone completely to pieces. He was horrible. It made you shudder to look at him and if Mr. Jones had not been so officious, at that moment the Controleur would certainly have ordered him to be deported.

"You've been a trouble ever since you came to the islands, Ginger. You're a disgrace. You're incorrigibly idle. You've been picked up in the street dead drunk time and time again. You've kicked up row after row. You're hopeless. I told you the last time you were brought here that if you were arrested again I should deal with you severely. You've gone the limit this time and you're for it. I sentence you to six months' hard labour."

"Me?"

"You."

"By God, I'll kill you when I come out."

He burst into a string of oaths both filthy and blasphemous. Mr. Gruyter listened scornfully. You can swear much better in Dutch than in English and there was nothing that Ginger Ted said that he could not have effectively capped.

"Be quiet," he ordered. "You make me tired."

The Controleur repeated his sentence in Malay and the prisoner was led struggling away.

Mr. Gruyter sat down to tiffin in high good humour. It was astonishing how amusing life could be if you exercised a little ingenuity. There were people in Amsterdam, and even in Batavia and Surabaya, who looked upon his island home as a place of exile. They little knew how agreeable it was and what fun he could extract from unpromising material. They asked him whether he did not miss the club and the races and the cinema, the dances that were held once a week at the Casino and the society of Dutch ladies. Not at all. He liked comfort. The substantial furniture of the room in which he sat had a satisfying solidity. He liked reading French novels of a frivolous nature and he appreciated the sensation of reading one after the other without the uneasiness occasioned by the thought that he was wasting his time. It seemed to him a great luxury to waste time. When his young man's fancy turned to thoughts of love his head boy brought to the house a little dark-skinned bright-eyed creature in a sarong. He took care to form no connection of a permanent nature. He thought that change kept the heart young. He enjoyed freedom and was not weighed down by a sense of responsibility. He did not mind the heat. It made a sluice over with cold water half a dozen times a day a pleasure that had almost an æsthetic quality. He played the piano. He wrote letters to his friends in Holland. He felt no need for the conversation of intellectual persons. He liked a good laugh, but he could get that out of a fool just as well as out of a professor of philosophy.

He had a notion that he was a very wise little man.

Like all good Dutchmen in the Far East he began his lunch with a small glass of Hollands gin. It has a musty acrid flavour, and the taste for it must be acquired, but Mr. Gruyter preferred it to any cocktail. When he drank it he felt besides that he was upholding the traditions of his race. Then he had *rystafel*. He had it every day. He heaped a soup-plate high with rice, and then, his three boys waiting on him, helped himself to the curry that one handed him, to the fried egg that another brought, and to the condiment presented by the third. Then each one brought another dish, of bacon, or bananas, or pickled fish, and presently his plate was piled high in a huge pyramid. He stirred it all together and began to eat. He ate slowly and with relish. He drank a bottle of beer.

He did not think while he was eating. His attention was applied to the mass in front of him and he consumed it with a happy concentration. It never palled on him. And when he had emptied the great plate it was a compensation to think that next day he would have *rystafel* again. He grew tired of it as little as the rest of us grow tired of bread. He finished his beer and lit his cigar. The boy brought him a cup of coffee. He leaned back in his chair then and allowed himself the luxury of reflection.

It tickled him to have sentenced Ginger Ted to the richly deserved punishment of six months' hard labour, and he smiled when he thought of him working on the roads with the other prisoners. It would have been silly to deport from the island the one man with whom he could occasionally have a heart-to-heart talk, and besides, the satisfaction it would have given the missionary would have been bad for that gentleman's character. Ginger Ted was a scamp and a scallywag, but the Controleur had a kindly feeling for him. They had drunk many a bottle of beer in one another's company and when the pearl fishers from Port Darwin came in and they all made a night of it, they had got gloriously tight together. The Controleur liked the reckless way in which Ginger Ted squandered the priceless treasure of life.

Ginger Ted had wandered in one day on the ship that was going up from Merauke to Macassar. The captain did not know how he had found his way there, but he had travelled steerage with the natives, and he stopped off at the Alas Islands because he liked the look of them. Mr. Gruyter had a suspicion that their attraction consisted perhaps in their being under the Dutch flag and so out of British jurisdiction. But his papers were in order, so there was no reason why he should not stay. He said that he was buying pearl-shell for an Australian firm, but it soon appeared that his commercial undertakings were not serious. Drink, indeed, took up so much of his time that he had little left over for other pursuits. He was in receipt of two pounds a week, paid monthly, which came regularly to him from England. The Controleur guessed that this sum was paid only so long as he kept well away from the persons who sent it. It was anyway too small to permit him any liberty of movement. Ginger Ted was reticent. The Controleur discovered that he was an Englishman, this he learnt from his passport, which described him as Edward Wilson, and that he had been in Australia. But why

he had left England and what he had done in Australia
he had no notion. Nor could he ever quite tell to what
class Ginger Ted belonged. When you saw him in a
filthy singlet and a pair of ragged trousers, a battered
topi on his head, with the pearl fishers and heard his
conversation, coarse, obscene and illiterate, you thought
he must be a sailor before the mast who had deserted his
ship, or a labourer, but when you saw his handwriting
you were surprised to find that it was that of a man not
without at least some education, and on occasion when
you got him alone, if he had had a few drinks but was
not yet drunk, he would talk of matters that neither a
sailor nor a labourer would have been likely to know
anything about. The Controleur had a certain sensitiveness and he realised that Ginger Ted did not speak to
him as an inferior to a superior but as an equal. Most
of his remittance was mortgaged before he received it,
and the Chinamen to whom he owed money were standing at his elbow when the monthly letter was delivered
to him, but with what was left he proceeded to get
drunk. It was then that he made trouble, for when
drunk he grew violent and was then likely to commit
acts that brought him into the hands of the police.
Hitherto Mr. Gruyter had contented himself with keeping him in gaol till he was sober and giving him a talking
to. When he was out of money he cadged what drink
he could from anyone who would give it him. Rum,
brandy, arak, it was all the same to him. Two or three
times Mr. Gruyter had got him work on plantations
run by Chinese in one or other of the islands, but he
could not stick to it, and in a few weeks was back again
at Baru on the beach. It was a miracle how he kept

body and soul together. He had, of course, a way with him. He picked up the various dialects spoken on the islands, and knew how to make the natives laugh. They despised him, but they respected his physical strength, and they liked his company. He was as a result never at a loss for a meal or a mat to sleep on. The strange thing was, and it was this that chiefly outraged the Rev. Owen Jones, that he could do anything he liked with a woman. The Controleur could not imagine what it was they saw in him. He was casual with them and rather brutal. He took what they gave him, but seemed incapable of gratitude. He used them for his pleasure and then flung them indifferently away. Once or twice this had got him into trouble, and Mr. Gruyter had had to sentence an angry father for sticking a knife in Ginger Ted's back one night, and a Chinese woman had sought to poison herself by swallowing opium because he had deserted her. Once Mr. Jones came to the Controleur in a great state because the beachcomber had seduced one of his converts. The Controleur agreed that it was very deplorable, but could only advise Mr. Jones to keep a sharp eye on these young persons. The Controleur liked it less when he discovered that a girl whom he fancied a good deal himself and had been seeing for several weeks had all the time been according her favours also to Ginger Ted. When he thought of this particular incident he smiled again at the thought of Ginger Ted doing six months' hard labour. It is seldom in this life that in the process of doing your bounden duty you can get back on a fellow who has played you a dirty trick.

A few days later Mr. Gruyter was taking a walk, partly for exercise and partly to see that some job he wanted done was being duly proceeded with, when he passed a gang of prisoners working under the charge of a warder. Among them he saw Ginger Ted. He wore the prison sarong, a dingy tunic called in Malay a baju, and his own battered topi. They were repairing the road, and Ginger Ted was wielding a heavy pick. The way was narrow and the Controleur saw that he must pass within a foot of him. He remembered his threats. He knew that Ginger Ted was a man of violent passion and the language he had used in the dock made it plain that he had not seen what a good joke it was of the Controleur's to sentence him to six months' hard labour. If Ginger Ted suddenly attacked him with the pick, nothing on God's earth could save him. It was true that the warder would immediately shoot him down, but meanwhile the Controleur's head would be bashed in. It was with a funny little feeling in the pit of his stomach that Mr. Gruyter walked through the gang of prisoners. They were working in pairs a few feet from one another. He set his mind on neither hastening his pace nor slackening it. As he passed Ginger Ted, the man swung his pick into the ground and looked up at the Controleur and as he caught his eye winked. The Controleur checked the smile that rose to his lips and with official dignity strode on. But that wink, so lusciously full of sardonic humour, filled him with satisfaction. If he had been the Caliph of Bagdad instead of a junior official in the Dutch Civil Service, he would forthwith have released Ginger Ted, sent slaves to bathe and perfume him, and having clothed him in a golden robe entertained him to a sumptuous repast.

Ginger Ted was an exemplary prisoner and in a month

or two the Controleur, having occasion to send a gang
to do some work on one of the outlying islands, included
him in it. There was no gaol there, so the ten fellows he
sent, under the charge of a warder, were billeted on the
natives and after their day's work lived like free men.
The job was sufficient to take up the rest of Ginger Ted's
sentence. The Controleur saw him before he left.

"Look here, Ginger," he said to him, "here's ten
guilder for you so that you can buy yourself tobacco
when you're gone."

"Couldn't you make it a bit more? There's eight
pounds a month coming in regularly."

"I think that's enough. I'll keep the letters that come
for you, and when you get back you'll have a tidy sum.
You'll have enough to take you anywhere you want to
go."

"I'm very comfortable here," said Ginger Ted.

"Well, the day you come back, clean yourself up and
come over to my house. We'll have a bottle of beer together."

"That'll be fine. I guess I'll be ready for a good crack
then."

Now chance steps in. The island to which Ginger
Ted had been sent was called Maputiti, and like all the
rest of them it was rocky, heavily wooded and surrounded by a reef. There was a village among coconuts
on the sea-shore opposite the opening of the reef and
another village on a brackish lake in the middle of the
island. Of this some of the inhabitants had been converted to Christianity. Communication with Baru was
effected by a launch that touched at the various islands
at irregular intervals. It carried passengers and produce.

But the villagers were seafaring folk, and if they had
to communicate urgently with Baru, manned a prahu
and sailed the fifty miles or so that separated them from
it. It happened that when Ginger Ted's sentence had
but another fortnight to run the Christian headman of
the village on the lake was taken suddenly ill. The native remedies availed him nothing and he writhed in
agony. Messengers were sent to Baru imploring the missionary's help; but as ill luck would have it Mr. Jones
was suffering at the moment from an attack of malaria.
He was in bed and unable to move. He talked the matter over with his sister.

"It sounds like acute appendicitis," he told her.

"You can't go, Owen," she said.

"I can't let the man die."

Mr. Jones had a temperature of a hundred and four.
His head was aching like mad. He had been delirious
all night. His eyes were shining strangely and his sister
felt that he was holding on to his wits by a sheer effort
of will.

"You couldn't operate in the state you're in."

"No, I couldn't. Then Hassan must go."

Hassan was the dispenser.

"You couldn't trust Hassan. He'd never dare to do
an operation on his own responsibility. And they'd never
let him. I'll go. Hassan can stay here and look after
you."

"You can't remove an appendix?"

"Why not? I've seen you do it. I've done lots of minor
operations."

Mr. Jones felt he didn't quite understand what she
was saying.

"Is the launch in?"

"No, it's gone to one of the islands. But I can go in the prahu the men came in."

"You? I wasn't thinking of you. You can't go."

"I'm going, Owen."

"Going where?" he said.

She saw that his mind was wandering already. She put her hand soothingly on his dry forehead. She gave him a dose of medicine. He muttered something and she realised that he did not know where he was. Of course she was anxious about him, but she knew that his illness was not dangerous, and she could leave him safely to the mission boy who was helping her nurse him and to the native dispenser. She slipped out of the room. She put her toilet things, a night-dress, and a change of clothes into a bag. A little chest with surgical instruments, bandages and antiseptic dressings was kept always ready. She gave them to the two natives who had come over from Maputiti, and telling the dispenser what she was going to do gave him instructions to inform her brother when he was able to listen. Above all he was not to be anxious about her. She put on her topi and sallied forth. The mission was about half a mile from the village. She walked quickly. At the end of the jetty the prahu was waiting. Six men manned it. She took her place in the stern and they set off with a rapid stroke. Within the reef the sea was calm, but when they crossed the bar they came upon a long swell. But this was not the first journey of the sort Miss Jones had taken and she was confident in the seaworthiness of the boat she was in. It was noon and the sun beat down from a sultry sky. The only thing that harassed her was that they could not arrive before dark, and if she found it necessary to operate at once she could count only on the light of hurricane lamps.

Miss Jones was a woman of hard on forty. Nothing in her appearance would have prepared you for such determination as she had just shown. She had an odd drooping gracefulness, which suggested that she might be swayed by every breeze; it was almost an affectation; and it made the strength of character which you soon discovered in her seem positively monstrous. She was flat-chested, tall and extremely thin. She had a long sallow face and she was much afflicted with prickly heat. Her lank brown hair was drawn back straight from her forehead. She had rather small eyes, grey in colour, and because they were somewhat too close they gave her face a shrewish look. Her nose was long and thin and a trifle red. She suffered a good deal from indigestion. But this infirmity availed nothing against her ruthless determination to look upon the bright side of things. Firmly persuaded that the world was evil and men unspeakably vicious, she extracted any little piece of decency she could find in them with the modest pride with which a conjurer extracts a rabbit from a hat. She was quick, resourceful and competent. When she arrived on the island she saw that there was not a moment to lose if she was to save the headman's life. Under the greatest difficulties, showing a native how to give the anæsthetic, she operated, and for the next three days nursed the patient with anxious assiduity. Everything went very well and she realised that her brother could not have made a better job of it. She waited long enough to take out the stitches and then prepared to go home.

She could flatter herself that she had not wasted her time. She had given medical attention to such as needed it, she had strengthened the small Christian community in its faith, admonished such as were lax and cast the good seed in places where it might be hoped under divine providence to take root.

The launch, coming from one of the other islands, put in somewhat late in the afternoon, but it was full moon and they expected to reach Baru before midnight. They brought her things down to the wharf and the people who were seeing her off stood about repeating their thanks. Quite a little crowd collected. The launch was loaded with sacks of copra, but Miss Jones was used to its strong smell and it did not incommode her. She made herself as comfortable a place to sit in as she could, and waiting for the launch to start, chatted with her grateful flock. She was the only passenger. Suddenly a group of natives emerged from the trees that embowered the little village on the lagoon and she saw that among them was a white man. He wore a prison sarong and a baju. He had long red hair. She at once recognised Ginger Ted. A policeman was with him. They shook hands and Ginger Ted shook hands with the villagers who accompanied him. They bore bundles of fruit and a jar which Miss Jones guessed contained native spirit, and these they put in the launch. She discovered to her surprise that Ginger Ted was coming with her. His term was up and instructions had arrived that he was to be returned to Baru in the launch. He gave her a glance, but did not nod—indeed Miss Jones turned away her head—and stepped in. The mechanic started his engine and in a moment they were jug-jugging through the channel in the lagoon. Ginger Ted clambered on to a pile of sacks and lit a cigarette.

Miss Jones ignored him. Of course she knew him very well. Her heart sank when she thought that he was going to be once more in Baru, creating a scandal and drinking, a peril to the women and a thorn in the flesh of all decent people. She knew the steps her brother had taken to have him deported and she had no patience with the Controleur, who would not see a duty that stared him so plainly in the face. When they had crossed the bar and were in the open sea Ginger Ted took the stopper out of the jar of arak and putting his mouth to it took a long pull. Then he handed the jar to the two mechanics who formed the crew. One was a middle-aged man and the other a youth.

"I do not wish you to drink anything while we are on the journey," said Miss Jones sternly to the elder one.

He smiled at her and drank.

"A little arak can do no one any harm," he answered. He passed the jar to his companion, who drank also.

"If you drink again I shall complain to the Controleur," said Miss Jones.

The elder man said something she could not understand, but which she suspected was very rude, and passed the jar back to Ginger Ted. They went along for an hour or more. The sea was like glass and the sun set radiantly. It set behind one of the islands and for a few minutes changed it into a mystic city of the skies. Miss Jones turned round to watch it and her heart was filled with gratitude for the beauty of the world.

"And only man is vile," she quoted to herself.

They went due east. In the distance was a little island which she knew they passed close by. It was uninhabited. A rocky islet thickly grown with virgin forest. The boatman lit his lamps. The night fell and immediately the sky was thick with stars. The moon had not yet risen. Suddenly there was a slight jar and the launch began to vibrate strangely. The engine rattled. The head mechanic, calling to his mate to take the helm, crept under the housing. They seemed to be going more slowly. The engine stopped. She asked the youth what was the matter, but he did not know. Ginger Ted got down from the top of the copra sacks and slipped under the housing. When he reappeared she would have liked to ask him what had happened, but her dignity prevented her. She sat still and occupied herself with her thoughts. There was a long swell and the launch rolled slightly. The mechanic emerged once more into view and started the engine. Though it rattled like mad they began to move. The launch vibrated from stem to stern. They went very slowly. Evidently something was amiss, but Miss Jones was exasperated rather than alarmed. The launch was supposed to do six knots, but now it was just crawling along; at that rate they would not get into Baru till long, long after midnight. The mechanic, still busy under the housing, shouted out something to the man at the helm. They spoke in Bugi, of which Miss Jones knew very little. But after a while she noticed that they had changed their course and seemed to be heading for the little uninhabited island a good deal to the lee of which they should have passed.

"Where are we going?" she asked the helmsman with sudden misgiving.

He pointed to the islet. She got up and went to the housing and called to the man to come out.

"You're not going there? Why? What's the matter?"

"I can't get to Baru," he said.

"But you must. I insist. I order you to go to Baru."

The man shrugged his shoulders. He turned his back on her and slipped once more under the housing. Then Ginger Ted addressed her.

"One of the blades of the propeller has broken off. He thinks he can get as far as that island. We shall have to stay the night there and he'll put on a new propeller in the morning when the tide's out."

"I can't spend the night on an uninhabited island with three men," she cried.

"A lot of women would jump at it."

"I insist on going to Baru. Whatever happens we must get there to-night."

"Don't get excited, old girl. We've got to beach the boat to put a new propeller on, and we shall be all right on the island."

"How dare you speak to me like that! I think you're very insolent."

"You'll be O.K. We've got plenty of grub and we'll have a snack when we land. You have a drop of arak and you'll feel like a house on fire."

"You're an impertinent man. If you don't go to Baru I'll have you all put in prison."

"We're not going to Baru. We can't. We're going to that island and if you don't like it you can get out and swim."

"Oh, you'll pay for this."

"Shut up, you old cow," said Ginger Ted.

Miss Jones gave a gasp of anger. But she controlled herself. Even out there, in the middle of the ocean, she had too much dignity to bandy words with that vile wretch. The launch, the engine rattling horribly, crawled on. It was pitch dark now, and she could no longer see the island they were making for. Miss Jones, deeply incensed, sat with lips tight shut and a frown on her brow; she was not used to being crossed. Then the moon rose and she could see the bulk of Ginger Ted sprawling on the top of the piled sacks of copra. The glimmer of his cigarette was strangely sinister. Now the island was vaguely outlined against the sky. They reached it and the boatman ran the launch on to the beach. Suddenly Miss Jones gave a gasp. The truth had dawned on her and her anger changed to fear. Her heart beat violently. She shook in every limb. She felt dreadfully faint. She saw it all. Was the broken propeller a put-up job or was it an accident? She could not be certain; anyhow, she knew that Ginger Ted would seize the opportunity. Ginger Ted would rape her. She knew his character. He was mad about women. That was what he had done, practically, to the girl at the mission, such a good little thing she was and an excellent sempstress; they would have prosecuted him for that and he would have been sentenced to years of imprisonment only very unfortunately the innocent child had gone back to him several times and indeed had only complained of his ill usage when he left her for somebody else. They had gone to the Controleur about it, but he had refused to take any steps, saying in that coarse way of his that even if what the girl said was true, it didn't look very much as though it had been an altogether unpleasant experience. Ginger Ted was a scoundrel. And she was a white woman. What chance was there that he would spare her? None. She knew men. But she must pull herself together. She must keep her wits about her. She must have courage. She was determined to sell her virtue dearly, and if he killed her—well, she would rather die than yield. And if she died she would rest in the arms of Jesus. For a moment a great light blinded her eyes and she saw the mansions of her Heavenly Father. They were a grand and sumptuous mixture of a picture palace and a railway station. The mechanics and Ginger Ted jumped out of the launch and, waist deep in water, gathered round the broken propeller. She took advantage of their preoccupation to get her case of surgical instruments out of the box. She took out the four scalpels it contained and secreted them in her clothing. If Ginger Ted touched her she would not hesitate to plunge a scalpel in his heart.

"Now then, miss, you'd better get out," said Ginger Ted. "You'll be better off on the beach than in the boat."

She thought so too. At least there she would have freedom of action. Without a word she clambered over the copra sacks. He offered her his hand.

"I don't want your help," she said coldly.

"You can go to hell," he answered.

It was a little difficult to get out of the boat without showing her legs, but by the exercise of considerable ingenuity she managed it.

"Damned lucky we've got something to eat. We'll

make a fire and then you'd better have a snack and a
nip of arak."

"I want nothing. I only want to be left alone."

"It won't hurt me if you go hungry."

She did not answer. She walked, with head erect,
along the beach. She held the largest scalpel in her
closed fist. The moon allowed her to see where she was
going. She looked for a place to hide. The thick forest
came down to the very edge of the beach; but, afraid
of its darkness (after all, she was but a woman), she
dared not plunge into its depth. She did not know what
animals lurked there or what dangerous snakes.
Besides, her instinct told her that it was better to keep
those three bad men in sight; then if they came towards
her she would be prepared. Presently she found a little
hollow. She looked round. They seemed to be occupied
with their own affairs and they could not see her.
She slipped in. There was a rock between them and
her so that she was hidden from them and yet could
watch them. She saw them go to and from the boat
carrying things. She saw them build a fire. It lit them
luridly and she saw them sit around it and eat, and she
saw the jar of arak passed from one to the other. They
were all going to get drunk. What would happen to
her then? It might be that she could cope with Ginger
Ted, though his strength terrified her, but against three
she would be powerless. A mad idea came to her to
go to Ginger Ted and fall on her knees before him and
beg him to spare her. He must have some spark of
decent feeling in him and she had always been so convinced that there was good even in the worst of men.

He must have had a mother. Perhaps he had a sister.
Ah, but how could you appeal to a man blinded with
lust and drunk with arak? She began to feel terribly
weak. She was afraid she was going to cry. That would
never do. She needed all her self-control. She bit her
lip. She watched them, like a tiger watching his prey;
no, not like that, like a lamb watching three hungry
wolves. She saw them put more wood on the fire and
Ginger Ted, in his sarong, silhouetted by the flames.
Perhaps after he had had his will of her he would pass
her on to the others. How could she go back to her
brother when such a thing had happened to her? Of
course he would be sympathetic, but would he ever feel
quite the same to her again? It would break his heart.
And perhaps he would think that she ought to have
resisted more. For his sake perhaps it would be better
if she said nothing about it, naturally the men would say
nothing. It would mean twenty years in prison for them.
But then supposing she had a baby. Miss Jones instinctively clenched her hands with horror and nearly cut
herself with the scalpel. Of course it would only infuriate
them if she resisted.

"What shall I do?" she cried. "What have I done to
deserve this?"

She flung herself down on her knees and prayed to
God to save her. She prayed long and earnestly. She
reminded God that she was a virgin and just mentioned,
in case it had slipped the divine memory, how much
St. Paul had valued that excellent state. And then she
peeped round the rock again. The three men appeared
to be smoking and the fire was dying down. Now was
the time that Ginger Ted's lewd thoughts might be

expected to turn to the woman who was at his mercy. She smothered a cry, for suddenly he got up and walked in her direction. She felt all her muscles grow taut, and though her heart was beating furiously she clenched the scalpel firmly in her hand. But it was for another purpose that Ginger Ted had got up. Miss Jones blushed and looked away. He strolled slowly back to the others and sitting down again raised the jar of arak to his lips. Miss Jones, crouching behind the rock, watched with straining eyes. The conversation round the fire grew less and presently she divined, rather than saw, that the two natives wrapped themselves in blankets and composed themselves to slumber. She understood. This was the moment Ginger Ted had been waiting for. When they were fast asleep he would get up cautiously and without a sound, in order not to wake the others, creep stealthily towards her. Was it that he was unwilling to share her with them or did he know that his deed was so dastardly that he did not wish them to know of it? After all, he was a white man and she was a white woman. He could not have sunk so low as to allow her to suffer the violence of natives. But his plan, which was so obvious to her, had given her an idea; when she saw him coming she would scream, she would scream so loudly that it would wake the two mechanics. She remembered now that the elder, though he had only one eye, had a kind face. But Ginger Ted did not move. She was feeling terribly tired. She began to fear that she would not have the strength now to resist him. She had gone through too much. She closed her eyes for a minute.

When she opened them it was broad daylight. She

must have fallen asleep and, so shattered was she by emotion, have slept till long after dawn. It gave her quite a turn. She sought to rise, but something caught in her legs. She looked and found that she was covered with two empty copra sacks. Someone had come in the night and put them over her. Ginger Ted. She gave a little scream. The horrible thought flashed through her mind that he had outraged her in her sleep. No. It was impossible. And yet he had had her at his mercy. Defenceless. And he had spared her. She blushed furiously. She raised herself to her feet, feeling a little stiff, and arranged her disordered dress. The scalpel had fallen from her hand and she picked it up. She took the two copra sacks and emerged from her hiding-place. She walked towards the boat. It was floating in the shallow water of the lagoon.

"Come on, Miss Jones," said Ginger Ted. "We've finished. I was just going to wake you up."

She could not look at him, but she felt herself as red as a turkey cock.

"Have a banana?" he said.

Without a word she took it. She was very hungry, and ate it with relish.

"Step on this rock and you'll be able to get in without wetting your feet."

Miss Jones felt as though she could sink into the ground with shame, but she did as he told her. He took hold of her arm—good heavens, his hand was like an iron vice, never, never could she have struggled with him—and helped her into the launch. The mechanic started the engine and they slid out of the lagoon. In three hours they were at Baru.

That evening, having been officially released, Ginger Ted went to the Controleur's house. He wore no longer the prison uniform, but the ragged singlet and the khaki shorts in which he had been arrested. He had had his hair cut and it fitted his head now like a little curly red cap. He was thinner. He had lost his bloated flabbiness and looked younger and better. Mr. Gruyter, a friendly grin on his round face, shook hands with him and asked him to sit down. The boy brought two bottles of beer.

"I'm glad to see you hadn't forgotten my invitation, Ginger," said the Controleur.

"Not likely. I've been looking forward to this for six months."

"Here's luck, Ginger Ted."

"Same to you, Controleur."

They emptied their glasses and the Controleur clapped his hands. The boy brought two more bottles.

"Well, you don't bear me any malice for the sentence I gave you, I hope."

"No bloody fear. I was mad for a minute, but I got over it. I didn't have half a bad time, you know. Nice lot of girls on that island, Controleur. You ought to give 'em a look over one of these days."

"You're a bad lot, Ginger."

"Terrible."

"Good beer, isn't it?"

"Fine."

"Let's have some more."

Ginger Ted's remittance had been arriving every month and the Controleur now had fifty pounds for him. When the damage he had done to the Chinaman's shop was paid for there would still be over thirty.

"That's quite a lot of money, Ginger. You ought to do something useful with it."

"I mean to," answered Ginger. "Spend it."

The Controleur sighed.

"Well, that's what money's for, I guess."

The Controleur gave his guest the news. Not much had happened during the last six months. Time on the Alas Islands did not matter very much and the rest of the world did not matter at all.

"Any wars anywhere?" asked Ginger Ted.

"No. Not that I've noticed. Harry Jervis found a pretty big pearl. He says he's going to ask a thousand quid for it."

"I hope he gets it."

"And Charlie McCormack's married."

"He always was a bit soft."

Suddenly the boy appeared and said Mr. Jones wished to know if he might come in. Before the Controleur could give an answer Mr. Jones walked in.

"I won't detain you long," he said. "I've been trying to get hold of this good man all day and when I heard he was here I thought you wouldn't mind my coming."

"How is Miss Jones?" asked the Controleur politely. "None the worse for her night in the open, I trust."

"She's naturally a bit shaken. She had a temperature and I've insisted on her going to bed, but I don't think it's serious."

The two men had got up on the missionary's entrance, and now the missionary went up to Ginger Ted and held out his hand.

"I want to thank you. You did a great and noble thing. My sister is right, one should always look for the good in their fellow men; I am afraid I misjudged you in the past: I beg your pardon."

He spoke very solemnly. Ginger Ted looked at him with amazement. He had not been able to prevent the missionary taking his hand. He still held it.

"What the hell are you talking about?"

"You had my sister at your mercy and you spared her. I thought you were all evil and I am ashamed. She was defenceless. She was in your power. You had pity on her. I thank you from the bottom of my heart. Neither my sister nor I will ever forget. God bless and guard you always."

Mr. Jones's voice shook a little and he turned his head away. He released Ginger Ted's hand and strode quickly to the door. Ginger Ted watched him with a blank face.

"What the blazes does he mean?" he asked.

The Controleur laughed. He tried to control himself, but the more he did the more he laughed. He shook and you saw the folds of his fat belly ripple under the sarong. He leaned back in his long chair and rolled from side to side. He did not laugh only with his face, he laughed with his whole body, and even the muscles of his podgy legs shook with mirth. He held his aching ribs. Ginger Ted looked at him frowning, and because he did not understand what the joke was he grew angry. He seized one of the empty beer bottles by the neck.

"If you don't stop laughing, I'll break your bloody head open," he said.

The Controleur mopped his face. He swallowed a mouthful of beer. He sighed and groaned because his sides were hurting him.

"He's thanking you for having respected the virtue of Miss Jones," he spluttered at last.

"Me?" cried Ginger Ted.

The thought took quite a long time to travel through his head, but when at last he got it he flew into a violent rage. There flowed from his mouth such a stream of blasphemous obscenities as would have startled a marine.

"That old cow," he finished. "What does he take me for?"

"You have the reputation of being rather hot stuff with the girls, Ginger," giggled the little Controleur.

"I wouldn't touch her with the fag end of a barge-pole. It never entered my head. The nerve. I'll wring his blasted neck. Look here, give me my money, I'm going to get drunk."

"I don't blame you," said the Controleur.

"That old cow," repeated Ginger Ted. "That old cow."

He was shocked and outraged. The suggestion really shattered his sense of decency.

The Controleur had the money at hand and having got Ginger Ted to sign the necessary papers gave it to him.

"Go and get drunk, Ginger Ted," he said, "but I warn you, if you get into mischief it'll be twelve months next time."

"I shan't get into mischief," said Ginger Ted sombrely. He was suffering from a sense of injury. "It's an insult," he shouted at the Controleur. "That's what it is, it's a bloody insult."

He lurched out of the house, and as he went he muttered to himself: "dirty swine, dirty swine." Ginger Ted remained drunk for a week. Mr. Jones went to see the Controleur again.

"I'm very sorry to hear that poor fellow has taken up his evil course again," he said. "My sister and I are dreadfully disappointed. I'm afraid it wasn't very wise to give him so much money at once."

"It was his own money. I had no right to keep it back."

"Not a legal right, perhaps, but surely a moral right."

He told the Controleur the story of that fearful night on the island. With her feminine instinct, Miss Jones had realised that the man, inflamed with lust, was determined to take advantage of her, and, resolved to defend herself to the last, had armed herself with a scalpel. He told the Controleur how she had prayed and wept and how she had hidden herself. Her agony was indescribable, and she knew that she could never have survived the shame. She rocked to and fro and every moment she thought he was coming. And there was no help anywhere and at last she had fallen asleep; she was tired out, poor thing, she had undergone more than any human being could stand, and then when she awoke she found that he had covered her with copra sacks. He had found her asleep, and surely it was her innocence, her very helplessness that had moved him, he hadn't the heart to touch her; he covered her gently with two copra sacks and crept silently away.

"It shows you that deep down in him there is something sterling. My sister feels it's our duty to save him. We must do something for him."

"Well, in your place I wouldn't try till he's got through all his money," said the Controleur, "and then if he's not in gaol you can do what you like."

But Ginger Ted didn't want to be saved. About a fortnight after his release from prison he was sitting on a stool outside a Chinaman's shop looking vacantly down the street when he saw Miss Jones coming along. He stared at her for a minute and once more amazement seized him. He muttered to himself and there can be little doubt that his mutterings were disrespectful. But then he noticed that Miss Jones had seen him and he quickly turned his head away; he was conscious, notwithstanding, that she was looking at him. She was walking briskly, but she sensibly diminished her pace as she approached him. He thought she was going to stop and speak to him. He got up quickly and went into the shop. He did not venture to come out for at least five minutes. Half an hour later Mr. Jones himself came along and he went straight up to Ginger Ted with outstretched hand.

"How do you do, Mr. Edward? My sister told me I should find you here."

Ginger Ted gave him a surly look and did not take the proffered hand. He made no answer.

"We'd be so very glad if you'd come to dinner with us next Sunday. My sister's a capital cook and she'll make you a real Australian dinner."

"Go to hell," said Ginger Ted.

"That's not very gracious," said the missionary, but with a little laugh to show that he was not affronted. "You go and see the Controleur from time to time, why shouldn't you come and see us? It's pleasant to

talk to white people now and then. Won't you let bygones be bygones? I can assure you of a very cordial
welcome."

"I haven't got clothes fit to go out in," said Ginger
Ted sulkily.

"Oh, never mind about that. Come as you are."

"I won't."

"Why not? You must have a reason."

Ginger Ted was a blunt man. He had no hesitation
in saying what we should all like to when we receive
unwelcome invitations.

"I don't want to."

"I'm sorry. My sister will be very disappointed."

Mr. Jones, determined to show that he was not in
the least offended, gave him a breezy nod and walked
on. Forty-eight hours later there mysteriously arrived
at the house in which Ginger Ted lodged a parcel
containing a suit of ducks, a tennis shirt, a pair of socks
and some shoes. He was unaccustomed to receiving
presents and next time he saw the Controleur asked
him if it was he who had sent the things.

"Not on your life," replied the Controleur. "I'm
perfectly indifferent to the state of your wardrobe."

"Well, then, who the hell can have?"

"Search me."

It was necessary from time to time for Miss Jones
to see Mr. Gruyter on business and shortly after this
she came to see him one morning in his office. She
was a capable woman and though she generally wanted
him to do something he had no mind to, she did not
waste his time. He was a little surprised then to discover
that she had come on a very trivial errand. When he

told her that he could not take cognizance of the matter in question, she did not as was her habit try to convince him, but accepted his refusal as definite. She got up to go and then as though it were an afterthought said:

"Oh, Mr. Gruyter, my brother is very anxious that we should have the man they call Ginger Ted to supper with us and I've written him a little note inviting him for the day after to-morrow. I think he's rather shy, and I wonder if you'd come with him."

"That's very kind of you."

"My brother feels that we ought to do something for the poor fellow."

"A woman's influence and all that sort of thing," said the Controleur demurely.

"Will you persuade him to come? I'm sure he will if you make a point of it, and when he knows the way he'll come again. It seems such a pity to let a young man like that go to pieces altogether."

The Controleur looked up at her. She was several inches taller than he. He thought her very unattractive. She reminded him strangely of wet linen hung on a clothes-line to dry. His eyes twinkled, but he kept a straight face.

"I'll do my best," he said.

"How old is he?" she asked.

"According to his passport he's thirty-one."

"And what is his real name?"

"Wilson."

"Edward Wilson," she said softly.

"It's astonishing that after the life he's led he should be so strong," murmured the Controleur. "He has the strength of an ox."

"Those red-headed men sometimes are very power-ful," said Miss Jones, but spoke as though she were choking.

"Quite so," said the Controleur.

Then for no obvious reason Miss Jones blushed. She hurriedly said good-bye to the Controleur and left his office.

"*Godverdomme!*" said the Controleur.

He knew now who had sent Ginger Ted the new clothes.

He met him during the course of the day and asked him whether he had heard from Miss Jones. Ginger Ted took a crumpled ball of paper out of his pocket and gave it to him. It was the invitation. It ran as follows:

Dear Mr. Wilson,—

My brother and I would be so very glad if you would come and have supper with us next Thursday at 7.30. The Controleur has kindly promised to come. We have some new records from Australia which I am sure you will like. I am afraid I was not very nice to you last time we met, but I did not know you so well then, and I am big enough to admit it when I have committed an error. I hope you will forgive me and let me be your friend.

Yours sincerely,

Martha Jones.

The Controleur noticed that she addressed him as Mr. Wilson and referred to his own promise to go, so that when she told him she had already invited Ginger Ted she had a little anticipated the truth.

"What are you going to do?"

"I'm not going, if that's what you mean. Damned nerve."

"You must answer the letter."

"Well, I won't."

"Now look here, Ginger, you put on those new clothes and you come as a favour to me. I've got to go, and damn it all, you can't leave me in the lurch. It won't hurt you just once."

Ginger Ted looked at the Controleur suspiciously, but his face was serious and his manner sincere; he could not guess that within him the Dutchman bubbled with laughter.

"What the devil do they want me for?"

"I don't know. The pleasure of your society, I suppose."

"Will there be any booze?"

"No, but come up to my house at seven, and we'll have a tiddly before we go."

"Oh, all right," said Ginger Ted sulkily.

The Controleur rubbed his little fat hands with joy. He was expecting a great deal of amusement from the party. But when Thursday came and seven o'clock Ginger Ted was dead drunk and Mr. Gruyter had to go alone. He told the missionary and his sister the plain truth. Mr. Jones shook his head.

"I'm afraid it's no good, Martha, the man's hopeless."

For a moment Miss Jones was silent and the Controleur saw two tears trickle down her long thin nose. She bit her lip.

"No one is hopeless. Everyone has some good in

him. I shall pray for him every night. It would be wicked to doubt the power of God."

Perhaps Miss Jones was right in this, but the divine providence took a very funny way of effecting its ends. Ginger Ted began to drink more heavily than ever. He was so troublesome that even Mr. Gruyter lost patience with him. He made up his mind that he could not have the fellow on the islands any more and resolved to deport him on the next boat that touched at Baru. Then a man died under mysterious circumstances after having been for a trip to one of the islands and the Controleur learnt that there had been several deaths on the same island. He sent the Chinese who was the official doctor of the group to look into the matter, and very soon received intelligence that the deaths were due to cholera. Two more took place at Baru and the certainty was forced upon him that there was an epidemic.

The Controleur cursed freely. He cursed in Dutch, he cursed in English and he cursed in Malay. Then he drank a bottle of beer and smoked a cigar. After that he took thought. He knew the Chinese doctor would be useless. He was a nervous little man from Java and the natives would refuse to obey his orders. The Controleur was efficient and knew pretty well what must be done, but he could not do everything single-handed. He did not like Mr. Jones, but just then he was thankful that he was at hand, and he sent for him at once. In ten minutes Mr. Jones was in the office. He was accompanied by his sister.

"You know what I want to see you about, Mr. Jones," he said abruptly.

"Yes. I've been expecting a message from you. That is why my sister has come with me. We are ready to put all our resources at your disposal. I need not tell you that my sister is as competent as a man."

"I know. I shall be very glad of her assistance."

They set to without further delay to discuss the steps that must be taken. Hospital huts would have to be erected and quarantine stations. The inhabitants of the various villages on the islands must be forced to take proper precautions. In a good many cases the infected villages drew their water from the same well as the uninfected, and in each case this difficulty would have to be dealt with according to circumstances. It was necessary to send round people to give orders and make sure that they were carried out. Negligence must be ruthlessly punished. The worst of it was that the natives would not obey other natives, and orders given by native policemen, themselves unconvinced of their efficacy, would certainly be disregarded. It was advisable for Mr. Jones to stay at Baru where the population was largest and his medical attention most wanted; and what with the official duties that forced him to keep in touch with his headquarters, it was impossible for Mr. Gruyter to visit all the other islands himself. Miss Jones must go; but the natives of some of the outlying islands were wild and treacherous; the Controleur had had a good deal of trouble with them. He did not like the idea of exposing her to danger.

"I'm not afraid," she said.

"I daresay. But if you have your throat cut I shall get into trouble, and besides, we're so short-handed I don't want to risk losing your help."

"Then let Mr. Wilson come with me. He knows the natives better than anyone and can speak all their dialects."

"Ginger Ted?" The Controleur stared at her. "He's just getting over an attack of D.T.'s."

"I know," she answered.

"You know a great deal, Miss Jones."

Even though the moment was so serious Mr. Gruyter could not but smile. He gave her a sharp look, but she met it coolly.

"There's nothing like responsibility for bringing out what there is in a man, and I think something like this may be the making of him."

"Do you think it would be wise to trust yourself for days at a time to a man of such infamous character?" said the missionary.

"I put my trust in God," she answered gravely.

"Do you think he'd be any use?" asked the Controleur. "You know what he is."

"I'm convinced of it." Then she blushed. "After all, no one knows better than I that he's capable of self-control."

The Controleur bit his lip.

"Let's send for him."

He gave a message to the sergeant and in a few minutes Ginger Ted stood before them. He looked ill. He had evidently been much shaken by his recent attack and his nerves were all to pieces. He was in rags and he had not shaved for a week. No one could have looked more disreputable.

"Look here, Ginger," said the Controleur, "it's about this cholera business. We've got to force the natives to take precautions and we want you to help us."

"Why the hell should I?"

"No reason at all. Except philanthropy."

"Nothing doing, Controleur. I'm not a philanthropist."

"That settles that. That was all. You can go."

But as Ginger Ted turned to the door Miss Jones stopped him.

"It was my suggestion, Mr. Wilson. You see, they want me to go to Labobo and Sakunchi, and the natives there are so funny I was afraid to go alone. I thought if you came I should be safer."

He gave her a look of extreme distaste.

"What do you suppose I care if they cut your throat?"

Miss Jones looked at him and her eyes filled with tears. She began to cry. He stood and watched her stupidly.

"There's no reason why you should." She pulled herself together and dried her eyes. "I'm being silly. I shall be all right. I'll go alone."

"It's damned foolishness for a woman to go to Labobo."

She gave him a little smile.

"I daresay it is, but you see, it's my job and I can't help myself. I'm sorry if I offended you by asking you. You must forget about it. I daresay it wasn't quite fair to ask you to take such a risk."

For quite a minute Ginger Ted stood and looked at her. He shifted from one foot to the other. His surly face seemed to grow black.

"Oh, hell, have it your own way," he said at last. "I'll come with you. When d'you want to start?"

They set out next day, with drugs and disinfectants, in the government launch. Mr. Gruyter as soon as he had put the necessary work in order was to start off in a prahu in the other direction. For four months the epidemic raged. Though everything possible was done to localise it one island after another was attacked. The Controleur was busy from morning to night. He had no sooner got back to Baru from one or other of the islands to do what was necessary there than he had to set off again. He distributed food and medicine. He cheered the terrified people. He supervised everything. He worked like a dog. He saw nothing of Ginger Ted, but he heard from Mr. Jones that the experiment was working out beyond all hopes. The scamp was behaving himself. He had a way with the natives; and by cajolery, firmness and on occasion the use of his fist, managed to make them take the steps necessary for their own safety. Miss Jones could congratulate herself on the success of the scheme. But the Controleur was too tired to be amused. When the epidemic had run its course he rejoiced because out of a population of eight thousand only six hundred had died.

Finally he was able to give the district a clean bill of health.

One evening he was sitting in his sarong on the verandah of his house and he read a French novel with the happy consciousness that once more he could take things easy. His head boy came in and told him that Ginger Ted wished to see him. He got up from his chair and shouted to him to come in. Company was just what he wanted. It had crossed the Controleur's mind that it would be pleasant to get drunk that night, but it is dull to get drunk alone, and he had regretfully put the thought aside. And heaven had sent Ginger Ted in the nick of time. By God, they would make a night of it. After four months they deserved a bit of fun. Ginger Ted entered. He was wearing a clean suit of white ducks. He was shaved. He looked another man.

"Why, Ginger, you look as if you'd been spending a month at a health resort instead of nursing a pack of natives dying of cholera. And look at your clothes. Have you just stepped out of a band-box?"

Ginger Ted smiled rather sheepishly. The head boy brought two bottles of beer and poured them out.

"Help yourself, Ginger," said the Controleur as he took his glass.

"I don't think I'll have any, thank you."

The Controleur put down his glass and looked at Ginger Ted with amazement.

"Why, what's the matter? Aren't you thirsty?"

"I don't mind having a cup of tea."

"A cup of what?"

"I'm on the wagon. Martha and I are going to be married."

"Ginger!"

The Controleur's eyes popped out of his head. He scratched his shaven pate.

"You can't marry Miss Jones," he said. "No one could marry Miss Jones."

"Well, I'm going to. That's what I've come to see you about. Owen's going to marry us in chapel, but we want to be married by Dutch law as well."

"A joke's a joke, Ginger. What's the idea?"

"She wanted it. She fell for me that night we spent on the island when the propeller broke. She's not a bad old girl when you get to know her. It's her last chance, if you understand what I mean, and I'd like to do something to oblige her. And she wants someone to take care of her, there's no doubt about that."

"Ginger, Ginger, before you can say knife she'll make you into a damned missionary."

"I don't know that I'd mind that so much if we had a little mission of our own. She says I'm a bloody marvel with the natives. She says I can do more with a native in five minutes than Owen can do in a year. She says she's never known anyone with the magnetism I have. It seems a pity to waste a gift like that."

The Controleur looked at him without speaking and slowly nodded his head three or four times. She'd nobbled him all right.

"I've converted seventeen already," said Ginger Ted.

"You? I didn't know you believed in Christianity."

"Well, I don't know that I did exactly, but when I talked to 'em and they just came into the fold like a lot of blasted sheep, well, it gave me quite a turn. Blimey, I said, I daresay there's something in it after all."

"You should have raped her, Ginger. I wouldn't have been hard on you. I wouldn't have given you more than three years and three years is soon over."

"Look here, Controleur, don't you ever let on that the thought never entered my head. Women are touchy, you know, and she'd be as sore as hell if she knew that."

"I guessed she'd got her eye on you, but I never thought it would come to this." The Controleur in an agitated manner walked up and down the verandah. "Listen to me, old boy," he said after an interval of reflection, "we've had some grand times together and a friend's a friend. I'll tell you what I'll do, I'll lend you the launch and you can go and hide on one of the islands till the next ship comes along and then I'll get 'em to slow down and take you on board. You've only got one chance now and that's to cut and run."

Ginger Ted shook his head.

"It's no good, Controleur, I know you mean well, but I'm going to marry the blasted woman, and that's that. You don't know the joy of bringing all them bleeding sinners to repentance, and Christ, that girl can make a treacle pudding. I haven't eaten a better one since I was a kid."

The Controleur was very much disturbed. The drunken scamp was his only companion on the islands and he did not want to lose him. He discovered that he had even a certain affection for him. Next day he went to see the missionary.

"What's this I hear about your sister marrying Ginger Ted?" he asked him. "It's the most extraordinary thing I've ever heard in my life."

"It's true nevertheless."

"You must do something about it. It's madness."

"My sister is of full age and entitled to do as she pleases."

"But you don't mean to tell me you approve of it. You know Ginger Ted. He's a bum and there are no two ways about it. Have you told her the risk she's running? I mean, bringing sinners to repentance and all that sort of thing's all right, but there are limits. And does the leopard ever change his spots?"

Then for the first time in his life the Controleur saw a twinkle in the missionary's eye.

"My sister is a very determined woman, Mr. Gruyter," he replied. "From that night they spent on the island he never had a chance."

The Controleur gasped. He was as surprised as the prophet when the Lord opened the mouth of the ass, and she said unto Balaam, "What have I done unto thee, that thou hast smitten me these three times?" Perhaps Mr. Jones was human after all.

"*Allejesus!*" muttered the Controleur.

Before anything more could be said Miss Jones swept into the room. She was radiant. She looked ten years younger. Her cheeks were flushed and her nose was hardly red at all.

"Have you come to congratulate me, Mr. Gruyter?" she cried, and her manner was sprightly and girlish. "You see, I was right after all. Everyone has some good in them. You don't know how splendid Edward has been all through this terrible time. He's a hero. He's a saint. Even I was surprised."

"I hope you'll be very happy, Miss Jones."

"I know I shall. Oh, it would be wicked of me to doubt it. For it is the Lord who has brought us together."

"Do you think so?"

"I know it. Don't you see? Except for the cholera Edward would never have found himself. Except for the cholera we should never have learnt to know one another. I have never seen the hand of God more plainly manifest."

The Controleur could not but think that it was rather a clumsy device to bring those two together that necessitated the death of six hundred innocent persons, but not being well versed in the ways of omnipotence he made no remark.

"You'll never guess where we're going for our honeymoon," said Miss Jones, perhaps a trifle archly.

"Java?"

"No, if you'll lend us the launch, we're going to that island where we were marooned. It has very tender recollections for both of us. It was there that I first guessed how fine and good Edward was. It's there I want him to have his reward."

The Controleur caught his breath. He left quickly, for he thought that unless he had a bottle of beer at once he would have a fit. He was never so shocked in his life.

THE BOOK-BAG

SOME people read for instruction, which is praise-worthy, and some for pleasure, which is innocent, but not a few read from habit, and I suppose that this is neither innocent nor praiseworthy. Of that lamentable company am I. Conversation after a time bores me, games tire me and my own thoughts, which we are told are the unfailing resource of a sensible man, have a tendency to run dry. Then I fly to my book as the opium-smoker to his pipe. I would sooner read the catalogue of the Army and Navy Stores or Bradshaw's Guide than nothing at all, and indeed I have spent many delightful hours over both these works. At one time I never went out without a second-hand book-seller's list in my pocket. I know no reading more fruity. Of course to read in this way is as reprehensible as doping, and I never cease to wonder at the imperti-nence of great readers who, because they are such, look down on the illiterate. From the standpoint of what eternity is it better to have read a thousand books than to have ploughed a million furrows? Let us admit that reading with us is just a drug that we cannot do without—who of this band does not know the restless-ness that attacks him when he has been severed from reading too long, the apprehension and irritability, and the sigh of relief which the sight of a printed page

extracts from him?—and so let us be no more vain-
glorious than the poor slaves of the hypodermic needle
or the pint-pot.

And like the dope-fiend who cannot move from place
to place without taking with him a plentiful supply of
his deadly balm I never venture far without a suffi-
ciency of reading matter. Books are so necessary to me
that when in a railway train I have become aware
that fellow-travellers have come away without a single
one I have been seized with a veritable dismay. But
when I am starting on a long journey the problem is
formidable. I have learnt my lesson. Once, imprisoned
by illness for three months in a hill-town in Java, I came
to the end of all the books I had brought with me, and
knowing no Dutch was obliged to buy the school-books
from which intelligent Javanese, I suppose, acquired
knowledge of French and German. So I read again
after five and twenty years the frigid plays of Goethe,
the fables of La Fontaine and the tragedies of the tender
and exact Racine. I have the greatest admiration for
Racine, but I admit that to read his plays one after
the other requires a certain effort in a person who is
suffering from colitis. Since then I have made a point
of travelling with the largest sack made for carrying
soiled linen and filling it to the brim with books to suit
every possible occasion and every mood. It weighs a
ton and strong porters reel under its weight. Custom-
house officials look at it askance, but recoil from it with
consternation when I give them my word that it contains nothing but books. Its inconvenience is that the
particular work I suddenly hanker to read is always at
the bottom and it is impossible for me to get it without

emptying the book-bag's entire contents upon the floor. Except for this, however, I should perhaps never have heard the singular history of Olive Hardy.

I was wandering about Malaya, staying here and there, a week or two if there was a rest-house or a hotel, and a day or so if I was obliged to inflict myself on a planter or a District Officer whose hospitality I had no wish to abuse; and at the moment I happened to be at Penang. It is a pleasant little town, with a hotel that has always seemed to me very agreeable, but the stranger finds little to do there and time hung a trifle heavily on my hands. One morning I received a letter from a man I knew only by name. This was Mark Featherstone. He was Acting Resident, in the absence on leave of the Resident, at a place called Tenggarah. There was a sultan there and it appeared that a water festival of some sort was to take place which Featherstone thought would interest me. He said that he would be glad if I would come and stay with him for a few days. I wired to tell him that I should be delighted and next day took the train to Tenggarah. Featherstone met me at the station. He was a man of about thirty-five, I should think, tall and handsome, with fine eyes and a strong, stern face. He had a wiry black moustache and bushy eyebrows. He looked more like a soldier than a government official. He was very smart in white ducks, with a white topi, and he wore his clothes with elegance. He was a little shy, which seemed odd in a strapping fellow of resolute mien, but I surmised that this was only because he was unused to the society of that strange fish, a writer, and I hoped in a little to put him at his ease.

"My boys'll look after your barang," he said. "We'll go down to the club. Give them your keys and they'll unpack before we get back."

I told him that I had a good deal of luggage and thought it better to leave everything at the station but what I particularly wanted. He would not hear of it.

"It doesn't matter a bit. It'll be safer at my house. It's always better to have one's barang with one."

"All right."

I gave my keys and the ticket for my trunk and my book-bag to a Chinese boy who stood at my host's elbow. Outside the station a car was waiting for us and we stepped in.

"Do you play bridge?" asked Featherstone.

"I do."

"I thought most writers didn't."

"They don't," I said. "It's generally considered among authors a sign of deficient intelligence to play cards."

The club was a bungalow, pleasing but unpretentious; it had a large reading-room, a billiard-room with one table, and a small card-room. When we arrived it was empty but for one or two persons reading the English weeklies, and we walked through to the tennis courts where a couple of sets were being played. A number of people were sitting on the verandah, looking on, smoking and sipping long drinks. I was introduced to one or two of them. But the light was failing and soon the players could hardly see the ball. Featherstone asked one of the men I had been introduced to if he would like a rubber. He said he would. Featherstone looked about for a fourth. He caught sight of a man sitting a little by himself, paused for a second, and went up to him. The two exchanged a few words and then came towards us. We strolled in to the card-room. We had a very nice game. I did not pay much attention to the two men who made up the four. They stood me drinks, and I, a temporary member of the club, returned the compliment. The drinks were very small, quarter whiskies, and in the two hours we played each of us was able to show his open-handedness without an excessive consumption of alcohol. When the advancing hour suggested that the next rubber must be the last we changed from whisky to gin pahits. The rubber came to an end. Featherstone called for the book and the winnings and losings of each one of us were set down. One of the men got up.

"Well, I must be going," he said.

"Going back to the Estate?" asked Featherstone.

"Yes," he nodded. He turned to me. "Shall you be here to-morrow?"

"I hope so."

He went out of the room.

"I'll collect my mem and get along home to dinner," said the other.

"We might be going too," said Featherstone.

"I'm ready whenever you are," I replied.

We got into the car and drove to his house. It was a longish drive. In the darkness I could see nothing much, but presently I realised that we were going up a rather steep hill. We reached the Residency.

It had been an evening like any other, pleasant, but

not at all exciting, and I had spent I don't know how many just like it. I did not expect it to leave any sort of impression on me.

Featherstone led me into his sitting-room. It looked comfortable, but it was a trifle ordinary. It had large basket arm-chairs covered with cretonne and on the walls were a great many framed photographs; the tables were littered with papers, magazines and official reports, with pipes, yellow tins of straight-cut cigarettes and pink tins of tobacco. In a row of shelves were untidily stacked a good many books, their bindings stained with damp and the ravages of white ants. Featherstone showed me my room and left me with the words:

"Shall you be ready for a gin pahit in ten minutes?"

"Easily," I said.

I had a bath and changed and went downstairs. Featherstone, ready before me, mixed our drink as he heard me clatter down the wooden staircase. We dined. We talked. The festival which I had been invited to see was the next day but one, but Featherstone told me he had arranged for me before that to be received by the Sultan.

"He's a jolly old boy," he said. "And the palace is a sight for sore eyes."

After dinner we talked a little more, Featherstone put on the gramophone, and we looked at the latest illustrated papers that had arrived from England. Then we went to bed. Featherstone came to my room to see that I had everything I wanted.

"I suppose you haven't any books with you," he said. "I haven't got a thing to read."

"Books?" I cried.

I pointed to my book-bag. It stood upright, bulging oddly, so that it looked like a humpbacked gnome somewhat the worse for liquor.

"Have you got books in there? I thought that was your dirty linen or a camp-bed or something. Is there anything you can lend me?"

"Look for yourself."

Featherstone's boys had unlocked the bag, but quailing before the sight that then discovered itself had done no more. I knew from long experience how to unpack it. I threw it over on its side, seized its leather bottom and, walking backwards, dragged the sack away from its contents. A river of books poured on to the floor. A look of stupefaction came upon Featherstone's face.

"You don't mean to say you travel with as many books as that? By George, what a snip."

He bent down and turning them over rapidly looked at the titles. There were books of all kinds. Volumes of verse, novels, philosophical works, critical studies (they say books about books are profitless, but they certainly make very pleasant reading), biographies, history; there were books to read when you were ill and books to read when your brain, all alert, craved for something to grapple with, there were books that you had always wanted to read, but in the hurry of life at home had never found time to, there were books to read at sea when you were meandering through narrow waters on a tramp steamer, and there were books for bad weather when your whole cabin creaked and you had to wedge yourself in your bunk in order not to fall out; there were books chosen solely for their length, which you **took** with you when on some expedition you had to travel light, and there were the books you could read when you could read nothing else. Finally Featherstone picked out a life of Byron that had recently appeared.

"Hullo, what's this?" he said. "I read a review of it some time ago."

"I believe it's very good," I replied. "I haven't read it yet."

"May I take it? It'll do me for to-night at all events."

"Of course. Take anything you like."

"No, that's enough. Well, good-night. Breakfast at eight-thirty."

When I came down next morning the head boy told me that Featherstone, who had been at work since six, would be in shortly. While I waited for him I glanced at his shelves.

"I see you've got a grand library of books on bridge," I remarked as we sat down to breakfast.

"Yes, I get every one that comes out. I'm very keen on it."

"That fellow we were playing with yesterday plays a good game."

"Which? Hardy?"

"I don't know. Not the one who said he was going to collect his wife. The other."

"Yes, that was Hardy. That was why I asked him to play. He doesn't come to the club very often."

"I hope he will to-night."

"I wouldn't bank on it. He has an estate about thirty miles away. It's a longish ride to come just for a rubber of bridge."

"Is he married?"

"No. Well, yes. But his wife is in England."

"It must be awfully lonely for those men who live by themselves on those estates," I said.

"Oh, he's not so badly off as some. I don't think he much cares about seeing people. I think he'd be just as lonely in London."

There was something in the way Featherstone spoke that struck me as a little strange. His voice had what I can only describe as a shuttered tone. He seemed suddenly to have moved away from me. It was as though one were passing along a street at night and paused for a second to look in at a lighted window that showed a comfortable room and suddenly an invisible hand pulled down a blind. His eyes, which habitually met those of the person he was talking to with frankness, now avoided mine and I had a notion that it was not only my fancy that read in his face an expression of pain. It was drawn for a moment as it might be by a twinge of neuralgia. I could not think of anything to say and Featherstone did not speak. I was conscious that his thoughts, withdrawn from me and what we were about, were turned upon a subject unknown to me. Presently he gave a little sigh, very slight, but unmistakable, and seemed with a deliberate effort to pull himself together.

"I'm going down to the office immediately after breakfast," he said. "What are you going to do with yourself?"

"Oh, don't bother about me. I shall slack around. I'll stroll down and look at the town."

"There's not much to see."

"All the better. I'm fed up with sights."

I found that Featherstone's verandah gave me sufficient entertainment for the morning. It had one of the
most enchanting views I had seen in the F.M.S. The
Residency was built on the top of a hill and the garden
was large and well-cared for. Great trees gave it almost
the look of an English park. It had vast lawns and
there Tamils, black and emaciated, were scything
with deliberate and beautiful gestures. Beyond and
below, the jungle grew thickly to the bank of a broad,
winding and swiftly flowing river, and on the other
side of this, as far as the eye could reach, stretched the
wooded hills of Tenggarah. The contrast between the
trim lawns, so strangely English, and the savage growth
of the jungle beyond pleasantly titillated the fancy.
I sat and read and smoked. It is my business to be
curious about people and I asked myself how the peace
of this scene, charged nevertheless with a tremulous
and dark significance, affected Featherstone who lived
with it. He knew it under every aspect: at dawn when
the mist rising from the river shrouded it with a ghostly
pall; in the splendour of noon; and at last when the
shadowy gloaming crept softly out of the jungle, like
an army making its way with caution in unknown
country, and presently enveloped the green lawns and
the great flowering trees and the flaunting cassias in
the silent night. I wondered whether, unbeknownst to
him, the tender and yet strangely sinister aspect of the
scene, acting on his nerves and his loneliness, imbued
him with some mystical quality so that the life he led,
the life of the capable administrator, the sportsman
and the good fellow, on occasion seemed to him not
quite real. I smiled at my own fancies, for certainly

the conversation we had had the night before had not indicated in him any stirrings of the soul. I had thought him quite nice. He had been at Oxford and was a member of a good London club. He seemed to attach a good deal of importance to social things. He was a gentleman and slightly conscious of the fact that he belonged to a better class than most of the Englishmen his life brought him in contact with. I gathered from the various silver pots that adorned his dining-room that he excelled in games. He played tennis and billiards. When he went on leave he hunted and, anxious to keep his weight down, he dieted carefully. He talked a good deal of what he would do when he retired. He hankered after the life of a country gentleman. A little house in Leicestershire, a couple of hunters and neighbours to play bridge with. He would have his pension and he had a little money of his own. But meanwhile he worked hard and did his work, if not brilliantly, certainly with competence. I have no doubt that he was looked upon by his superiors as a reliable officer. He was cut upon a pattern that I knew too well to find very interesting. He was like a novel that is careful, honest and efficient, yet a little ordinary, so that you seem to have read it all before, and you turn the pages listlessly knowing that it will never afford you a surprise or move you to excitement.

But human beings are incalculable and he is a fool who tells himself that he knows what a man is capable of.

In the afternoon Featherstone took me to see the Sultan. We were received by one of his sons, a shy, smiling youth who acted as his A.D.C. He was dressed in a neat blue suit, but round his waist he wore a sarong, white flowers on a yellow ground, on his head a red fez, and on his feet knobby American shoes. The palace, built in the Moorish style, was like a very big doll's house and it was painted bright yellow, which is the royal colour. We were led into a spacious room, furnished with the sort of furniture you would find in an English lodging-house at the seaside, but the chairs were covered with yellow silk. On the floor was a Brussels carpet and on the walls photographs in very grand gilt frames of the Sultan at various state functions. In a cabinet was a large collection of all kinds of fruit done entirely in crochet work. The Sultan came in with several attendants. He was a man of fifty, perhaps, short and stout, dressed in trousers and tunic of a large white and yellow check; round his middle he wore a very beautiful yellow sarong and on his head a white fez. He had large, handsome, friendly eyes. He gave us coffee to drink, sweet cakes to eat and cheroots to smoke. Conversation was not difficult, for he was affable, and he told me that he had never been to a theatre or played cards, for he was very religious, and he had four wives and twenty-four children. The only bar to the happiness of his life seemed to be that common decency obliged him to divide his time equally between his four wives. He said that an hour with one was a month and with another five minutes. I remarked that Professor Einstein—or was it Bergson?—had made similar observations upon time and indeed on this question had given the world much to ponder over. Presently we took our leave and the Sultan presented me with some beautiful white Malaccas.

In the evening we went to the club. One of the men we had played with the day before got up from his chair as we entered.

"Ready for a rubber?" he said.

"Where's our fourth?" I asked.

"Oh, there are several fellows here who'll be glad to play."

"What about that man we played with yesterday?" I had forgotten his name.

"Hardy? He's not here."

"It's not worth while waiting for him," said Featherstone.

"He very seldom comes to the club. I was surprised to see him last night."

I did not know why I had the impression that behind the very ordinary words of these two men there was an odd sense of embarrassment. Hardy had made no impression on me and I did not even remember what he looked like. He was just a fourth at the bridge table. I had a feeling that they had something against him. It was no business of mine and I was quite content to play with a man who at that moment joined us. We certainly had a more cheerful game than before. A good deal of chaff passed from one side of the table to the other. We played less serious bridge. We laughed. I wondered if it was only that they were less shy of the stranger who had happened in upon them or if the presence of Hardy had caused in the other two a certain constraint. At half-past eight we broke up and Featherstone and I went back to dine at his house.

After dinner we lounged in arm-chairs and smoked cheroots. For some reason our conversation did not flow easily. I tried topic after topic, but could not get Featherstone to interest himself in any of them. I began to think that in the last twenty-four hours he had said all he had to say. I fell somewhat discouraged into silence. It prolonged itself and again, I did not know why, I had a faint sensation that it was charged with a significance that escaped me. I felt slightly uncomfortable. I had that queer feeling that one sometimes has when sitting in an empty room that one is not by oneself. Presently I was conscious that Featherstone was steadily looking at me. I was sitting by a lamp, but he was in shadow so that the play of his features was hidden from me. But he had very large brilliant eyes and in the half darkness they seemed to shine dimly. They were like new boot-buttons that caught a reflected light. I wondered why he looked at me like that. I gave him a glance and catching his eyes insistently fixed upon me faintly smiled.

"Interesting book that one you lent me last night," he said suddenly, and I could not help thinking his voice did not sound quite natural. The words issued from his lips as though they were pushed from behind.

"Oh, the Life of Byron?" I said breezily. "Have you read it already?"

"A good deal of it. I read till three."

"I've heard it's very well done. I'm not sure that Byron interests me so much as all that. There was so much in him that was so frightfully second-rate. It makes one rather uncomfortable."

"What do you think is the real truth of that story about him and his sister?"

"Augusta Leigh? I don't know very much about it. I've never read Astarte."

"Do you think they were really in love with one another?"

"I suppose so. Isn't it generally believed that she was the only woman he ever genuinely loved?"

"Can you understand it?"

"I can't really. It doesn't particularly shock me. It just seems to me very unnatural. Perhaps 'unnatural' isn't the right word. It's incomprehensible to me. I can't throw myself into the state of feeling in which such a thing seems possible. You know, that's how a writer gets to know the people he writes about, by standing himself in their shoes and feeling with their hearts."

I knew I did not make myself very clear, but I was trying to describe a sensation, an action of the subconscious, which from experience was perfectly familiar to me, but which no words I knew could precisely indicate. I went on.

"Of course she was only his half-sister, but just as habit kills love I should have thought habit would prevent its arising. When two persons have known one another all their lives and lived together in close contact I can't imagine how or why that sudden spark should flash that results in love. The probabilities are that they would be joined by mutual affection and I don't know anything that is more contrary to love than affection."

I could just see in the dimness the outline of a smile flicker for a moment on my host's heavy, and it seemed to me then, somewhat saturnine face.

"You only believe in love at first sight?"

"Well, I suppose I do, but with the proviso that people may have met twenty times before seeing one another. 'Seeing' has an active side and a passive one. Most people we run across mean so little to us that we never bestir ourselves to look at them. We just suffer the impression they make on us."

"Oh, but one's often heard of couples who've known one another for years and it's never occurred to one they cared two straws for each other and suddenly they go and get married. How do you explain that?"

"Well, if you're going to bully me into being logical and consistent, I should suggest that their love is of a different kind. After all, passion isn't the only reason for marriage. It may not even be the best one. Two people may marry because they're lonely or because they're good friends or for convenience' sake. Though I said that affection was the greatest enemy of love, I would never deny that it's a very good substitute. I'm not sure that a marriage founded on it isn't the happiest."

"What did you think of Tim Hardy?"

I was a little surprised at the sudden question, which seemed to have nothing to do with the subject of our conversation.

"I didn't think of him very much. He seemed quite nice. Why?"

"Did he seem to you just like everybody else?"

"Yes. Is there anything peculiar about him? If you'd told me that I'd have paid more attention to him."

"He's very quiet, isn't he? I suppose no one who

knew nothing about him would give him a second thought."

I tried to remember what he looked like. The only thing that had struck me when we were playing cards was that he had fine hands. It passed idly through my mind that they were not the sort of hands I should have expected a planter to have. But why a planter should have different hands from anybody else I did not trouble to ask myself. His were somewhat large, but very well formed, with peculiarly long fingers, and the nails were of an admirable shape. They were virile and yet oddly sensitive hands. I noticed this and thought no more about it. But if you are a writer, instinct and the habit of years enable you to store up impressions that you are not aware of. Sometimes of course they do not correspond with the facts and a woman for example may remain in your subconsciousness as a dark, massive and ox-eyed creature when she is indeed rather small and of a nondescript colouring. But that is of no consequence. The impression may very well be more exact than the sober truth. And now, seeking to call up from the depths of me a picture of this man I had a feeling of some ambiguity. He was clean-shaven and his face, oval but not thin, seemed strangely pale under the tan of long exposure to the tropical sun. His features were vague. I did not know whether I remembered it or only imagined now that his rounded chin gave one the impression of a certain weakness. He had thick brown hair, just turning grey, and a long wisp fell down constantly over his forehead. He pushed it back with a gesture that had become habitual. His brown eyes were rather large and gentle, but perhaps a little sad; they had a melting softness which, I could imagine, might be very appealing.

After a pause Featherstone continued:

"It's rather strange that I should run across Tim Hardy here after all these years. But that's the way of the F.M.S. People move about and you find yourself in the same place as a man you'd known years before in another part of the country. I first knew Tim when he had an estate near Sibuku. Have you ever been there?"

"No. Where is it?"

"Oh, it's up north. Towards Siam. It wouldn't be worth your while to go. It's just like every other place in the F.M.S. But it was rather nice. It had a very jolly little club and there were some quite decent people. There was the schoolmaster and the head of the police, the doctor, the padre and the government engineer. The usual lot, you know. A few planters. Three or four women. I was A.D.O. It was one of my first jobs. Tim Hardy had an estate about twenty-five miles away. He lived there with his sister. They had a bit of money of their own and he'd bought the place. Rubber was pretty good then and he wasn't doing at all badly. We rather cottoned on to one another. Of course it's a toss-up with planters. Some of them are very good fellows, but they're not exactly . . ." he sought for a word or a phrase that did not sound snobbish. "Well, they're not the sort of people you'd be likely to meet at home. Tim and Olive were of one's own class, if you understand what I mean."

"Olive was the sister?"

"Yes. They'd had a rather unfortunate past. Their

parents had separated when they were quite small,
seven or eight, and the mother had taken Olive and the
father had kept Tim. Tim went to Clifton, they were
West Country people, and only came home for the
holidays. His father was a retired naval man who lived
at Fowey. But Olive went with her mother to Italy.
She was educated in Florence; she spoke Italian perfectly and French too. For all those years Tim and Olive
never saw one another once, but they used to write to
one another regularly. They'd been very much attached
when they were children. As far as I could understand,
life when their people were living together had been
rather stormy with all sorts of scenes and upsets, you
know the sort of thing that happens when two people
who are married don't get on together, and that had
thrown them on their own resources. They were left a
good deal to themselves. Then Mrs. Hardy died and
Olive came home to England and went back to her
father. She was eighteen then and Tim was seventeen.
A year later the war broke out. Tim joined up and his
father, who was over fifty, got some job at Portsmouth.
I take it he had been a hard liver and a heavy drinker.
He broke down before the end of the war and died after
a lingering illness. They don't seem to have had any
relations. They were the last of a rather old family; they
had a fine old house in Dorsetshire that had belonged to
them for a good many generations, but they had never
been able to afford to live in it and it was always let. I
remember seeing photographs of it. It was very much a
gentleman's house, of grey stone and rather stately, with
a coat of arms carved over the front door and mullioned
windows. Their great ambition was to make enough

money to be able to live in it. They used to talk about it a lot. They never spoke as though either of them would marry, but always as though it were a settled thing that they would remain together. It was rather funny considering how young they were."

"How old were they then?" I asked.

"Well, I suppose he was twenty-five or twenty-six and she was a year older. They were awfully kind to me when I first went up to Sibuku. They took a fancy to me at once. You see, we had more in common than most of the people there. I think they were glad of my company. They weren't particularly popular."

"Why not?" I asked.

"They were rather reserved and you couldn't help seeing that they liked their own society better than other people's. I don't know if you've noticed it, but that always seems to put people's backs up. They resent it somehow if they have a feeling that you can get along very well without them."

"It's tiresome, isn't it?" I said.

"It was rather a grievance to the other planters that Tim was his own master and had private means. They had to put up with an old Ford to get about in, but Tim had a real car. Tim and Olive were very nice when they came to the club and they played in the tennis tournaments and all that sort of thing, but you had an impression that they were always glad to get away again. They'd dine out with people and make themselves very pleasant, but it was pretty obvious that they'd just as soon have stayed at home. If you had any sense you couldn't blame them. I don't know if you've been much to planters' houses. They're a bit dreary. A lot of gimcrack furniture and silver ornaments and tiger skins. And the food's uneatable. But the Hardys had made their bungalow rather nice. There was nothing very grand in it; it was just easy and homelike and comfortable. Their living-room was like a drawing-room in an English country house. You felt that their things meant something to them and that they had had them a long time. It was a very jolly house to stay at. The bungalow was in the middle of the estate, but it was on the brow of a little hill and you looked right over the rubber trees to the sea in the distance. Olive took a lot of trouble with her garden and it was really topping. I never saw such a show of cannas. I used to go there for week-ends. It was only about half an hour's drive to the sea and we'd take our lunch with us and bathe and sail. Tim kept a small boat there. Those days were grand. I never knew one could enjoy oneself so much. It's a beautiful bit of coast and it was really extraordinarily romantic. Then in the evenings we'd play patience and chess or turn on the gramophone. The cooking was damned good too. It was a change from what one generally got. Olive had taught their cook to make all sorts of Italian dishes and we used to have great wallops of macaroni and risotto and gnocchi and things like that. I couldn't help envying them their life, it was so jolly and peaceful, and when they talked of what they'd do when they went back to England for good I used to tell them they'd always regret what they'd left.

"'We've been very happy here,' said Olive.

"She had a way of looking at Tim, with a slow, sidelong glance from under her long eyelashes, that was rather engaging.

"In their own house they were quite different from what they were when they went out. They were so easy and cordial. Everybody admitted that and I'm bound to say that people enjoyed going there. They often asked people over. They had the gift of making you feel at home. It was a very happy house, if you know what I mean. Of course no one could help seeing how attached they were to one another. And whatever people said about their being standoffish and self-centred, they were bound to be rather touched by the affection they had for one another. People said they couldn't have been more united if they were married, and when you saw how some couples got on you couldn't help thinking they made most marriages look rather like a wash-out. They seemed to think the same things at the same time. They had little private jokes that made them laugh like children. They were so charming with one another, so gay and happy, that really to stay with them was, well, a spiritual refreshment. I don't know what else you could call it. When you left them, after a couple of days at the bungalow, you felt that you'd absorbed some of their peace and their sober gaiety. It was as though your soul had been sluiced with cool clear water. You felt strangely purified."

It was singular to hear Featherstone talking in this exalted strain. He looked so spruce in his smart white coat, technically known as a bum-freezer, his moustache was so trim, his thick curly hair so carefully brushed, that his high-flown language made me a trifle uncomfortable. But I realised that he was trying to express in his clumsy way a very sincerely felt emotion.

"What was Olive Hardy like?" I asked.

"I'll show you. I've got quite a lot of snapshots."

He got up from his chair and going to a shelf brought me a large album. It was the usual thing, indifferent photographs of people in groups and unflattering likenesses of single figures. They were in bathing dress or in shorts or tennis things, generally with their faces all screwed up because the sun blinded them, or puckered by the distortion of laughter. I recognised Hardy, not much changed after ten years, with his wisp of hair hanging across his forehead. I remembered him better now that I saw the snapshots. In them he looked nice and fresh and young. He had an alertness of expression that was attractive and that I certainly had not noticed when I saw him. In his eyes was a sort of eagerness for life that danced and sparkled through the fading print. I glanced at the photographs of his sister. Her bathing dress showed that she had a good figure, well-developed, but slender; and her legs were long and slim.

"They look rather alike," I said.

"Yes, although she was a year older they might have been twins, they were so much alike. They both had the same oval face and that pale skin without any colour in the cheeks, and they both had those soft brown eyes, very liquid and appealing, so that you felt whatever they did you could never be angry with them. And they both had a sort of careless elegance that made them look charming whatever they wore and however untidy they were. He's lost that now, I suppose, but he certainly had it when I first knew him. They always rather reminded me of the brother and sister in Twelfth Night. You know whom I mean."

"Viola and Sebastian."

"They never seemed to belong quite to the present. There was something Elizabethan about them. I don't think it was only because I was very young then that I couldn't help feeling they were strangely romantic somehow. I could see them living in Illyria."

I gave one of the snapshots another glance.

"The girl looks as though she had a good deal more character than her brother," I remarked.

"She had. I don't know if you'd have called Olive beautiful, but she was awfully attractive. There was something poetic in her, a sort of lyrical quality as it were, that coloured her movements, her acts and everything about her. It seemed to exalt her above common cares. There was something so candid in her expression, so courageous and independent in her bearing, that—oh, I don't know, it made mere beauty just flat and dull."

"You speak as if you'd been in love with her," I interrupted.

"Of course I was. I should have thought you'd guessed that at once. I was frightfully in love with her."

"Was it love at first sight?" I smiled.

"Yes, I think it was, but I didn't know it for a month or so. When it suddenly struck me that what I felt for her—I don't know how to explain it, it was a sort of shattering turmoil that affected every bit of me—that that was love, I knew I'd felt it all along. It was not only her looks, though they were awfully alluring, the smoothness of her pale skin and the way her hair fell over her forehead and the grave sweetness of her brown eyes, it was more than that; you had a sensation of well-being when you were with her, as though you **could** relax and be quite natural and needn't pretend to be anything you weren't. You felt she was incapable of meanness. It was impossible to think of her as envious of other people or catty. She seemed to have a natural generosity of soul. One could be silent with her for an hour at a time and yet feel that one had had a good time."

"A rare gift," I said.

"She was a wonderful companion. If you made a suggestion to do something she was always glad to fall in with it. She was the least exacting girl I ever knew. You could throw her over at the last minute and however disappointed she was it made no difference. Next time you saw her she was just as cordial and serene as ever."

"Why didn't you marry her?"

Featherstone's cheroot had gone out. He threw the stub away and deliberately lit another. He did not answer for a while. It may seem strange to persons who live in a highly civilised state that he should confide these intimate things to a stranger; it did not seem strange to me. I was used to it. People who live so desperately alone, in the remote places of the earth, find it a relief to tell someone whom in all probability they will never meet again the story that has burdened perhaps for years their waking thoughts and their dreams at night. And I have an inkling that the fact of your being a writer attracts their confidence. They feel that what they tell you will excite your interest in an impersonal way that makes it easier for them to discharge their souls. Besides, as we all know from our own experience, it is never unpleasant to talk about oneself.

"Why didn't you marry her?" I had asked him.

"I wanted to badly enough," Featherstone answered at length. "But I hesitated to ask her. Although she was always so nice to me and so easy to get on with, and we were such good friends, I always felt that there was something a little mysterious in her. Although she was so simple, so frank and natural, you never quite got over the feeling of an inner kernel of aloofness, as if deep in her heart she guarded, not a secret, but a sort of privacy of the soul that not a living person would ever be allowed to know. I don't know if I make myself clear."

"I think so."

"I put it down to her upbringing. They never talked of their mother, but somehow I got the impression that she was one of those neurotic, emotional women who wreck their own happiness and are a pest to everyone connected with them. I had a suspicion that she'd led rather a hectic life in Florence and it struck me that Olive owed her beautiful serenity to a disciplined effort of her own will and that her aloofness was a sort of citadel she'd built to protect herself from the knowledge of all sorts of shameful things. But of course that aloofness was awfully captivating. It was strangely exciting to think that if she loved you, and you were married to her, you would at last pierce right into the hidden heart of that mystery; and you felt that if you could share that with her it would be as it were a consummation of all you'd ever desired in your life. Heaven wouldn't be in it. You know, I felt about it just like Bluebeard's wife about the forbidden chamber in the castle. Every room was open to me, but I should never rest till I had gone into that last one that was locked against me."

My eye was caught by a chik-chak, a little brown house lizard with a large head, high up on the wall. It is a friendly little beast and it is good to see it in a house. It watched a fly. It was quite still. On a sudden it made a dart and then as the fly flew away fell back with a sort of jerk into a strange immobility.

"And there was another thing that made me hesitate. I couldn't bear the thought that if I proposed to her and she refused me she wouldn't let me come to the bungalow in the same old way. I should have hated that, I enjoyed going there so awfully. It made me so happy to be with her. But you know, sometimes one can't help oneself. I did ask her at last, but it was almost by accident. One evening, after dinner, when we were sitting on the verandah by ourselves, I took her hand. She withdrew it at once.

"'Why did you do that?' I asked her.

"'I don't very much like being touched,' she said. She turned her head a little and smiled. 'Are you hurt? You mustn't mind, it's just a funny feeling I have. I can't help it.'

"'I wonder if it's ever occurred to you that I'm frightfully fond of you,' I said.

"I expect I was terribly awkward about it, but I'd never proposed to anyone before." Featherstone gave a little sound that was not quite a chuckle and not quite a sigh. "For the matter of that, I've never proposed to anyone since. She didn't say anything for a minute. Then she said:

"'I'm very glad, but I don't think I want you to be anything more than that.'

"'Why not?' I asked.

"'I could never leave Tim.'

"'But supposing he marries?'

"'He never will.'

"I'd gone so far then that I thought I'd better go on. But my throat was so dry that I could hardly speak. I was shaking with nervousness.

"'I'm frightfully in love with you, Olive. I want to marry you more than anything in the world.'

"She put her hand very gently on my arm. It was like a flower falling to the ground.

"'No, dear, I can't,' she said.

"I was silent. It was difficult for me to say what I wanted to. I'm naturally rather shy. She was a girl. I couldn't very well tell her that it wasn't quite the same thing living with a husband and living with a brother. She was normal and healthy; she must want to have babies; it wasn't reasonable to starve her natural instincts. It was such waste of her youth. But it was she who spoke first.

"'Don't let's talk about this any more,' she said. 'D'you mind? It did strike me once or twice that perhaps you cared for me. Tim noticed it. I was sorry because I was afraid it would break up our friendship. I don't want it to do that, Mark. We do get on so well together, the three of us, and we have such jolly times. I don't know what we should do without you now.'

"'I thought of that too,' I said.

"'D'you think it need?' she asked me.

"'My dear, I don't want it to,' I said. 'You must know how much I love coming here. I've never been so happy anywhere before!'

"'You're not angry with me?'

"'Why should I be? It's not your fault. It only means that you're not in love with me. If you were you wouldn't care a hang about Tim.'

"'You are rather sweet,' she said.

"She put her arm round my neck and kissed me lightly on the cheek. I had a notion that in her mind it settled our relation. She adopted me as a second brother.

"A few weeks later Tim went back to England. The tenant of their house in Dorset was leaving and though there was another in the offing, he thought he ought to be on the spot to conduct negotiations. And he wanted some new machinery for the estate. He thought he'd get it at the same time. He didn't expect to be gone more than three months and Olive made up her mind not to go. She knew hardly anyone in England, and it was practically a foreign country to her, she didn't mind being left alone, and she wanted to look after the estate. Of course they could have put a manager in charge, but that wasn't the same thing. Rubber was falling and in case of accidents it was just as well that one or other of them should be there. I promised Tim I'd look after her and if she wanted me she could always call me up. My proposal hadn't changed anything. We carried on as though nothing had happened. I don't know whether she'd told Tim. He made no sign that he knew. Of course I loved her as much as ever, but I kept it to myself. I have a good deal of self-control, you know. I had a sort of feeling I hadn't a chance. I hoped eventually my love would change into something else and we could just be wonderful friends. It's funny, it never has, you know. I suppose I was hit too badly ever to get quite over it.

"She went down to Penang to see Tim off and when she came back I met her at the station and drove her home. I couldn't very well stay at the bungalow while Tim was away, but I went over every Sunday and had tiffin and we'd go down to the sea and have a bathe. People tried to be kind to her and asked her to stay with them, but she wouldn't. She seldom left the estate. She had plenty to do. She read a lot. She was never bored. She seemed quite happy in her own company, and when she had visitors it was only from a sense of duty. She didn't want them to think her ungracious. But it was an effort and she told me she heaved a sigh of relief when she saw the last of them and could again enjoy without disturbance the peaceful loneliness of the bungalow. She was a very curious girl. It was strange that at her age she should be so indifferent to parties and the other small gaieties the station afforded. Spiritually, if you know what I mean, she was entirely self-supporting. I don't know how people found out that I was in love with her; I thought I'd never given myself away in anything, but I had hints here and there that they knew. I gathered they thought Olive hadn't gone home with her brother on my account. One woman, a Mrs. Sergison, the policeman's wife, actually asked me when they were going to be able to congratulate me. Of course I pretended I didn't know what she was talking about, but it didn't go down very well. I couldn't help being amused. I meant so little to Olive in that way that I really believe she'd entirely forgotten that I'd asked her to marry me. I can't say she was unkind to me, I don't think she could have been unkind to anyone; but she treated me with just the casualness with which a sister might treat a younger brother. She was two or three years older than I. She was always terribly glad to see me, but it never occurred to her to put herself out for me, she was almost amazingly intimate with me; but unconsciously, you know, as you might be with a person you'd known so well all your life that you never thought of putting on frills with him. I might not have been a man at all, but an old coat that she wore all the time because it was easy and comfortable and she didn't mind what she did in it. I should have been crazy not to see that she was a thousand miles away from loving me.

"Then one day, three or four weeks before Tim was due back, when I went to the bungalow I saw she'd been crying. I was startled. She was always so composed. I'd never seen her upset over anything.

"'Hullo, what's the matter?' I said.

"'Nothing.'

"'Come off it, darling,' I said. 'What have you been crying about?'

"She tried to smile.

"'I wish you hadn't got such sharp eyes,' she said. 'I think I'm being silly. I've just had a cable from Tim to say he's postponed his sailing.'

"'Oh, my dear, I am sorry,' I said. 'You must be awfully disappointed.'

"'I've been counting the days. I want him back so badly.'

"'Does he say why he's postponing?' I asked.

"'No, he says he's writing. I'll show you the cable.'

"I saw that she was very nervous. Her slow quiet eyes were filled with apprehension and there was a little frown of anxiety between her brows. She went into her bedroom and in a moment came back with the cable. I felt that she was watching me anxiously as I read. So far as I remember it ran: *Darling, I cannot sail on the seventh after all. Please forgive me. Am writing fully. Fondest love. Tim.*

"'Well, perhaps the machinery he wanted isn't ready and he can't bring himself to sail without it,' I said.

"'What could it matter if it came by a later ship? Anyhow, it'll be hung up at Penang.'

"'It may be something about the house.'

"'If it is why doesn't he say so? He must know how frightfully anxious I am.'

"'It wouldn't occur to him,' I said. 'After all, when you're away you don't realise that the people you've left behind don't know something that you take as a matter of course.'

"She smiled again, but now more happily.

"'I daresay you're right. In point of fact Tim is a little like that. He's always been rather slack and casual. I daresay I've been making a mountain out of a molehill. I must just wait patiently for his letter.'

"Olive was a girl with a lot of self-control and I saw her by an effort of will pull herself together. The little line between her eyebrows vanished and she was once more her serene, smiling and kindly self. She was always gentle: that day she had a mildness so heavenly that it was shattering. But for the rest of the time I could see that she kept her restlessness in check only by the deliberate exercise of her common sense. It was as though she had a foreboding of ill. I was with her the day before the mail was due. Her anxiety was all the more pitiful to see because she took such pains to hide it. I was always busy on mail day, but I promised to go up to the estate later on and hear the news. I was just thinking of starting when Hardy's seis came along in the car with a message from the amah asking me to go at once to her mistress. The amah was a decent, elderly woman to whom I had given a dollar or two and said that if anything went wrong on the estate she was to let me know at once. I jumped into my car. When I arrived I found the amah waiting for me on the steps.

"'A letter came this morning,' she said.

"I interrupted her. I ran up the steps. The sitting-room was empty.

"'Olive,' I called.

"I went into the passage and suddenly I heard a sound that froze my heart. The amah had followed me and now she opened the door of Olive's room. The sound I had heard was the sound of Olive crying. I went in. She was lying on her bed, on her face, and her sobs shook her from head to foot. I put my hand on her shoulder.

"'Olive, what is it?' I asked.

"'Who's that?' she cried. She sprang to her feet suddenly, as though she were scared out of her wits. And then: 'Oh, it's you,' she said. She stood in front of me, with her head thrown back and her eyes closed, and the tears streamed from them. It was dreadful. 'Tim's married,' she gasped, and her face screwed up in a sort of grimace of pain.

"I must admit that for one moment I had a thrill of exultation, it was like a little electric shock tingling through my heart; it struck me that now I had a chance, she might be willing to marry me; I know it was terribly selfish of me; you see, the news had taken me by surprise; but it was only for a moment, after that I was melted by her awful distress and the only thing I felt was deep sorrow because she was unhappy. I put my arm round her waist.

"'Oh, my dear, I'm so sorry,' I said. 'Don't stay here. Come into the sitting-room and sit down and we'll talk about it. Let me give you something to drink.'

"She let me lead her into the next room and we sat down on the sofa. I told the amah to fetch the whisky and syphon and I mixed her a good strong stengah and made her drink a little. I took her in my arms and rested her head on my shoulder. She let me do what I liked with her. The great tears streamed down her poor face.

"'How could he?' she moaned. 'How could he?'

"'My darling,' I said, 'it was bound to happen sooner or later. He's a young man. How could you expect him never to marry? It's only natural.'

"'No, no, no,' she gasped.

"Tight-clenched in her hand I saw that she had a letter and I guessed that it was Tim's.

"'What does he say?' I asked.

"She gave a frightened movement and clutched the letter to her heart as though she thought I would take it from her.

"'He says he couldn't help himself. He says he had to. What does it mean?'

"'Well, you know, in his way he's just as attractive as you are. He has so much charm. I suppose he just fell madly in love with some girl and she with him.'

"'He's so weak,' she moaned.

"'Are they coming out?' I asked.

"'They sailed yesterday. He says it won't make any difference. He's insane. How *can* I stay here?'

"She began to cry hysterically. It was torture to see that girl, usually so calm, utterly shattered by her emotion. I had always felt that her lovely serenity masked a capacity for deep feeling. But the abandon of her distress simply broke me up. I held her in my arms and kissed her, her eyes and her wet cheek and her hair. I don't think she knew what I was doing. I was hardly conscious of it myself. I was so deeply moved.

"'What shall I do?' she wailed.

"'Why won't you marry me?' I said.

"She tried to withdraw herself from me, but I wouldn't let her go.

"'After all, it would be a way out,' I said.

"'How can I marry you?' she moaned. 'I'm years older than you are.'

"'Oh, what nonsense, two or three. What do I care?'

"'No, no.'

"'Why not?' I said.

"'I don't love you,' she said.

"'What does that matter? I love you.'

"I don't know what I said. I told her that I'd try to make her happy. I said I'd never ask anything from her but what she was prepared to give me. I talked and talked. I tried to make her see reason. I felt that she didn't want to stay there, in the same place as Tim, and

I told her that I'd be moved soon to some other district. I thought that might tempt her. She couldn't deny that we'd always got on awfully well together. After a time she did seem to grow a little quieter. I had a feeling that she was listening to me. I had even a sort of feeling that she knew that she was lying in my arms and that it comforted her. I made her drink a drop more whisky. I gave her a cigarette. At last I thought I might be just mildly facetious.

"'You know, I'm not a bad sort really,' I said. 'You might do worse.'

"'You don't know me,' she said. 'You know nothiug whatever about me.'

"'I'm capable of learning,' I said.

"She smiled a little.

"'You're awfully kind, Mark,' she said.

"'Say yes, Olive,' I begged.

"She gave a deep sigh. For a long time she stared at the ground. But she did not move and I felt the softness of her body in my arms. I waited. I was frightfully nervous and the minutes seemed endless.

"'All right,' she said at last, as though she were not conscious that any time had passed between my prayer and her answer.

"I was so moved that I had nothing to say. But when I wanted to kiss her lips, she turned her face away, and wouldn't let me. I wanted us to be married at once, but she was quite firm that she wouldn't. She insisted on waiting till Tim came back. You know how some-times you see so clearly in people's thoughts that you're more certain of them than if they'd spoken them; I saw that she couldn't quite believe that what Tim had written was true and that she had a sort of miserable hope that it was all a mistake and he wasn't married after all. It gave me a pang, but I loved her so much, I just bore it. I was willing to bear anything. I adored her. She wouldn't even let me tell anyone that we were engaged. She made me promise not to say a word till Tim's return. She said she couldn't bear the thought of the congratulations and all that. She wouldn't even let me make any announcement of Tim's marriage. She was obstinate about it. I had a notion that she felt if the fact were spread about it gave it a certainty that she didn't want it to have.

"But the matter was taken out of her hands. News travels mysteriously in the East. I don't know what Olive had said in the amah's hearing when first she received the news of Tim's marriage; anyhow, the Hardys' seis told the Sergisons' and Mrs. Sergison attacked me the next time I went into the club.

"'I hear Tim Hardy's married,' she said.

"'Oh?' I answered, unwilling to commit myself.

"She smiled at my blank face, and told me that her amah having told her the rumour she had rung up Olive and asked her if it was true. Olive's answer had been rather odd. She had not exactly confirmed it, but said that she had received a letter from Tim telling her he was married.

"'She's a strange girl,' said Mrs. Sergison. 'When I asked her for details she said she had none to give and when I said: "Aren't you thrilled?" she didn't answer.'

"'Olive's devoted to Tim, Mrs. Sergison,' I said. 'His marriage has naturally been a shock to her. She knows nothing about Tim's wife. She's nervous about her.'

"'And when are you two going to be married?' she asked me abruptly.

"'What an embarrassing question!' I said, trying to laugh it off.

"She looked at me shrewdly.

"'Will you give me your word of honour that you're not engaged to her?'

"I didn't like to tell her a deliberate lie, nor to ask her to mind her own business, and I'd promised Olive faithfully that I would say nothing till Tim got back. I hedged.

"'Mrs. Sergison,' I said, 'when there's anything to tell I promise that you'll be the first person to hear it. All I can say to you now is that I do want to marry Olive more than anything in the world.'

"'I'm very glad that Tim's married,' she answered. 'And I hope she'll marry you very soon. It was a morbid and unhealthy life that they led up there, those two, they kept far too much to themselves and they were far too much absorbed in one another.'

"I saw Olive practically every day. I felt that she didn't want me to make love to her, and I contented myself with kissing her when I came and when I went. She was very nice to me, kindly and thoughtful; I knew she was glad to see me and sorry when it was time for me to go. Ordinarily, she was apt to fall into silence, but during this time she talked more than I had ever heard her talk before. But never of the future and never of Tim and his wife. She told me a lot about her life in Florence with her mother. She had led a strange lonely life, mostly with servants and governesses, while her mother, I suspected, engaged in one affair after another with vague Italian counts and Russian princes. I guessed that by the time she was fourteen there wasn't much she didn't know. It was natural for her to be quite unconventional: in the only world she knew till she was eighteen conventions weren't mentioned because they didn't exist. Gradually, Olive seemed to regain her serenity and I should have thought that she was beginning to accustom herself to the thought of Tim's marriage if it hadn't been that I couldn't but notice how pale and tired she looked. I made up my mind that the moment he arrived I'd press her to marry me at once. I could get short leave whenever I asked for it, and by the time that was up I thought I could manage a transfer to some other post. What she wanted was change of air and fresh scenes.

"We knew, of course, within a day when Tim's ship would reach Penang, but it was a question whether she'd get in soon enough for him to catch the train and I wrote to the P. & O. agent asking him to telegraph as soon as he had definite news. When I got the wire and took it up to Olive I found that she'd just received one from Tim. The ship had docked early and he was arriving next day. The train was supposed to get in at eight o'clock in the morning, but it was liable to be anything from one to six hours late, and I bore with me an invitation from Mrs. Sergison asking Olive to come back with me to stay the night with her so that she would be on the spot and need not go to the station till the news came through that the train was coming.

"I was immensely relieved. I thought that when the blow at last fell Olive wouldn't feel it so much. She had worked herself up into such a state that I couldn't help thinking that she must have a reaction now. She might take a fancy to her sister-in-law. There was no reason why they shouldn't all three get on very well together. To my surprise Olive said she wasn't coming down to the station to meet them.

"'They'll be awfully disappointed,' I said.

"'I'd rather wait here,' she answered. She smiled a little. 'Don't argue with me, Mark, I've quite made up my mind.'

"'I've ordered breakfast in my house,' I said.

"'That's all right. You meet them and take them to your house and give them breakfast, and then they can come along here afterwards. Of course I'll send the car down.'

"'I don't suppose they'll want to breakfast if you're not there,' I said.

"'Oh, I'm sure they will. If the train gets in on time they wouldn't have thought of breakfasting before it arrived and they'll be hungry. They won't want to take this long drive without anything to eat.'

"I was puzzled. She had been looking forward so intensely to Tim's coming, it seemed strange that she should want to wait all by herself while the rest of us were having a jolly breakfast. I supposed she was nervous and wanted to delay as long as possible meeting the strange woman who had come to take her place. It seemed unreasonable. I couldn't see that an hour sooner or an hour later could make any difference, but I knew women were funny, and anyhow I felt Olive wasn't in the mood for me to press it.

"'Telephone when you're starting so that I shall know when to expect you,' she said.

"'All right,' I said, 'but you know I shan't be able to come with them. It's my day for going to Lahad.'

"This was a town that I had to go to once a week to take cases. It was a good way off and one had to ferry across a river, which took some time, so that I never got back till late. There were a few Europeans there and a club. I generally had to go on there for a bit to be sociable and see that things were getting along all right.

"'Besides,' I added, 'with Tim bringing his wife home for the first time I don't suppose he'll want me about. But if you'd like to ask me to dinner I'll be glad to come to that.'

"Olive smiled.

"'I don't think it'll be my place to issue any more invitations, will it?' she said. 'You must ask the bride.'

"She said this so lightly that my heart leaped. I had a feeling that at last she had made up her mind to accept the altered circumstances and, what was more, was accepting them with cheerfulness. She asked me to stay to dinner. Generally I left about eight and dined at home. She was very sweet, almost tender, and I was happier than I'd been for weeks. I had never been more desperately in love with her. I had a couple of gin pahits and I think I was in rather good form at dinner. I know I made her laugh. I felt that at last she was casting away the load of misery that had oppressed her. That was why I didn't let myself be very much disturbed by what happened at the end.

"'Don't you think it's about time you were leaving a presumably maiden lady?' she said.

"She spoke in a manner that was so quietly gay that I answered without hesitation:

"'Oh, my dear, if you think you've got a shred of reputation left you deceive yourself. You're surely not under the impression that the ladies of Sibuku don't know that I've been coming to see you every day for a month. The general feeling is that if we're not married it's high time we were. Don't you think it would be just as well if I broke it to them that we're engaged?'

"'Oh, Mark, you mustn't take our engagement very seriously,' she said.

"I laughed.

"'How else do you expect me to take it? It is serious.'

"She shook her head a little.

"'No. I was upset and hysterical that day. You were being very sweet to me. I said yes because I was too miserable to say no. But now I've had time to collect myself. Don't think me unkind. I made a mistake. I've been very much to blame. You must forgive me'

"'Oh, darling, you're talking nonsense. You've got nothing against me.'

"She looked at me steadily. She was quite calm. She had even a little smile at the back of her eyes.

"'I can't marry you. 1 can't marry anyone. It was absurd of me ever to think I could.'

"I didn't answer at once. She was in a queer state and I thought it better not to insist.

"'I suppose I can't drag you to the altar by main force,' I said.

"I held out my hand and she gave me hers. I put my arm round her, and she made no attempt to withdraw. She suffered me to kiss her as usual on her cheek.

"Next morning I met the train. For once in a way it was punctual. Tim waved to me as his carriage passed the place where I was standing, and by the time I had walked up he had already jumped out and was handing down his wife. He grasped my hand warmly.

"'Where's Olive?' he said, with a glance along the platform. 'This is Sally.'

"I shook hands with her and at the same time explained why Olive was not there.

"'It was frightfully early, wasn't it?' said Mrs. Hardy.

"I told them that the plan was for them to come and have a bit of breakfast at my house and then drive home.

"'I'd love a bath,' said Mrs. Hardy.

"'You shall have one,' I said.

"She was really an extremely pretty little thing, very fair, with enormous blue eyes and a lovely little straight nose. Her skin, all milk and roses, was exquisite. A little of the chorus girl type, of course, and you may happen to think that rather namby-pamby, but in that style she was enchanting. We drove to my house, they both had a bath and Tim a shave; I just had two minutes alone with him. He asked me how Olive had taken his marriage. I told him she'd been upset.

"'I was afraid so,' he said, frowning a little. He gave a short sigh. 'I couldn't do anything else.'

"I didn't understand what he meant. At that moment Mrs. Hardy joined us and slipped her arm through her husband's. He took her hand in his and gently pressed it. He gave her a look that had in it something pleased and humorously affectionate, as though he didn't take her quite seriously, but enjoyed his sense of proprietorship and was proud of her beauty. She really was lovely. She was not at all shy, she asked me to call her Sally before we'd known one another ten minutes, and she was quick in the uptake. Of course, just then she was excited at arriving. She'd never been East and everything thrilled her. It was quite obvious that she was head over heels in love with Tim. Her eyes never left him and she hung on his words. We had a jolly breakfast and then we parted. They got into their car to go home and I into mine to go to Lahad. I promised to go straight to the estate from there and in point of fact it was out of my way to pass by my house. I took a change with me. I didn't see why Olive shouldn't like Sally very much, she was frank and gay, and ingenuous; she was extremely young, she couldn't have been more than nineteen, and her wonderful prettiness couldn't fail to appeal to Olive. I was just as glad to have had a reasonable excuse to leave the three of them by themselves for the day, but as I started out from Lahad I had a notion that by the time I arrived they would all be pleased to see me. I drove up to the bungalow and blew my horn two or three times, expecting someone to appear. Not a soul. The place was in total darkness. I was surprised. It was absolutely silent. I couldn't make it out. They must be in. Very odd, I thought. I waited a moment, then got out of the car and walked up the steps. At the top of them I stumbled over something. I swore and bent down to see what it was; it had felt like a body. There was a cry and I saw it was the amah. She shrank back cowering as I touched her and broke into loud wails.

"'What the hell's the matter?' I cried, and then I felt a hand on my arm and heard a voice. Tuan, Tuan. I turned and in the darkness recognised Tim's head boy. He began to speak in little frightened gasps. I listened to him with horror. What he told me was unspeakable. I pushed him aside and rushed into the house. The sitting-room was dark. I turned on the light. The first thing I saw was Sally huddled up in an armchair. She was startled by my sudden appearance and cried out. I could hardly speak. I asked her if it was true. When she told me it was I felt the room suddenly going round and round me. I had to sit down. As the car that bore Tim and Sally drove up the road that led to the house and Tim sounded the claxon to announce their arrival and the boys and the amah ran out to greet them there was the sound of a shot. They ran to Olive's room and found her lying in front of the looking-glass in a pool of blood. She had shot herself with Tim's revolver.

"'Is she dead?' I said.

"'No, they sent for the doctor, and he took her to the hospital.'

"I hardly knew what I was doing. I didn't even trouble to tell Sally where I was going. I got up and staggered to the door. I got into the car and told my seis to drive like hell to the hospital. I rushed in. I asked where she was. They tried to bar my way, but I pushed them aside. I knew where the private rooms were. Someone clung to my arm, but I shook him off. I vaguely understood that the doctor had given instructions that no one was to go into the room. I didn't care about that. There was an orderly at the door; he put out his arm to prevent me from passing. I swore at him and told him to get out of my way. I suppose I made a row, I was beside myself; the door was opened and the doctor came out.

"'Who's making all this noise?' he said. 'Oh, it's you. What do you want?'

"'Is she dead?' I asked.

"'No. But she's unconscious. She never regained consciousness. It's only a matter of an hour or two.'

"'I want to see her.'

"'You can't.'

"'I'm engaged to her.'

"'You?' he cried, and even at that moment I was aware that he looked at me strangely. 'That's all the more reason.'

"I didn't know what he meant. I was stupid with horror.

"'Surely you can do something to save her,' I cried.

"He shook his head.

"'If you saw her you wouldn't wish it,' he said.

"I stared at him aghast. In the silence I heard a man's convulsive sobbing.

"'Who's that?' I asked.

"'Her brother.'

"Then I felt a hand on my arm. I looked round and saw it was Mrs. Sergison.

"'My poor boy,' she said, 'I'm so sorry for you.'

"'What on earth made her do it?' I groaned.

"'Come away, my dear,' said Mrs. Sergison. 'You can do no good here.'

"'No, I must stay,' I said.

"'Well, go and sit in my room,' said the doctor.

"I was so broken that I let Mrs. Sergison take me by

the arm and lead me into the doctor's private room. She made me sit down. I couldn't bring myself to realise that it was true. I thought it was a horrible nightmare from which I must awake. I don't know how long we sat there. Three hours. Four hours. At last the doctor came in.

"'It's all over,' he said.

"Then I couldn't help myself, I began to cry. I didn't care what they thought of me. I was so frightfully unhappy.

"We buried her next day.

"Mrs. Sergison came back to my house and sat with me for a while. She wanted me to go to the club with her. I hadn't the heart. She was very kind, but I was glad when she left me by myself. I tried to read, but the words meant nothing to me. I felt dead inside. My boy came in and turned on the lights. My head was aching like mad. Then he came back and said that a lady wished to see me. I asked who it was. He wasn't quite sure, but he thought it must be the new wife of the tuan at Putatan. I couldn't imagine what she wanted. I got up and went to the door. He was right. It was Sally. I asked her to come in. I noticed that she was deathly white. I felt sorry for her. It was a frightful experience for a girl of that age and for a bride a miserable home-coming. She sat down. She was very nervous. I tried to put her at her ease by saying conventional things. She made me very uncomfortable because she stared at me with those enormous blue eyes of hers, and they were simply ghastly with horror. She interrupted me suddenly.

"'You're the only person here I know,' she said. 'I

had to come to you. I want you to get me away from
here.'

"I was dumbfounded.

"'What *do* you mean?' I said.

"'I don't want you to ask me any questions. I just
want you to get me away. At once. I want to go back
to England!'

"'But you can't leave Tim like that just now,' I said.
'My dear, you must pull yourself together. I know it's
been awful for you. But think of Tim. I mean, he'll be
miserable. If you have any love for him the least you
can do is to try and make him a little less unhappy.'

"'Oh, you don't know,' she cried. 'I can't tell you.
It's too horrible. I beseech you to help me. If there's a
train to-night let me get on it. If I can only get to
Penang I can get a ship. I can't stay in this place another night. I shall go mad.'

"I was absolutely bewildered.

"'Does Tim know?' I asked her.

"'I haven't seen Tim since last night. I'll never see
him again. I'd rather die.'

"I wanted to gain a little time.

"'But how can you go without your things? Have
you got any luggage?'

"'What does that matter?' she cried impatiently.
'I've got what I want for the journey.'

"'Have you any money?'

"'Enough. Is there a train to-night?'

"'Yes,' I said. 'It's due just after midnight.'

"'Thank God. Will you arrange everything? Can I
stay here till then?'

"'You're putting me in a frightful position,' I said.

'I don't know what to do for the best. You know, it's an awfully serious step you're taking.'

"'If you knew everything you'd know it was the only possible thing to do.'

"'It'll create an awful scandal here. I don't know what people'll say. Have you thought of the effect on Tim?' I was worried and unhappy. 'God knows I don't want to interfere in what isn't my business. But if you want me to help you I ought to know enough to feel justified in doing so. You must tell me what's happened.'

"'I can't. I can only tell you that I know everything.'

"She hid her face with her hands and shuddered. Then she gave herself a shake as though she were recoiling from some frightful sight.

"'He had no right to marry me. It was monstrous.'

"And as she spoke her voice rose shrill and piercing. I was afraid she was going to have an attack of hysterics. Her pretty doll-like face was terrified and her eyes stared as though she could never close them again.

"'Don't you love him any more?' I asked.

"'After that?'

"'What will you do if I refuse to help you?' I said.

"'I suppose there's a clergyman here or a doctor. You can't refuse to take me to one of them.'

"'How did you get here?'

"'The head boy drove me. He got a car from somewhere.'

"'Does Tim know you've gone?'

"'I left a letter for him.'

"'He'll know you're here.'

"'He won't try to stop me. I promise you that. He

daren't. For God's sake don't you try either. I tell you
I shall go mad if I stay here another night.'

"I sighed. After all she was of an age to decide for
herself."

I, the writer of this, hadn't spoken for a long time.

"Did you know what she meant?" I asked Featherstone.

He gave me a long, haggard look.

"There was only one thing she could mean. It was
unspeakable. Yes, I knew all right. It explained everything. Poor Olive. Poor sweet. I suppose it was unreasonable of me, at that moment I only felt a horror
of that little pretty fair-haired thing with her terrified
eyes. I hated her. I didn't say anything for a while.
Then I told her I'd do as she wished. She didn't even
say thank you. I think she knew what I felt about her.
When it was dinner time I made her eat something and
then she asked me if there was a room she could go
and lie down in till it was time to go to the station.
I showed her into my spare room and left her. I sat in
the sitting-room and waited. My God, I don't think
the time has ever passed so slowly for me. I thought
twelve would never strike. I rang up the station and
was told the train wouldn't be in till nearly two. At
midnight she came back to the sitting-room and we
sat there for an hour and a half. We had nothing to
say to one another and we didn't speak. Then I took
her to the station and put her on the train."

"Was there an awful scandal?"

Featherstone frowned.

"I don't know. I applied for short leave. After that
I was moved to another post. I heard that Tim had

sold his estate and bought another. But I didn't know where. It was a shock to me at first when I found him here."

Featherstone, getting up, went over to a table and mixed himself a whisky and soda. In the silence that fell now I heard the monotonous chorus of the croaking frogs. And suddenly the bird that is known as the fever-bird, perched in a tree close to the house, began to call. First, three notes in a descending, chromatic scale, then five, then four. The varying notes of the scale succeeded one another with maddening persist-ence. One was compelled to listen and to count them, and because one did not know how many there would be it tortured one's nerves.

"Blast that bird," said Featherstone. "That means no sleep for me to-night."

THE BACK OF BEYOND

GEORGE MOON was sitting in his office. His work was
finished, and he lingered there because he hadn't the
heart to go down to the club. It was getting on towards
tiffin time, and there would be a good many fellows
hanging about the bar. Two or three of them would
offer him a drink. He could not face their heartiness.
Some he had known for thirty years. They had bored
him, and on the whole he disliked them, but now that
he was seeing them for the last time it gave him a
pang. To-night they were giving him a farewell dinner.
Everyone would be there and they were presenting
him with a silver tea-service that he did not in the least
want. They would make speeches in which they would
refer eulogistically to his work in the colony, express
their regret at his departure and wish him long life
to enjoy his well-earned leisure. He would reply suit-
ably. He had prepared a speech in which he surveyed
the changes that had taken place in the F.M.S., since
first, a raw cadet, he had landed at Singapore. He would
thank them for their loyal co-operation with him during
the term which it had been his privilege to serve as
Resident at Timbang Belud, and draw a glowing picture of the future that awaited the country as a whole,
and Timbang Belud in particular. He would remind
them that he had known it as a poverty-stricken village

with a few Chinese shops and left it now a prosperous town with paved streets down which ran trams, with stone houses, a rich Chinese settlement and a club-house second in splendour only to that of Singapore. They would sing For he's a jolly good fellow and Auld Lang Syne. Then they would dance and a good many of the younger men would get drunk. The Malays had already given him a farewell party and the Chinese an interminable feast. To-morrow a vast concourse would see him off at the station and that would be the end of him. He wondered what they would say of him. The Malays and the Chinese would say that he had been stern, but acknowledge that he had been just. The planters had not liked him. They thought him hard because he would not let them ride roughshod over their labour. His subordinates had feared him. He drove them. He had no patience with slackness or in-efficiency. He had never spared himself and saw no reason why he should spare others. They thought him inhuman. It was true that there was nothing come-hither in him. He could not throw off his official position when he went to the club and laugh at bawdy stories, chaff and be chaffed. He was conscious that his arrival cast a gloom, and to play bridge with him (he liked to play every day from six to eight) was looked upon as a privilege rather than an entertainment. When at some other table a young man's four as the evening wore on grew hilarious, he caught glances thrown in his direction and sometimes an older member would stroll up to the noisy ones and in an undertone advise them to be quiet. George Moon sighed a little. From an official standpoint his career had been a success,

he had been the youngest Resident ever appointed in
the F.M.S., and for exceptional services a C.M.G. had
been conferred upon him; but from the human it had
perhaps been otherwise. He had earned respect, respect for his ability, industry and trustworthiness, but
he was too clear-sighted to think for a moment that he
had inspired affection. No one would regret him. In a
few months he would be forgotten.

He smiled grimly. He was not sentimental. He had
enjoyed his authority, and it gave him an austere satisfaction to know that he had kept everyone up to the
mark. It did not displease him to think that he had been
feared rather than loved. He saw his life as a problem in
higher mathematics, the working-out of which had
required intense application of all his powers, but of
which the result had not the least practical consequence.
Its interest lay in its intricacy and its beauty in its
solution. But like pure beauty it led nowhither. His
future was blank. He was fifty-five, and full of energy,
and to himself his mind seemed as alert as ever, his
experience of men and affairs was wide: all that remained to him was to settle down in a country town in
England or in a cheap part of the Riviera and play
bridge with elderly ladies and golf with retired colonels.
He had met, when on leave, old chiefs of his, and had
observed with what difficulty they adapted themselves
to the change in their circumstances. They had looked
forward to the freedom that would be theirs when they
retired and had pictured the charming uses to which
they would put their leisure. Mirage. It was not very
pleasant to be obscure after having been distinguished,
to live in a poky villa after having dwelt in a spacious

residency, to make do with a couple of maids when you had been accustomed to the service of half a dozen Chinese boys; and above all, it was not pleasant to realise that you did not matter a row of beans to any-one when you had grown used to the delicate flattery of knowing that a word of praise could delight and a frown humiliate all sorts and conditions of men.

George Moon stretched out his hand and helped himself to a cigarette from the box on his desk. As he did so he noticed all the little lines on the back of his hand and the thinness of his shrivelled fingers. He frowned with distaste. It was the hand of an old man. There was in his office a Chinese mirror-picture that he had bought long ago and that he was leaving behind. He got up and looked at himself in it. He saw a thin yellow face, wrinkled and tight-lipped, thin grey hair and grey tired eyes. He was tallish, very spare, with narrow shoulders, and he held himself erect. He had always played polo and even now could beat most of the younger men at tennis. When you talked to him he kept his eyes fixed on your face, listening attentively, but his expression did not change, and you had no notion what effect your words had on him. Perhaps he did not realise how disconcerting this was. He seldom smiled.

An orderly came in with a name written on a chit. George Moon looked at it and told him to show the visitor in. He sat down once more in his chair and looked with his cold eyes at the door through which in a mo-ment the visitor would come. It was Tom Saffary, and he wondered what he wanted. Presumably something to do with the festivity that night. It had amused him to hear that Tom Saffary was the head of the committee that had organised it, for their relations during the last year had been far from cordial. Saffary was a planter and one of his Tamil overseers had lodged a complaint against him for assault. The Tamil had been grossly insolent to him and Saffary had given him a thrashing. George Moon realised that the provocation was great, but he had always set his face against the planters taking the law in their own hands, and when the case was tried he sentenced Saffary to a fine. But when the court rose, to show that there was no ill-feeling he asked Saffary to luncheon: Saffary, resentful of what he thought an unmerited affront, curtly refused and since then had declined to have any social relations with the Resident. He answered when George Moon, casually, but resolved not to be affronted, spoke to him; but would neither play bridge nor tennis with him. He was manager of the largest rubber estate in the district, and George Moon asked himself sardonically whether he had arranged the dinner and collected subscriptions for the presentation, because he thought his dignity required it or whether, now that his Resident was leaving, it appealed to his sentimentality to make a noble gesture. It tickled George Moon's frigid sense of humour to think that it would fall to Tom Saffary to make the principal speech of the evening, in which he would enlarge upon the departing Resident's admirable qualities, and voice the community's regret at their irreparable loss.

Tom Saffary was ushered in. The Resident rose from his chair, shook hands with him and thinly smiled.

"How do you do? Sit down. Won't you have a cigarette?"

"How do you do?"

Saffary took the chair to which the Resident motioned him, and the Resident waited for him to state his business. He had a notion that his visitor was embarrassed. He was a big, burly stout fellow, with a red face and a double chin, curly black hair and blue eyes. He was a fine figure of a man, strong as a horse, but it was plain that he did himself too well. He drank a good deal and ate too heartily. But he was a good business man and a hard worker. He ran his estate efficiently. He was popular in the community. He was generally known as a good chap. He was free with his money and ready to lend a helping hand to anyone in distress. It occurred to the Resident that Saffary had come in order, before the dinner, to compose the difference between them. The emotion that might have occasioned such a desire excited in the Resident's sensibility a very faint, good-humoured contempt. He had no enemies because individuals did not mean enough to him for him to hate any of them, but if he had, he thought, he would have hated them to the end.

"I daresay you're a bit surprised to see me here this morning, and I expect, as it's your last day and all that, you're pretty busy."

George Moon did not answer, and the other went on.

"I've come on rather an awkward business. The fact is that my wife and I won't be able to come to the dinner to-night, and after that unpleasantness we had together last year I thought it only right to come and tell you that it has nothing to do with that. I think you treated me very harshly; it's not the money I minded, it was the indignity, but bygones are bygones. Now that you're leaving I don't want you to think that I bear any more ill-feeling towards you."

"I realised that when I heard that you were chiefly responsible for the send-off you're giving me," answered the Resident civilly. "I'm sorry that you won't be able to come to-night."

"I'm sorry, too. It's on account of Knobby Clarke's death." Saffary hesitated for a moment. "My wife and I were very much upset by it."

"It was very sad. He was a great friend of yours, wasn't he?"

"He was the greatest friend I had in the colony."

Tears shone in Tom Saffary's eyes. Fat men are very emotional, thought George Moon.

"I quite understand that in that case you should have no heart for what looks like being a rather uproarious party," he said kindly. "Have you heard anything of the circumstances?"

"No, nothing but what appeared in the paper."

"He seemed all right when he left here."

"As far as I know he'd never had a day's illness in his life."

"Heart, I suppose. How old was he?"

"Same age as me. Thirty-eight."

"That's young to die."

Knobby Clarke was a planter and the estate he managed was next door to Saffary's. George Moon had liked him. He was a rather ugly man, sandy, with high cheekbones and hollow temples, large pale eyes in deep sockets and a big mouth. But he had an attractive smile and an easy manner. He was amusing and could tell a good story. He had a careless good humour that people found pleasing. He played games well. He was no fool. George Moon would have said he was somewhat colourless. In the course of his career he had known a good many men like him. They came and went. A fortnight before he had left for England on leave and the Resident knew that the Saffarys had given a large dinner-party on his last night. He was married and his wife of course went with him.

"I'm sorry for her," said George Moon. "It must have been a terrible blow. He was buried at sea, wasn't he?"

"Yes. That's what it said in the paper."

The news had reached Timbang the night before. The Singapore papers arrived at six, just as people were getting to the club, and a good many men waited to play bridge or billiards till they had had a glance at them. Suddenly one fellow had called out:

"I say, do you see this? Knobby's dead."

"Knobby who? Not Knobby Clarke?"

There was a three-line paragraph in a column of general intelligence.

"*Messrs. Star, Moseley & Co. have received a cable informing them that Mr. Harold Clarke of Timbang Batu died suddenly on his way home and was buried at sea.*"

A man came up and took the paper from the speaker's hand, and incredulously read the note for himself. Another peered over his shoulder. Such as happened to be reading the paper turned to the page in question and read the three indifferent lines.

"By George," cried one.

"I say, what tough luck," said another.

"He was as fit as a fiddle when he left here."

A shiver of dismay pierced those hearty, jovial, careless men, and each one for a moment remembered that he too was mortal. Other members came in and as they entered, braced by the thought of the six o'clock drink, and eager to meet their friends, they were met by the grim tidings.

"I say, have you heard? Poor Knobby Clarke's dead."

"No? I say, how awful!"

"Rotten luck, isn't it?"

"Rotten."

"Damned good sort."

"One of the best."

"It gave me quite a turn when I saw it in the paper just by chance."

"I don't wonder."

One man with the paper in his hand went into the billiard-room to break the news. They were playing off the handicap for the Prince of Wales's Cup. That august personage had presented it to the club on the occasion of his visit to Timbang Belud. Tom Saffary was playing against a man called Douglas, and the Resident, who had been beaten in the previous round, was seated with about a dozen others watching the game. The marker was monotonously calling out the score. The newcomer waited for Saffary to finish his break and then called out to him.

"I say, Tom, Knobby's dead."

"Knobby? It's not true."

The other handed him the paper. Three or four gathered round to read with him.

"Good God!"

There was a moment's awed silence. The paper was passed from hand to hand. It was odd that none seemed willing to believe till he saw it for himself in black and white.

"Oh, I am sorry."

"I say, it's awful for his wife," said Tom Saffary. "She was going to have a baby. My poor missus'll be upset."

"Why, it's only a fortnight since he left here."

"He was all right then."

"In the pink."

Saffary, his fat red face sagging a little, went over to a table and, seizing his glass, drank deeply.

"Look here, Tom," said his opponent, "would you like to call the game off?"

"Can't very well do that." Saffary's eye sought the score board and he saw that he was ahead. "No, let's finish. Then I'll go home and break it to Violet."

Douglas had his shot and made fourteen. Tom Saffary missed an easy in-off, but left nothing. Douglas played again, but did not score and again Saffary missed a shot that ordinarily he could have been sure of. He frowned a little. He knew his friends had betted on him pretty heavily and he did not like the idea of failing them. Douglas made twenty-two. Saffary emptied his glass and by an effort of will that was quite patent to the sympathetic onlookers settled down to concentrate on the game. He made a break of eighteen and when he just failed to do a long Jenny they gave him a round

of applause. He was sure of himself now and began to
score quickly. Douglas was playing well too, and the
match grew exciting to watch. The few minutes during
which Saffary's attention wandered had allowed his
opponent to catch up with him, and now it was anybody's game.

"Spot two hundred and thirty-five," called the
Malay, in his queer clipped English. "Plain two hundred and twenty-eight. Spot to play."

Douglas made eight, and then Saffary, who was plain,
drew up to two hundred and forty. He left his opponent
a double balk. Douglas hit neither ball, and so gave
Saffary another point.

"Spot two hundred and forty-three," called the marker. "Plain two hundred and forty-one. Plain to play."

Saffary played three beautiful shots off the red and
finished the game.

"A popular victory," the bystanders cried.

"Congratulations, old man," said Douglas.

"Boy," called Saffary, "ask these gentlemen what
they'll have. Poor old Knobby."

He sighed heavily. The drinks were brought and
Saffary signed the chit. Then he said he'd be getting
along. Two others had already begun to play.

"Sporting of him to go on like that," said someone
when the door was closed on Saffary.

"Yes, it shows grit."

"For a while I thought his game had gone all to
pieces."

"He pulled himself together in grand style. He knew
there were a lot of bets on him. He didn't want to let
his backers down."

"Of course it's a shock, a thing like that."

"They were great pals. I wonder what he died of."

"Good shot, sir."

George Moon, remembering this scene, thought it strange that Tom Saffary, who on hearing of his friend's death had shown such self-control, should now apparently take it so hard. It might be that just as in the war a man when hit often did not know it till some time afterwards, Saffary had not realised how great a blow to him Harold Clarke's death was till he had had time to think it over. It seemed to him, however, more probable that Saffary, left to himself, would have carried on as usual, seeking sympathy for his loss in the company of his fellows, but that his wife's conventional sense of propriety had insisted that it would be bad form to go to a party when the grief they were suffering from made it only decent for them to eschew, for a little, festive gatherings. Violet Saffary was a nice little woman, three or four years younger than her husband; not very pretty, but pleasant to look at and always becomingly dressed; amiable, ladylike and unassuming. In the days when he had been on friendly terms with the Saffarys the Resident had from time to time dined with them. He had found her agreeable, but not very amusing. They had never talked but of commonplace things. Of late he had seen little of her. When they chanced to meet she always gave him a friendly smile, and on occasion he said one or two civil words to her. But it was only by an effort of memory that he distinguished her from half a dozen of the other ladies in the community whom his official position brought him in contact with.

Saffary had presumably said what he had come to say and the Resident wondered why he did not get up and go. He sat heaped up in his chair oddly, so that it gave you the feeling that his skeleton had ceased to support him and his considerable mass of flesh was falling in on him. He looked dully at the desk that separated him from the Resident. He sighed deeply.

"You must try not to take it too hard, Saffary," said George Moon. "You know how uncertain life is in the East. One has to resign oneself to losing people one's fond of."

Saffary's eyes slowly moved from the desk, and he fixed them on George Moon's. They stared unwinking. George Moon liked people to look him in the eyes. Perhaps he felt that when he thus held their vision he held them in his power. Presently two tears formed themselves in Saffary's blue eyes and slowly ran down his cheeks. He had a strangely puzzled look. Something had frightened him. Was it death? No. Something that he thought worse. He looked cowed. His mien was cringing so that he made you think of a dog unjustly beaten.

"It's not that," he faltered. "I could have borne that."

George Moon did not answer. He held that big, powerful man with his cold level gaze and waited. He was pleasantly conscious of his absolute indifference. Saffary gave a harassed glance at the papers on the desk.

"I'm afraid I'm taking up too much of your time."

"No, I have nothing to do at the moment."

Saffary looked out of the window. A little shudder passed between his shoulders. He seemed to hesitate.

"I wonder if I might ask your advice," he said at last.

"Of course," said the Resident, with the shadow of a smile, "that's one of the things I'm here for."

"It's a purely private matter."

"You may be quite sure that I shan't betray any confidence you place in me."

"No, I know you wouldn't do that, but it's rather an awkward thing to speak about, and I shouldn't feel very comfortable meeting you afterwards. But you're going away to-morrow, and that makes it easier, if you understand what I mean."

"Quite."

Saffary began to speak, in a low voice, sulkily, as though he were ashamed, and he spoke with the awkwardness of a man unused to words. He went back and said the same thing over again. He got mixed up. He started a long, elaborate sentence and then broke off abruptly because he did not know how to finish it. George Moon listened in silence, his face a mask, smoking, and he only took his eyes off Saffary's face to reach for another cigarette from the box in front of him and light it from the stub of that which he was just finishing. And while he listened he saw, as it were a background, the monotonous round of the planter's life. It was like an accompaniment of muted strings that threw into sharper relief the calculated dissonances of an unexpected melody.

With rubber at so low a price every economy had to be exercised and Tom Saffary, notwithstanding the size of the estate, had to do work which in better times he had had an assistant for. He rose before dawn and went down to the lines where the coolies were assembled.

When there was just enough light to see he read out the names, ticking them off according to the answers, and assigned the various squads to their work. Some tapped, some weeded, and others tended the ditches. Saffary went back to his solid breakfast, lit his pipe and sallied forth again to inspect the coolies' quarters. Children were playing and babies sprawling here and there. On the sidewalks Tamil women cooked their rice. Their black skins shone with oil. They were draped about in dull red cotton and wore gold ornaments in their hair. There were handsome creatures among them, upright of carriage, with delicate features and small, exquisite hands; but Saffary looked upon them only with distaste. He set out on his rounds. On his well-grown estate the trees planted in rows gave one a charming feeling of the prim forest of a German fairy-tale. The ground was thick with dead leaves. He was accompanied by a Tamil overseer, his long black hair done in a chignon, barefooted, in sarong and baju, with a showy ring on his finger. Saffary walked hard, jumping the ditches when he came to them, and soon he dripped with sweat. He examined the trees to see that they were properly tapped, and when he came across a coolie at work looked at the shavings and if they were too thick swore at him and docked him half a day's pay. When a tree was not to be tapped any more he told the overseer to take away the cup and the wire that held it to the trunk. The weeders worked in gangs.

At noon Saffary returned to the bungalow and had a drink of beer which, because there was no ice, was lukewarm. He stripped the khaki shorts, the flannel shirt, the heavy boots and stockings in which he had been

walking, and shaved and bathed. He lunched in a
sarong and baju. He lay off for half an hour, and then
went down to his office and worked till five; he had tea
and went to the club. About eight he started back for
the bungalow, dined, and half an hour after went to bed.

But last night he went home immediately he had
finished his match. Violet had not accompanied him
that day. When the Clarkes were there they had met at
the club every afternoon, but now they had gone home
she came less often. She said there was no one there
who much amused her and she had heard everything
everyone had to say till she was fed to the teeth. She
did not play bridge and it was dull for her to wait about
while he played. She told Tom he need not mind leaving her alone. She had plenty of things to do in the
house.

As soon as she saw him back so early she guessed that
he had come to tell her that he had won his match. He
was like a child in his self-satisfaction over one of these
small triumphs. He was a kindly, simple creature and
she knew that his pleasure at winning was not only on
his own account, but because he thought it must give
her pleasure too. It was rather sweet of him to hurry
home in order to tell her all about it without delay.

"Well, how did your match go?" she said as soon
as he came lumbering into the sitting-room.

"I won."

"Easily?"

"Well, not as easily as I should have. I was a bit
ahead, and then I stuck, I couldn't do a thing, and you
know what Douglas is, not at all showy, but steady, and
he pulled up with me. Then I said to myself, well, if I

don't buck up I shall get a licking. I had a bit of luck
here and there, and then, to cut a long story short, I beat
him by seven."

"Isn't that splendid? You ought to win the cup now,
oughtn't you?"

"Well, I've got three matches more. If I can get into
the semi-finals I ought to have a chance."

Violet smiled. She was anxious to show him that she
was as much interested as he expected her to be.

"What made you go to pieces when you did?"

His face sagged.

"That's why I came back at once. I'd have scratched
only I thought it wasn't fair on the fellows who'd
backed me. I don't know how to tell you, Violet."

She gave him a questioning look.

"Why, what's the matter? Not bad news?"

"Rotten. Knobby's dead."

For a full minute she stared at him, and her face, her
neat friendly little face, grew haggard with horror. At
first it seemed as though she could not understand.

"What *do* you mean?" she cried.

"It was in the paper. He died on board. They buried
him at sea."

Suddenly she gave a piercing cry and fell headlong to
the floor. She had fainted dead away.

"Violet," he cried, and threw himself down on his
knees and took her head in his arms. "Boy, boy."

A boy, startled by the terror in his master's voice,
rushed in and Saffary shouted to him to bring brandy.
He forced a little between Violet's lips. She opened her
eyes, and as she remembered they grew dark with
anguish. Her face was screwed up like a little child's

when it is just going to burst into tears. He lifted her up in his arms and laid her on the sofa. She turned her head away.

"Oh, Tom, it isn't true. It can't be true."

"I'm afraid it is."

"No, no, no."

She burst into tears. She wept convulsively. It was dreadful to hear her. Saffary did not know what to do. He knelt beside her and tried to soothe her. He sought to take her in his arms, but with a sudden gesture she repelled him.

"Don't touch me," she cried, and she said it so sharply that he was startled.

He rose to his feet.

"Try not to take it too hard, sweetie," he said. "I know it's been an awful shock. He was one of the best."

She buried her face in the cushions and wept despairingly. It tortured him to see her body shaken by those uncontrollable sobs. She was beside herself. He put his hand gently on her shoulder.

"Darling, don't give way like that. It's so bad for you."

She shook herself free from his hand.

"For God's sake leave me alone," she cried. "Oh, Hal, Hal." He had never heard her call the dead man that before. Of course his name was Harold, but everyone called him Knobby. "What shall I do?" she wailed. "I can't bear it. I can't bear it."

Saffary began to grow a trifle impatient. So much grief did seem to him exaggerated. Violet was not normally so emotional. He supposed it was the damned climate. It made women nervous and high-strung. Violet hadn't been home for four years. She was not hiding her face now. She lay, almost falling off the sofa, her mouth open in the extremity of her pain, and the tears streamed from her staring eyes. She was distraught.

"Have a little more brandy," he said. "Try and pull yourself together, darling. You can't do Knobby any good by getting in such a state."

With a sudden gesture she sprang to her feet and pushed him aside. She gave him a look of hatred.

"Go away, Tom. I don't want your sympathy. I want to be left alone."

She walked swiftly over to an armchair and threw herself down in it. She flung back her head and her poor white face was wrenched into a grimace of agony.

"Oh, it's not fair," she moaned. "What's to become of me now? Oh, God, I wish I were dead."

"Violet."

His voice quavered with pain. He was very nearly crying too. She stamped her foot impatiently.

"Go away, I tell you. Go away."

He started. He stared at her and suddenly gasped. A shudder passed through his great bulk. He took a step towards her and stopped, but his eyes never left her white, tortured face; he stared as though he saw in it something that appalled him. Then he dropped his head and without a word walked out of the room. He went into a little sitting-room they had at the back, but seldom used, and sank heavily into a chair. He thought. Presently the gong sounded for dinner. He had not had his bath. He gave his hands a glance.

He could not be bothered to wash them. He walked slowly into the dining-room. He told the boy to go and tell Violet that dinner was ready. The boy came back and said she did not want any.

"All right. Let me have mine then," said Saffary.

He sent Violet in a plate of soup and a piece of toast, and when the fish was served put some on a plate for her and gave it to the boy. But the boy came back with it at once.

"Mem, she say no wantchee," he said.

Saffary ate his dinner alone. He ate from habit, stolidly, through the familiar courses. He drank a bottle of beer. When he had finished the boy brought him a cup of coffee and he lit a cheroot. Saffary sat still till he had finished it. He thought. At last he got up and went back into the large verandah which was where they always sat. Violet was still huddled in the chair in which he had left her. Her eyes were closed, but she opened them when she heard him come. He took a light chair and sat down in front of her.

"What *was* Knobby to you, Violet?" he said.

She gave a slight start. She turned away her eyes, but did not speak.

"I can't quite make out why you should have been so frightfully upset by the news of his death."

"It was an awful shock."

"Of course. But it seems very strange that anyone should go simply all to pieces over the death of a friend."

"I don't understand what you mean," she said.

She could hardly speak the words and he saw that her lips were trembling.

"I've never heard you call him Hal. Even his wife called him Knobby."

She did not say anything. Her eyes, heavy with grief, were fixed on vacancy.

"Look at me, Violet."

She turned her head slightly and listlessly gazed at him.

"Was he your lover?"

She closed her eyes and tears flowed from them. Her mouth was strangely twisted.

"Haven't you got anything to say at all?"

She shook her head.

"You must answer me, Violet."

"I'm not fit to talk to you now," she moaned. "How can you be so heartless?"

"I'm afraid I don't feel very sympathetic at the moment. We must get this straight now. Would you like a drink of water?"

"I don't want anything."

"Then answer my question."

"You have no right to ask it. It's insulting."

"Do you ask me to believe that a woman like you who hears of the death of someone she knew is going to faint dead away and then, when she comes to, is going to cry like that? Why, one wouldn't be so upset over the death of one's only child. When we heard of your mother's death you cried of course, anyone would, and I know you were utterly miserable, but you came to me for comfort and you said you didn't know what you'd have done without me."

"This was so frightfully sudden."

"Your mother's death was sudden, too."

"Naturally I was very fond of Knobby."

"How fond? So fond that when you heard he was dead you didn't know and you didn't care what you said? Why did you say it wasn't fair? Why did you say, 'What's going to become of me now?'"

She sighed deeply. She turned her head this way and that like a sheep trying to avoid the hands of the butcher.

"You mustn't take me for an utter fool, Violet. I tell you it's impossible that you should be so shattered by the blow if there hadn't been something between you."

"Well, if you think that why do you torture me with questions?"

"My dear, it's no good shilly-shallying. We can't go on like this. What d'you think I'm feeling?"

She looked at him when he said this. She hadn't thought of him at all. She had been too much absorbed in her own misery to be concerned with his.

"I'm so tired," she sighed.

He leaned forward and roughly seized her wrist.

"Speak," he cried.

"You're hurting me."

"And what about me? D'you think you're not hurting me? How can you have the heart to let me suffer like this?"

He let go of her arm and sprang to his feet. He walked to the end of the room and back again. It looked as though the movement had suddenly roused him to fury. He caught her by the shoulders and dragged her to her feet. He shook her.

"If you don't tell me the truth I'll kill you," he cried.

"I wish you would," she said.

"He was your lover?"

"Yes."

"You swine."

With one hand still on her shoulder so that she could not move he swung back his other arm and with a flat palm struck her repeatedly, with all his strength, on the side of her face. She quivered under the blows, but did not flinch or cry out. He struck her again and again. All at once he felt her strangely inert, he let go of her and she sank unconscious to the floor. Fear seized him. He bent down and touched her, calling her name. She did not move. He lifted her up and put her back into the chair from which a little while before he had pulled her. The brandy that had been brought when first she fainted was still in the room and he fetched it and tried to force it down her throat. She choked and it spilt over her chin and neck. One side of her pale face was livid from the blows of his heavy hand. She sighed a little and opened her eyes. He held the glass again to her lips, supporting her head, and she sipped a little of the neat spirit. He looked at her with penitent, anxious eyes.

"I'm sorry, Violet. I didn't mean to do that. I'm dreadfully ashamed of myself. I never thought I could sink so low as to hit a woman."

Though she was feeling very weak and her face was hurting, the flicker of a smile crossed her lips. Poor Tom. He did say things like that. He felt like that. And how scandalised he would be if you asked him why a man shouldn't hit a woman. But Saffary, seeing the wan smile, put it down to her indomitable courage. By God, she's a plucky little woman, he thought. Game isn't the word.

"Give me a cigarette," she said.

He took one out of his case and put it in her mouth. He made two or three ineffectual attempts to strike his lighter. It would not work.

"Hadn't you better get a match?" she said.

For the moment she had forgotten her heart-rending grief and was faintly amused at the situation. He took a box from the table and held the lighted match to her cigarette. She inhaled the first puff with a sense of infinite relief.

"I can't tell you how ashamed I am, Violet," he said. "I'm disgusted with myself. I don't know what came over me."

"Oh, that's all right. It was very natural. Why don't you have a drink? It'll do you good."

Without a word, his shoulders all hunched up as though the burden that oppressed him were material, he helped himself to a brandy and soda. Then, still silent, he sat down. She watched the blue smoke curl into the air.

"What are you going to do?" she said at last.

He gave a weary gesture of despair.

"We'll talk about that to-morrow. You're not in a fit state to-night. As soon as you've finished your cigarette you'd better go to bed."

"You know so much, you'd better know everything."

"Not now, Violet."

"Yes, now."

She began to speak. He heard her words, but could hardly make sense of them. He felt like a man who has built himself a house with loving care and thought to live in it all his life, and then, he does not understand why, sees the housebreakers come and with their picks and heavy hammers destroy it room by room, till what was a fair dwelling-place is only a heap of rubble. What made it so awful was that it was Knobby Clarke who had done this thing. They had come out to the F.M.S. on the same ship and had worked at first on the same estate. They call the young planter a creeper and you can tell him in the streets of Singapore by his double felt hat and his khaki coat turned up at the wrists. Callow youths who saunter about staring and are inveigled by wily Chinese into buying worthless truck from Birmingham which they send home as Eastern curios, sit in the lounges of cheap hotels drinking innumerable stengahs, and after an evening at the pictures get into rickshaws and finish the night in the Chinese quarter. Tom and Knobby were inseparable. Tom, a big, powerful fellow, simple, very honest, hard-working; and Knobby, ungainly, but curiously attractive, with his deep-set eyes, hollow cheeks and large humorous mouth. It was Knobby who made the jokes and Tom who laughed at them. Tom married first. He met Violet when he went on leave. The daughter of a doctor killed in the war, she was governess in the house of some people who lived in the same place as his father. He fell in love with her because she was alone in the world, and his tender heart was touched by the thought of the drab life that lay before her. But Knobby married, because Tom had and he felt lost without him, a girl who had come East to spend the winter with relations. Enid Clarke had been very pretty then in her blonde way, and full face she was pretty still, though her skin, once so clear and fresh, was already faded; but she had a very weak,

small, insignificant chin and in profile reminded you
of a sheep. She had pretty flaxen hair, straight, because
in the heat it would not keep its wave, and china-blue
eyes. Though but twenty-six, she had already a tired
look. A year after marriage she had a baby, but it died
when only two years old. It was after this that Tom
Saffary managed to get Knobby the post of manager of
the estate next his own. The two men pleasantly re-
sumed their old familiarity, and their wives, who till
then had not known one another very well, soon made
friends. They copied one another's frocks and lent one
another servants and crockery when they gave a party.
The four of them met every day. They went everywhere
together. Tom Saffary thought it grand.

The strange thing was that Violet and Knobby
Clarke lived on these terms of close intimacy for three
years before they fell in love with one another. Neither
saw love approaching. Neither suspected that in the
pleasure each took in the other's company there was
anything more than the casual friendship of two persons
thrown together by the circumstances of life. To be
together gave them no particular happiness, but merely
a quiet sense of comfort. If by chance a day passed
without their meeting they felt unaccountably bored.
That seemed very natural. They played games together.
They danced together. They chaffed one another. The
revelation came to them by what looked like pure accident. They had all been to a dance at the club and
were driving home in Saffary's car. The Clarkes' estate
was on the way and he was dropping them at their
bungalow. Violet and Knobby sat in the back. He had
had a good deal to drink, but was not drunk; their hands

touched by chance, and he took hers and held it. They did not speak. They were all tired. But suddenly the exhilaration of the champagne left him and he was cold sober. They knew in a flash that they were madly in love with one another and at the same moment they realised that they had never been in love before. When they reached the Clarkes' Tom said:

"You'd better hop in beside me, Violet."

"I'm too exhausted to move," she said.

Her legs seemed so weak that she thought she would never be able to stand.

When they met next day neither referred to what had happened, but each knew that something inevitable had passed. They behaved to one another as they had always done, they continued to behave so for weeks, but they felt that everything was different. At last flesh and blood could stand it no longer and they became lovers. But the physical tie seemed to them the least important element in their relation, and indeed their way of living made it impossible for them, except very seldom, to enjoy any intimate connection. It was enough that they saw one another, though in the company of others, every day; a glance, a touch of the hand, assured them of their love, and that was all that mattered. The sexual act was no more than an affirmation of the union of their souls.

They very seldom talked of Tom or Enid. If sometimes they laughed together at their foibles it was not unkindly. It might have seemed odd to them to realise how completely these two people whom they saw so constantly had ceased to matter to them if they had given them enough thought to consider the matter.

Their relations with them fell into the routine of life that nobody notices, like shaving oneself, dressing and eating three meals a day. They felt tenderly towards them. They even took pains to please them, as you would with a bed-ridden invalid, because their own happiness was so great that in charity they must do what they could for others less fortunate. They had no scruples. They were too much absorbed in one another to be touched even for a moment by remorse. Beauty now excitingly kindled the pleasant humdrum life they had led so long.

But then an event took place that filled them with consternation. The company for which Tom worked entered into negotiations to buy extensive rubber plantations in British North Borneo and invited Tom to manage them. It was a better job than his present one, with a higher salary, and since he would have assistants under him he would not have to work so hard. Saffary welcomed the offer. Both Clarke and Saffary were due for leave and the two couples had arranged to travel home together. They had already booked their passages. This changed everything. Tom would not be able to get away for at least a year. By the time the Clarkes came back the Saffarys would be settled in Borneo. It did not take Violet and Knobby long to decide that there was only one thing to do. They had been willing enough to go on as they were, notwithstanding the hindrances to the enjoyment of their love, when they were certain of seeing one another continually; they felt that they had endless time before them and the future was coloured with a happiness that seemed to have no limit; but neither could suffer for an instant the thought of separation. They made up their minds to run away together, and then it seemed to them on a sudden that every day that passed before they could be together always and all the time was a day lost. Their love took another guise. It flamed into a devouring passion that left them no emotion to waste on others. They cared little for the pain they must cause Tom and Enid. It was unfortunate, but inevitable. They made their plans deliberately. Knobby on the pretence of business would go to Singapore and Violet, telling Tom that she was going to spend a week with friends on an estate down the line, would join him there. They would go over to Java and thence take ship to Sydney. In Sydney Knobby would look for a job. When Violet told Tom that the Mackenzies had asked her to spend a few days with them, he was pleased.

"That's grand. I think you want a change, darling," he said. "I've fancied you've been looking a bit peaked lately."

He stroked her cheek affectionately. The gesture stabbed her heart.

"You've always been awfully good to me, Tom," she said, her eyes suddenly filled with tears.

"Well, that's the least I could be. You're the best little woman in the world."

"Have you been happy with me these eight years?"

"Frightfully."

"Well, that's something, isn't it? No one can ever take that away from you."

She had told herself that he was the kind of man who would soon console himself. He liked women for themselves and it would not be long after he had regained

his freedom before he found someone that he would
wish to marry. And he would be just as happy with his
new wife as he had been with her. Perhaps he would
marry Enid. Enid was one of those dependent little
things that somewhat exasperated her and she did not
think her capable of deep feeling. Her vanity would
be hurt; her heart would not be broken. But now that
the die was cast, everything settled and the day fixed,
she had a qualm. Remorse beset her. She wished that
it had been possible not to cause those two people such
fearful distress. She faltered.

"We've had a very good time here, Tom," she said.
"I wonder if it's wise to leave it all. We're giving up a
certainty for we don't know what."

"My dear child, it's a chance in a million and much
better money."

"Money isn't everything. There's happiness."

"I know that, but there's no reason why we shouldn't
be just as happy in B.N.B. And besides, there was no
alternative. I'm not my own master. The directors
want me to go and I must, and that's all there is to it."

She sighed. There was no alternative for her either.
She shrugged her shoulders. It was hateful to cause
others pain; sometimes you couldn't help yourself. Tom
meant no more to her than the casual man on the voy-
age out who was civil to you: it was absurd that she
should be asked to sacrifice her life for him.

The Clarkes were due to sail for England in a fortnight and this determined the date of their elopement.
The days passed. Violet was restless and excited. She
looked forward with a joy that was almost painful to
the peace that she anticipated when they were once on

board the ship and could begin the life which she was
sure would give her at last perfect happiness.

She began to pack. The friends she was supposed to
be going to stay with entertained a good deal and this
gave her an excuse to take quite a lot of luggage. She
was starting next day. It was eleven o'clock in the
morning and Tom was making his round of the estate.
One of the boys came to her room and told her that
Mrs. Clarke was there and at the same moment she
heard Enid calling her. Quickly closing the lid of her
trunk, she went out on to the verandah. To her astonishment Enid came up to her, flung her arms round her
neck and kissed her eagerly. She looked at Enid and
saw that her cheeks, usually pale, were flushed and
that her eyes were shining. Enid burst into tears.

"What on earth's the matter, darling?" she cried.

For one moment she was afraid that Enid knew
everything. But Enid was flushed with delight and not
with jealousy or anger.

"I've just seen Dr. Harrow," she said. "I didn't want
to say anything about it. I've had two or three false
alarms, but this time he says it's all right."

A sudden coldness pierced Violet's heart.

"What do you mean? You're not going to . . ."

She looked at Enid and Enid nodded.

"Yes, he says there's no doubt about it at all. He
thinks I'm at least three months gone. Oh, my dear,
I'm so wildly happy."

She flung herself again into Violet's arms and clung
to her, weeping.

"Oh, darling, don't."

Violet felt herself grow pale as death and knew that

if she didn't keep a tight hold of herself she would faint.

"Does Knobby know?"

"No, I didn't say a word. He was so disappointed before. He was so frightfully cut up when baby died. He's wanted me to have another so badly."

Violet forced herself to say the things that were expected of her, but Enid was not listening. She wanted to tell the whole story of her hopes and fears, of her symptoms, and then of her interview with the doctor. She went on and on.

"When are you going to tell Knobby?" Violet asked at last. "Now, when he gets in?"

"Oh, no, he's tired and hungry when he gets back from his round. I shall wait till to-night after dinner."

Violet repressed a movement of exasperation; Enid was going to make a scene of it and was choosing her moment; but after all, it was only natural. It was lucky, for it would give her the chance to see Knobby first. As soon as she was rid of her she rang him up. She knew that he always looked in at his office on his way home, and she left a message asking him to call her. She was only afraid that he would not do so till Tom was back, but she had to take her chance of that. The bell rang and Tom had not yet come in.

"Hal?"

"Yes."

"Will you be at the hut at three?"

"Yes. Has anything happened?"

"I'll tell you when I see you. Don't worry."

She rang off. The hut was a little shelter on Knobby's estate which she could get to without difficulty and where they occasionally met. The coolies passed it while they worked and it had no privacy; but it was a convenient place for them without exciting comment to exchange a few minutes' conversation. At three Enid would be resting and Tom at work in his office.

When Violet walked up Knobby was already there. He gave a gasp.

"Violet, how white you are."

She gave him her hand. They did not know what eyes might be watching them and their behaviour here was always such as anyone could observe.

"Enid came to see me this morning. She's going to tell you to-night. I thought you ought to be warned. She's going to have a baby."

"Violet!"

He looked at her aghast. She began to cry. They had never talked of the relations they had, he with his wife and she with her husband. They ignored the subject because it was to each exquisitely painful. Violet knew what her own life was; she satisfied her husband's appetite; but, with a woman's strange nonchalance, because to do so gave her no pleasure, attached no importance to it; but somehow she had persuaded herself that with Hal it was different. He felt now instinctively how bitterly what she had learned wounded her. He tried to excuse himself.

"Darling, I couldn't help myself."

She cried silently and he watched her with miserable eyes.

"I know it seems beastly," he said, "but what could I do? It wasn't as if I had any reason to . . ."

She interrupted him.

"I don't blame you. It was inevitable. It's only because I'm stupid that it gives me such a frightful pain
in my heart."

"Darling!"

"We ought to have gone away together two years
ago. It was madness to think we could go on like this."

"Are you sure Enid's right? She thought she was in
the family way three or four years ago."

"Oh, yes, she's right. She's frightfully happy. She
says you wanted a child so badly."

"It's come as such an awful surprise. I don't seem
able to realise it yet."

She looked at him. He was staring at the leaf-strewn
earth with harassed eyes. She smiled a little.

"Poor Hal." She sighed deeply. "There's nothing to
be done about it. It's the end of us."

"What do you mean?" he cried.

"Oh, my dear, you can't very well leave her now,
can you? It was all right before. She would have been
unhappy, but she would have got over it. But now it's
different. It's not a very nice time for a woman anyhow. For months she feels more or less ill. She wants
affection. She wants to be taken care of. It would be
frightful to leave her to bear it all alone. We couldn't
be such beasts."

"Do you mean to say you want me to go back to
England with her?"

She nodded gravely.

"It's lucky you're going. It'll be easier when you get
away and we don't see one another every day."

"But I can't live without you now."

"Oh, yes, you can. You must. I can. And it'll be worse for me, because I stay behind and I shall have nothing."

"Oh, Violet, it's impossible."

"My dear, it's no good arguing. The moment she told me I saw it meant that. That's why I wanted to see you first. I thought the shock might lead you to blurt out the whole truth. You know I love you more than anything in the world. She's never done me any harm. I couldn't take you away from her now. It's bad luck on both of us, but there it is, I simply wouldn't dare to do a filthy thing like that."

"I wish I were dead," he moaned.

"That wouldn't do her any good, or me either," she smiled.

"What about the future? Have we got to sacrifice our whole lives?"

"I'm afraid so. It sounds rather grim, darling, but I suppose sooner or later we shall get over it. One gets over everything."

She looked at her wrist-watch.

"I ought to be getting back. Tom will be in soon. We're all meeting at the club at five."

"Tom and I are supposed to be playing tennis." He gave her a pitiful look. "Oh, Violet, I'm so frightfully unhappy."

"I know. So am I. But we shan't do any good by talking about it."

She gave him her hand, but he took her in his arms and kissed her, and when she released herself her cheeks were wet with his tears. But she was so desperate she could not cry.

Ten days later the Clarkes sailed.

While George Moon was listening to as much of this story as Tom Saffary was able to tell him, he reflected in his cool, detached way how odd it was that these commonplace people, leading lives so monotonous should have been convulsed by such a tragedy. Who would have thought that Violet Saffary, so neat and demure, sitting in the club reading the illustrated papers or chatting with her friends over a lemon squash, should have been eating her heart out for love of that ordinary man? George Moon remembered seeing Knobby at the club the evening before he sailed. He seemed in great spirits. Fellows envied him because he was going home. Those who had recently come back told him by no means to miss the show at the Pavilion. Drink flowed freely. The Resident had not been asked to the farewell party the Saffarys gave for the Clarkes, but he knew very well what it had been like, the good cheer, the cordiality, the chaff, and then after dinner the gramophone turned on and everyone dancing. He wondered what Violet and Clarke had felt as they danced together. It gave him an odd sensation of dismay to think of the despair that must have filled their hearts while they pretended to be so gay.

And with another part of his mind George Moon thought of his own past. Very few knew that story. After all, it had happened twenty-five years ago.

"What are you going to do now, Saffary?" he asked.

"Well, that's what I wanted you to advise me about. Now that Knobby's dead I don't know what's going to happen to Violet if I divorce her. I was wondering if I oughtn't to let her divorce me."

"Oh, you want to divorce?"

"Well, I must."

George Moon lit another cigarette and watched for a moment the smoke that curled away into the air.

"Did you ever know that I'd been married?"

"Yes, I think I'd heard. You're a widower, aren't you?"

"No, I divorced my wife. I have a son of twenty-seven. He's farming in New Zealand. I saw my wife the last time I was home on leave. We met at a play. At first we didn't recognise one another. She spoke to me. I asked her to lunch at the Berkeley."

George Moon chuckled to himself. He was alone. It was a musical comedy. He found himself sitting next to a large fat dark woman whom he vaguely thought he had seen before, but the play was just beginning and he did not give her a second look. When the curtain fell after the first act she looked at him with bright eyes and spoke.

"How are you, George?"

He gave a start. It was his wife. She had a bold, friendly manner and was very much at her ease.

"It's a long time since we met," she said.

"It is."

"How has life been treating you?"

"Oh, all right."

"I suppose you're a Resident now. You're still in the Service, aren't you?"

"Yes. I'm retiring soon, worse luck."

"Why? You look very fit."

"I'm reaching the age limit. I'm supposed to be an old buffer and no good any more."

"You're lucky to have kept so thin. I'm terrible, aren't I?"

"You don't look as though you were wasting away."

"I know. I'm stout and I'm growing stouter all the time. I can't help it and I love food. I can't resist cream and bread and potatoes."

George Moon laughed, but not at what she said; at his own thoughts. In years gone by it had sometimes occurred to him that he might meet her, but he had never thought that the meeting would take this turn. When the play was ended and with a smile she bade him good-night, he said:

"I suppose you wouldn't lunch with me one day?"

"Any day you like."

They arranged a date and duly met. He knew that she had married the man on whose account he had divorced her, and he judged by her clothes that she was in comfortable circumstances. They drank a cocktail. She ate the *hors-d'œuvres* with gusto. She was fifty if she was a day, but she carried her years with spirit. There was something jolly and careless about her, she was quick in the uptake, chatty, and she had the hearty, infectious laugh of the fat woman who has let herself go. If he had not known that her family had for a century been in the Indian Civil Service he would have thought that she had been a chorus girl. She was not flashy, but she had a sort of flamboyance of nature that suggested the stage. She was not in the least embarrassed.

"You never married again, did you?" she asked him.

"No."

"Pity. Because it wasn't a success the first time

there's no reason why it shouldn't have been the second."

"There's no need for me to ask if you've been happy."

"I've got nothing to complain of. I think I've got a happy nature. Jim's always been very good to me; he's retired now, you know, and we live in the country, and I adore Betty."

"Who's Betty?"

"Oh, she's my daughter. She got married two years ago. I'm expecting to be a grandmother almost any day."

"That ages us a bit."

She gave a laugh.

"Betty's twenty-two. It was nice of you to ask me to lunch, George. After all, it would be silly to have any feelings about something that happened so long ago as all that."

"Idiotic."

"We weren't fitted to one another and it's lucky we found it out before it was too late. Of course I was foolish, but then I was very young. Have you been happy too?"

"I think I can say I've been a success."

"Oh, well, that's probably all the happiness you were capable of."

He smiled in appreciation of her shrewdness. And then, putting the whole matter aside easily, she began to talk of other things. Though the courts had given him custody of their son, he, unable to look after him, had allowed his mother to have him. The boy had emigrated at eighteen and was now married. He was a stranger to George Moon, and he was aware that if he met him in the street he would not recognise him. He was too sincere to pretend that he took much interest in him. They talked of him, however, for a while, and then they talked of actors and plays.

"Well," she said at last, "I must be running away. I've had a lovely lunch. It's been fun meeting you, George. Thanks so much."

He put her into a taxi and taking off his hat walked down Piccadilly by himself. He thought her quite a pleasant, amusing woman: he laughed to think that he had ever been madly in love with her. There was a smile on his lips when he spoke again to Tom Saffary.

"She was a damned good-looking girl when I married her. That was the trouble. Though, of course, if she hadn't been I'd never have married her. They were all after her like flies round a honey-pot. We used to have awful rows. And at last I caught her out. Of course I divorced her."

"Of course."

"Yes, but I know I was a damned fool to do it." He leaned forward. "My dear Saffary, I know now that if I'd had any sense I'd have shut my eyes. She'd have settled down and made me an excellent wife."

He wished he were able to explain to his visitor how grotesque it had seemed to him when he sat and talked with that jolly, comfortable and good-humoured woman that he should have made so much fuss about what now seemed to him to matter so little.

"But one has one's honour to think of," said Saffary.

"Honour be damned. One has one's happiness to think of. Is one's honour really concerned because one's wife hops into bed with another man? We're not crusaders, you and I, or Spanish grandees. I *liked* my wife. I don't say I haven't had other women. I have. But she had just that something that none of the others could give me. What a fool I was to throw away what I wanted more than anything in the world because I couldn't enjoy exclusive possession of it!"

"You're the last man I should ever have expected to hear speak like that."

George Moon smiled thinly at the embarrassment that was so clearly expressed on Saffary's fat troubled face.

"I'm probably the first man you've heard speak the naked truth," he retorted.

"Do you mean to say that if it were all to do over again you would act differently?"

"If I were twenty-seven again I suppose I should be as big a fool as I was then. But if I had the sense I have now I'll tell you what I'd do if I found my wife had been unfaithful to me. I'd do just what you did last night: I'd give her a damned good hiding and let it go at that."

"Are you asking me to forgive Violet?"

The Resident shook his head slowly and smiled.

"No. You've forgiven her already. I'm merely advising you not to cut off your nose to spite your face."

Saffary gave him a worried look. It disconcerted him to know that this cold precise man should see in his heart emotions which seemed so unnatural to himself that he thrust them out of his consciousness.

"You don't know the circumstances," he said. "Knobby and I were almost like brothers. I got him this job. He owed everything to me. And except for me Violet might have gone on being a governess for the rest of her life. It seemed such a waste; I couldn't help feeling sorry for her. If you know what I mean, it was pity that first made me take any notice of her. Don't you think it's a bit thick that when you've been thoroughly decent with people they should go out of their way to do the dirty on you? It's such awful ingratitude."

"Oh, my dear boy, one mustn't expect gratitude. It's a thing that no one has a right to. After all, you do good because it gives you pleasure. It's the purest form of happiness there is. To expect thanks for it is really asking too much. If you get it, well, it's like a bonus on shares on which you've already received a dividend; it's grand, but you mustn't look upon it as your due."

Saffary frowned. He was perplexed. He could not quite make it out that George Moon should think so oddly about things that it had always seemed to him there were no two ways of thinking about. After all there were limits. I mean, if you had any sense of decency you had to behave like a tuan. There was your own self-respect to think of. It was funny that George Moon should give reasons that looked so damned plausible for doing something that, well, damn it, you had to admit you'd be only too glad to do if you could see your way to it. Of course George Moon was queer. No one ever quite understood him.

"Knobby Clarke is dead, Saffary. You can't be jealous of him any more. No one knows a thing except you and me and your wife, and to-morrow I'm going away for ever. Why don't you let bygones be bygones?"

"Violet would only despise me."

George Moon smiled, and unexpectedly on that prim, fastidious face, his smile had a singular sweetness.

"I know her very little. I always thought her a very nice woman. Is she as detestable as that?"

Saffary gave a start and reddened to his ears.

"No, she's an angel of goodness. It's me who's detestable for saying that of her." His voice broke and he gave a little sob. "God knows I only want to do the right thing."

"The right thing is the kind thing."

Saffary covered his face with his hands. He could not curb the emotion that shook him.

"I seem to be giving, giving all the time, and no one does a God-damned thing for me. It doesn't matter if my heart is broken, I must just go on." He drew the back of his hand across his eyes and sighed deeply. "I'll forgive her."

George Moon looked at him reflectively for a little.

"I wouldn't make too much of a song and dance about it, if I were you," he said. "You'll have to walk warily. She'll have a lot to forgive too."

"Because I hit her, you mean? I know, that was awful of me."

"Not a bit. It did her a power of good. I didn't mean that. You're behaving very generously, old boy, and you know, one needs a devil of a lot of tact to get people to forgive one one's generosity. Fortunately women are frivolous and they very quickly forget the benefits conferred upon them. Otherwise, of course, there'd be no living with them."

Saffary looked at him open-mouthed.

"Upon my word you're a rum 'un, Moon," he said. "Sometimes you seem as hard as nails and then you talk so that one thinks you're almost human, and then, just as one thinks one's misjudged you and you have a heart after all, you come out with something that just shocks one. I suppose that's what they call a cynic."

"I haven't deeply considered the matter," smiled George Moon, "but if to look truth in the face and not resent it when it's unpalatable, and take human nature as you find it, smiling when it's absurd and grieved without exaggeration when it's pitiful, is to be cynical, then I suppose I'm a cynic. Mostly human nature is both absurd and pitiful, but if life has taught you tolerance you find in it more to smile at than to weep."

When Tom Saffary left the room the Resident lit himself with deliberation the last cigarette he meant to smoke before tiffin. It was a new rôle for him to reconcile an angry husband with an erring wife and it caused him a discreet amusement. He continued to reflect upon human nature. A wintry smile hovered upon his thin and pallid lips. He recalled with what interest in the dry creeks of certain places along the coast he had often stood and watched the Jumping Johnnies. There were hundreds of them sometimes, from little things of a couple of inches long to great fat fellows as long as your foot. They were the colour of the mud they lived in. They sat and looked at you with large round eyes and then with a sudden dash buried themselves in their holes. It was extraordinary to see them scudding on their flappers over the surface of the mud. It teemed with them. They gave you a fearful feeling that the mud itself was mysteriously become alive and an atavistic terror froze your heart when you remembered that such creatures, but gigantic and terrible, were once the only inhabitants of the earth. There was something uncanny about them, but something amusing too. They reminded you very much of human beings. It was quite entertaining to stand there for half an hour and observe their gambols.

George Moon took his topi off the peg and not displeased with life stepped out into the sunshine.

NEIL MacADAM

CAPTAIN BREDON was good-natured. When Angus Munro, the Curator of the museum at Kuala Solor, told him that he had advised Neil MacAdam, his new assistant, on his arrival at Singapore to put up at the Van Dyke Hotel, and asked him to see that the lad got into no mischief during the few days he must spend there, he said he would do his best. Captain Bredon commanded the Sultan Ahmed, and when he was at Singapore always stayed at the Van Dyke. He had a Japanese wife and kept a room there. It was his home. When he got back after his fortnight's trip along the coast of Borneo the Dutch manager told him that Neil had been there for two days. The boy was sitting in the little dusty garden of the hotel reading old numbers of The Straits Times. Captain Bredon took a look at him first and then went up.

"You're MacAdam, aren't you?"

Neil rose to his feet, flushed to the roots of his hair and answered shyly: "I am."

"My name's Bredon. I'm skipper of the Sultan Ahmed. You're sailing with me next Tuesday. Munro asked me to look after you. What about a stengah? I suppose you've learned what that means by now."

"Thank you very much, but I don't drink." He spoke with a broad Scots accent.

"I don't blame you. Drink's been the ruin of many a good man in this country."

He called the Chinese boy and ordered himself a double whisky and a small soda.

"What have you been doing with yourself since you got in?"

"Walking about."

"There's nothing much to see in Singapore."

"I've found plenty."

Of course the first thing he had done was to go to the museum. There was little that he had not seen at home, but the fact that those beasts and birds, those reptiles, moths, butterflies and insects, were native to the country excited him. There was one section devoted to that part of Borneo of which Kuala Solor was the capital, and since these were the creatures that for the next three years would chiefly concern him, he examined them with attention. But it was outside, in the streets, that it was most thrilling, and except that he was a grave and sober young man he would have laughed aloud with joy. Everything was new to him. He walked till he was footsore. He stood at the corner of a busy street and wondered at the long line of rickshaws and the little men between the shafts running with dogged steps. He stood on a bridge over a canal, and looked at the sampans wedged up against one another like sardines in a tin. He peered into the Chinese shops in Victoria Road where so many strange things were sold. Bombay merchants, fat and exuberant, stood at their shop doors and sought to sell him silks and tinsel jewellery. He watched the Tamils, pensive and forlorn, who walked with a sinister grace, and the bearded

Arabs, in white skull-caps, who bore themselves with scornful dignity. The sun shone upon the varied scene with a hard, acrid brilliance. He was confused. He thought it would take him years to find his bearings in this multi-coloured and excessive world.

After dinner that night Captain Bredon asked him if he would like to go round the town.

"You ought to see a bit of life while you're here," he said.

They stepped into rickshaws and drove to the Chinese quarter. The Captain, who never drank at sea, had been making up for his abstinence during the day. He was feeling good. The rickshaws stopped at a house in a side street and they knocked at the door. It was opened and they passed through a narrow passage into a large room with benches all round it covered with red plush. A number of women were sitting about. French, Italian and American. A mechanical piano was grinding out harsh music and a few couples were dancing. Captain Bredon ordered drinks. Two or three women, waiting for an invitation, gave them inciting glances.

"Well, young feller, is there anyone you fancy here?" the Captain asked facetiously.

"To sleep with, d'you mean? No."

"No white girls where you're going, you know."

"Oh, well."

"Like to go an' see some natives?"

"I don't mind."

The Captain paid for the drinks and they strolled on. They went to another house. Here the girls were Chinese, small and dainty, with tiny feet and hands like flowers, and they wore suits of flowered silk. But their painted faces were like masks. They looked at the strangers with black derisive eyes. They were strangely inhuman.

"I brought you here because I thought you ought to see the place," said Captain Bredon, with the air of a man doing his bounden duty, "but just look see is all. They don't like us for some reason. In some of these Chinese joints they won't even let a white man in. Fact is, they say we stink. Funny, ain't it? They say we smell of corpses."

"We?"

"Give me Japs," said the Captain. "They're fine. My wife's a Jap, you know. You come along with me and I'll take you to a place where they have Japanese girls, and if you don't see something you like there I'm a Dutchman."

Their rickshaws were waiting and they stepped into them. Captain Bredon gave a direction and the boys started off. They were let into the house by a stout middle-aged Japanese woman, who bowed low as they entered. She took them into a neat, clean room furnished only with mats on the floor; they sat down and presently a little girl came in with a tray on which were two bowls of pale tea. With a shy bow she handed one to each of them. The Captain spoke to the middle-aged woman and she looked at Neil and giggled. She said something to the child, who went out, and presently four girls tripped in. They were sweet in their kimonos, with their shining black hair artfully dressed; they were small and plump, with round faces and laughing eyes. They bowed low as they came in and with good manners murmured polite greetings. Their speech sounded like the twittering of birds. Then they knelt, one on each side of the two men, and charmingly flirted with them. Captain Bredon soon had his arms round two slim waists. They all talked nineteen to the dozen. They were very gay. It seemed to Neil that the Captain's girls were mocking him, for their gleaming eyes were mischievously turned towards him, and he blushed. But the other two cuddled up to him, smiling, and spoke in Japanese as though he understood every word they said. They seemed so happy and guileless that he laughed. They were very attentive. They handed him the bowl so that he should drink his tea, and then took it from him so that he should not have the trouble of holding it. They lit his cigarette for him and one put out a small, delicate hand to take the ash so that it should not fall on his clothes. They stroked his smooth face and looked with curiosity at his large young hands. They were as playful as kittens.

"Well, which is it to be?" said the Captain after a while. "Made your choice yet?"

"What d'you mean?"

"I'll just wait and see you settled and then I'll fix myself up."

"Oh, I don't want either of them. I'm going home to bed."

"Why, what's the matter? You're not scared, are you?"

"No, I just don't fancy it. But don't let me stand in your way. I'll get back to the hotel all right."

"Oh, if you're not going to do anything I won't either. I only wanted to be matey."

He spoke to the middle-aged woman and what he

said caused the girls to look at Neil with sudden surprise. She answered and the Captain shrugged his
shoulders. Then one of the girls made a remark that
set them all laughing.

"What does she say?" asked Neil.

"She's pulling your leg," replied the Captain, smiling.

But he gave Neil a curious look. The girl, having
made them laugh once, now said something directly
to Neil. He could not understand, but the mockery of
her eyes made him blush and frown. He did not like
to be made fun of. Then she laughed outright and
throwing her arm round his neck lightly kissed him.

"Come on, let's be going," said the Captain.

When they dismissed their rickshaws and walked
into the hotel Neil asked him:

"What was it that girl said that made them all
laugh?"

"She said you were a virgin."

"I don't see anything to laugh in at that," said Neil,
with his slow Scots accent.

"Is it true?"

"I suppose it is."

"How old are you?"

"Twenty-two."

"What are you waiting for?"

"Till I marry."

The Captain was silent. At the top of the stairs he
held out his hand. There was a twinkle in his eyes when
he bade the lad good-night, but Neil met it with a level,
candid and untroubled gaze.

Three days later they sailed. Neil was the only white
passenger. When the Captain was busy he read. He

was reading again Wallace's Malay Archipelago. He had read it as a boy, but now it had a new and absorbing interest for him. When the Captain was at leisure they played cribbage or sat in long chairs on the deck, smoking, and talked. Neil was the son of a country doctor, and he could not remember when he had not been interested in natural history. When he had done with school he went to the University of Edinburgh and there took a B.Sc. with Honours. He was looking out for a job as demonstrator in biology when he chanced to see in Nature an advertisement for an assistant curator of the museum at Kuala Solor. The Curator, Angus Munro, had been at Edinburgh with his uncle, a Glasgow merchant, and his uncle wrote to ask him if he would give the boy a trial. Though Neil was especially interested in entomology he was a trained taxidermist, which the advertisement said was essential; he enclosed certificates from Neil's old teachers; he added that Neil had played football for his university. In a few weeks a cable arrived engaging him and a fortnight later he sailed.

"What's Mr. Munro like?" asked Neil.

"Good fellow. Everybody likes him."

"I looked out his papers in the scientific journals. He had one in the last number of The Ibis on the Gymnathidæ."

"I don't know anything about that. I know he's got a Russian wife. They don't like her much."

"I got a letter from him at Singapore saying they'd put me up for a bit till I could look round and see what I wanted to do."

Now they were steaming up the river. At the mouth

was a straggling fishermen's village standing on piles
in the water; on the bank grew thickly nipah palm and
the tortured mangrove; beyond stretched the dense
green of the virgin forest. In the distance, darkly
silhouetted against the blue sky, was the rugged outline
of a mountain. Neil, his heart beating with the excitement that possessed him, devoured the scene with eager
eyes. He was surprised. He knew his Conrad almost by
heart and he was expecting a land of brooding mystery.
He was not prepared for the blue milky sky. Little white
clouds on the horizon, like sailing boats becalmed,
shone in the sun. The green trees of the forest glittered
in the brilliant light. Here and there, on the banks,
were Malay houses with thatched roofs, and they
nestled cosily among fruit trees. Natives in dugouts
rowed, standing, up the river. Neil had no feeling of
being shut in, nor in that radiant morning, of gloom,
but of space and freedom. The country offered him a
gracious welcome. He knew he was going to be happy
in it. Captain Bredon from the bridge threw a friendly
glance at the lad standing below him. He had taken
quite a fancy to him during the four days the journey
had lasted. It was true he did not drink, and when you
made a joke he was as likely as not to take you seriously, but there was something very taking in his
seriousness; everything was interesting and important
to him—that, of course, was why he did not find your
jokes amusing; but even though he didn't see them he
laughed, because he felt you expected it. He laughed because life was grand. He was grateful for every little
thing you told him. He was very polite. He never asked
you to pass him anything without saying "please" and

always said "thank you" when you gave it. And he was a good-looking fellow, no one could deny that. Neil was standing with his hands on the rail, bare-headed, looking at the passing bank. He was tall, six foot two, with long, loose limbs, broad shoulders and narrow hips; there was something charmingly coltish about him, so that you expected him at any moment to break into a caper. He had brown curly hair with a peculiar shine in it; sometimes when the light caught it, it glittered like gold. His eyes, large and very blue, shone with good humour. They reflected his happy disposition. His nose was short and blunt and his mouth big, his chin determined; his face was rather broad. But his most striking feature was his skin; it was very white and smooth, with a lovely patch of red on either cheek. It would have been a beautiful skin even for a woman. Captain Bredon made the same joke to him every morning.

"Well, my lad, have you shaved to-day?"

Neil passed his hand over his chin.

"No, d'you think I need it?"

The Captain always laughed at this.

"Need it? Why, you've got a face like a baby's bottom."

And invariably Neil reddened to the roots of his hair.

"I shave once a week," he retorted.

But it wasn't only his looks that made you like him. It was his ingenuousness, his candour and the freshness with which he confronted the world. For all his intentness and the solemn way in which he took everything, and his inclination to argue upon every point that came up, there was something strangely simple in him that gave you quite an odd feeling. The Captain couldn't make it out.

"I wonder if it's because he's never had a woman," he said to himself. "Funny. I should have thought the girls never left him alone. With a complexion like that."

But the Sultan Ahmed was nearing the bend after rounding which Kuala Solor would be in sight and the Captain's reflections were interrupted by the necessities of his work. He rang down to the engine room. The ship slackened to half speed. Kuala Solor straggled along the left bank of the river, a white neat and trim little town, and on the right on a hill were the fort and the Sultan's Palace. There was a breeze and the Sultan's flag, at the top of a tall staff, waved bravely against the sky. They anchored in midstream. The doctor and a police officer came on board in the government launch. They were accompanied by a tall thin man in white ducks. The Captain stood at the head of the gangway and shook hands with them. Then he turned to the last comer.

"Well, I've brought you your young hopeful safe and sound." And with a glance at Neil: "This is Munro."

The tall thin man held out his hand and gave Neil an appraising look. Neil flushed a little and smiled. He had beautiful teeth.

"How do you do, sir?"

Munro did not smile with his lips, but faintly with his grey eyes. His cheeks were hollow and he had a thin aquiline nose and pale lips. He was deeply sunburned. His face looked tired, but his expression was very gentle, and Neil immediately felt confidence in him. The

Captain introduced him to the doctor and the policeman and suggested that they should have a drink. When they sat down and the boy brought bottles of beer Munro took off his topi. Neil saw that he had close-cropped brown hair turning grey. He was a man of forty, quiet, self-possessed in manner, with an intellectual air that distinguished him from the brisk little doctor and the heavy swaggering police officer.

"MacAdam doesn't drink," said the Captain when the boy poured out four glasses of beer.

"All the better," said Munro. "I hope you haven't been trying to lure him into evil ways."

"I tried to in Singapore," returned the Captain, with a twinkle in his eyes, "but there was nothing doing."

When he had finished his beer Munro turned to Neil.

"Well, we'll be getting ashore, shall we?"

Neil's baggage was put in charge of Munro's boy and the two men got into a sampan. They landed.

"Do you want to go straight up to the bungalow or would you like to have a look round first? We've got a couple of hours before tiffin."

"Couldn't we go to the museum?" said Neil.

Munro's eyes smiled gently. He was pleased. Neil was shy and Munro not by nature talkative, so they walked in silence. By the river were the native huts and here, living their immemorial lives, dwelt the Malays. They were busy, but without haste, and you were conscious of a happy, normal activity. There was a sense of the rhythm of life of which the pattern was birth and death, love and the affairs common to mankind. They came to the bazaars, narrow streets with arcades, when the teeming Chinese, working and eating, noisily talking, as is their way, indefatigably strove with eternity.

"It's not much after Singapore," said Munro, "but I always think it's rather picturesque."

He spoke with an accent less broad than Neil's, but the Scots burr was there and it put Neil at his ease. He could never quite get it out of his head that the English of English people was affected.

The museum was a handsome stone building and as they entered its portals Munro instinctively straightened himself. The attendant at the door saluted and Munro spoke to him in Malay, evidently explaining who Neil was, for the attendant gave him a smile and saluted again. It was cool in there in comparison with the heat without and the light was pleasant after the glare of the street.

"I'm afraid you'll be disappointed," said Munro. "We haven't got half the things we ought to have, but up to now we've been handicapped by lack of money. We've had to do the best we could. So you must make allowances."

Neil stepped in like a swimmer diving confidently into a summer sea. The specimens were admirably arranged. Munro had sought to please as well as to instruct, and birds and beasts and reptiles were presented, as far as possible in their natural surroundings, in such a way as to give a vivid impression of life. Neil lost his shyness and began with boyish enthusiasm to talk of this and that. He asked an infinity of questions. He was excited. Neither of them was conscious of the passage of time, and when Munro glanced at his watch he was surprised to see what the hour was. They got into rickshaws and drove to the bungalow.

Munro led the young man into a drawing-room. A woman was lying on a sofa reading a book and as they came in she slowly rose.

"This is my wife. I'm afraid we're dreadfully late, Darya."

"What does it matter?" she smiled. "What is more unimportant than time?"

She held out her hand, a rather large hand, to Neil and gave him a long, reflective, but friendly look.

"I suppose you've been showing him the museum."

She was a woman of five and thirty, of medium height, with a pale brown face of a uniform colour and pale blue eyes. Her hair, parted in the middle and wound into a knot on the nape of her neck, was untidy; it had a moth-like quality and was of a curious pale brown. Her face was broad, with high cheek-bones, and she had a rather fleshy nose. She was not a pretty woman, but there was in her slow movements a sensual grace and in her manner as it were a physical casualness that only very dull people could have failed to find interesting. She wore a frock of green cotton. She spoke English perfectly, but with a slight accent.

They sat down to tiffin. Neil was overcome once more with shyness, but Darya did not seem to notice it. She talked freely and easily. She asked him about his journey and what he had thought of Singapore. She told him about the people he would have to meet. That afternoon Munro was to take him to call on the Resident, the Sultan being away, and later they would go to the club. There he would see everybody.

"You will be popular," she said, her pale blue eyes resting on him with attention. A man less ingenuous than Neil might have noticed that she took stock of his size and youthful virility, his shiny, curling hair and his lovely skin. "They don't think much of us."

"Oh, nonsense, Darya. You're too sensitive. They're English, that's all."

"They think it's rather funny of Angus to be a scientist and they think it's rather vulgar of me to be a Russian. I don't care. They're fools. They're the most commonplace, the most narrow-minded, the most conventional people it has ever been my misfortune to live amongst."

"Don't put MacAdam off the moment he arrives. He'll find them kind and hospitable."

"What is your first name?" she asked the boy.

"Neil."

"I shall call you by it. And you must call me Darya. I hate being called Mrs. Munro. It makes me feel like a minister's wife."

Neil blushed. He was embarrassed that she should ask him so soon to be so familiar. She went on.

"Some of the men are not bad."

"They do their jobs competently and that's what they're here for," said Munro.

"They shoot. They play football and tennis and cricket. I get on with them quite well. The women are intolerable. They are jealous and spiteful and lazy. They can talk of nothing. If you introduce an intellectual subject they look down their noses as though you were indecent. What can they talk about? They're interested in nothing. If you speak of the body they think you improper, and if you speak of the soul they think you priggish."

"You mustn't take what 'my wife says too literally," smiled Munro, in his gentle, tolerant way. "The community here is just like any other in the East, neither very clever, nor very stupid, but amiable and kindly. And that's a good deal."

"I don't want people to be amiable and kindly. I want them to be vital and passionate. I want them to be interested in mankind. I want them to attach more importance to the things of the spirit than to a gin pahit or a curry tiffin. I want art to matter to them and literature." She addressed herself abruptly to Neil: "Have you got a soul?"

"Oh, I don't know. I don't know exactly what you mean."

"Why do you blush when I ask you? Why should you be ashamed of your soul? It is what is important in you. Tell me about it. I am interested in you and I want to know."

It seemed very awkward to Neil to be tackled in this way by a perfect stranger. He had never met anyone like this. But he was a serious young man and when he was asked a question straight out he did his best to answer it. It was Munro's presence that embarrassed him.

"I don't know what you mean by the soul. If you mean an immaterial or spiritual entity, separately produced by the creator, in temporary conjunction with the material body, then my answer is in the negative. It seems to me that such a radically dualistic view of human personality cannot be defended by anyone who is able to take a calm view of the evidence. If, on the other hand, you mean by soul the aggregate of psychic elements which form what we know as the personality of the individual, then, of course, I have."

"You're very sweet and you're wonderfully handsome," she said, smiling. "No, I mean the heart with its longings and the body with its desires and the infinite in us. Tell me, what did you read on the journey, or did you only play deck tennis?"

Neil was taken aback at the inconsequence of her reply. He would have been a little affronted except for the good humour in her eyes and the naturalness in her manner. Munro smiled quietly at the young man's bewilderment. When he smiled the lines that ran from the wings of his nostrils to the corners of his mouth became deep furrows.

"I read a lot of Conrad."

"For pleasure or to improve your mind?"

"Both. I admire him awfully."

Darya threw up her arms in an extravagant gesture of protest.

"That Pole," she cried. "How can you English ever have let yourselves be taken in by that wordy mountebank? He has all the superficiality of his countrymen. That stream of words, those involved sentences, the showy rhetoric, that affectation of profundity: when you get through all that to the thought at the bottom, what do you find but a commonplace? He was like a second-rate actor who puts on a romantic dress and declaims a play by Victor Hugo. For five minutes you say this is heroic, and then your whole soul revolts and you cry, no, this is false, false, false."

She spoke with a passion that Neil had never known anyone show when speaking of art or literature. Her cheeks, usually colourless, flushed and her pale eyes glowed.

"There's no one who got atmosphere like Conrad," said Neil. "I can smell and see and feel the East when I read him."

"Nonsense. What do you know about the East? Everyone will tell you that he made the grossest blunders. Ask Angus."

"Of course he was not always accurate," said Munro, in his measured, reflective way. "The Borneo he described is not the Borneo we know. He saw it from the deck of a merchant vessel and he was not an acute observer even of what he saw. But does it matter? I don't know why fiction should be hampered by fact. I don't think it's a mean achievement to have created a country, a dark, sinister, romantic and heroic country of the soul."

"You're a sentimentalist, my poor Angus." And then again to Neil: "You must read Turgeniev, you must read Tolstoi, you must read Dostoevsky."

Neil did not in the least know what to make of Darya Munro. She skipped over the first stages of acquaintance and treated him at once like someone she had known intimately all her life. It puzzled him. It seemed so reckless. When he met anyone his own instinct was to go cautiously. He was amiable, but he did not like to step too far before he saw his way before him. He did not want to give anyone his confidence before he thought himself justified. But with Darya you could not help yourself; she forced your confidence.

She poured out the feelings and thoughts that most people keep to themselves like a prodigal flinging gold pieces to a scrambling crowd. She did not talk, she did not act like anyone he had ever known. She did not mind what she said. She would speak of the natural functions of the human animal in a way that brought the blushes coursing to his cheeks. They excited her ridicule.

"Oh, what a prig you are! What is there indecent in it? When I'm going to take a purge, why shouldn't I say so and when I think you want one, why shouldn't I tell you?"

"Theoretically I daresay you're right," said Neil, always judicious and reasonable.

She made him tell her of his father and mother, his brothers, his life at school and at the university. She told him about herself. Her father was a general killed in the war and her mother a Princess Lutchkov. They were in Eastern Russia when the Bolsheviks seized power, and fled to Yokohama. Here they had subsisted miserably on the sale of their jewels and such objects of art as they had been able to save, and here she married a fellow exile. She was unhappy with him and in two years divorced him. Her mother died and, penniless, she was driven to earn her living as best she could. She was employed by an American relief organisation. She taught in a mission school. She worked in a hospital. She made Neil's blood boil, and at the same time embarrassed him very much, when she spoke of the men who tried to take advantage of her defencelessness and her poverty. She spared him no details.

"Brutes," he said.

"Oh, all men are like that," she replied, with a shrug of her shoulders.

She told him how once she protected her virtue at the point of her revolver.

"I swore I'd kill him if he took another step, and if he had I'd have shot him like a dog."

"Gosh!" said Neil.

It was at Yokohama that she met Angus. He was spending his leave in Japan. She was captivated by his straightforwardness, the decency which was so obvious in him, his tenderness and his consideration. He was not a business man; he was a scientist, and science is milk brother to art. He offered her peace. He offered her security. And she was tired of Japan. Borneo was a land of mystery. They had been married for five years.

She gave Neil the Russian novelists to read. She gave him Fathers and Sons, Anna Karenina and The Brothers Karamazoff.

"Those are the three peaks of our literature. Read them. They are the greatest novels the world has ever seen."

Like many of her countrymen she talked as though no other literature counted, and as though a few novels and stories, some indifferent poetry and a half a dozen good plays had made whatever else the world has produced negligible. Neil was fascinated and overwhelmed.

"You're rather like Alyosha yourself, Neil," she said, looking at him with eyes that were now so soft and tender, "an Alyosha with a Scotch dourness, suspicious and prudent, that will not let the soul in you, the spiritual beauty, come out."

"I'm not a bit like Alyosha," he answered self-consciously.

"You don't know what you're like. You don't know anything about yourself. Why are you a naturalist? Is it for money? You could have made much more money by going into your uncle's office in Glasgow. I feel in you something strange and unearthly. I could bow down at your feet as Father Zossima did to Dimitri."

"Please don't," he said, smiling, but flushing a little too.

But the novels he read made her seem a little less strange to him. They gave her an environment and he recognised in her traits which, however unusual in the women he knew in Scotland, his mother and the daughters of his uncle in Glasgow, were common to many of the characters in Russian fiction. He no longer wondered that she should like to sit up so late, drinking innumerable cups of tea, and lie on the sofa nearly all day long reading and incessantly smoking cigarettes. She could do nothing at all for days on end without being bored. She had a curious mixture of languor and zest. She often said, with a shrug of her shoulders, that she was an Oriental and a European only by chance. She had a feline grace that indeed suggested the Oriental. She was immensely untidy and it did not seem to affect her that cigarette ends, old papers and empty tins should lie about their living-room. But he thought she had something of Anna Karenina in her, and he transferred to her the sympathy he felt for that pathetic creature. He understood her arrogance. It was not unnatural that she despised the women of the community, whose acquaintance little by little he made; they *were* commonplace; her mind was quicker than theirs, she had a wider culture, and she had above all a sort of tremulous sensitiveness that made *them* extraordinarily colourless. She certainly took no pains to conciliate them. Though at home she slopped about in a sarong and baju, when she and Angus went out to dinner she dressed with a splendour that was somewhat out of place. She liked to display her ample bosom and her shapely back. She painted her cheeks and made up her eyes like an actress for the footlights. Though it made Neil angry to see the amused or outraged glances that her appearance provoked, he could not in his heart but think it a pity that she should make such an object of herself. She looked grand, of course, but if you hadn't known who she was you would have thought she wasn't respectable. There were things about her that he could never get over. She had an enormous appetite and it fashed him that she ate more than he and Angus put together. He could never quite get used to the bluntness with which she discussed sexual matters. She took it for granted that at home and in Edinburgh he had had affairs with a host of women. She pressed him for details of his adventures. His Scotch pawkiness helped him to parry her thrusts and he evaded her questions with native caution. She laughed at his reticence.

Sometimes she shocked him. He grew accustomed to the frankness with which she admired his looks, and when she told him that he was as beautiful as a young Norse god he did not turn a hair. Flattery fell off him like water from a duck's back. But he did not like it when she ran her hand, though large, very soft, with caressing fingers, through his curly hair or, a smile on her lips, stroked his smooth face. He couldn't bear being mussed about. One day she wanted a drink of tonic water and began pouring some out in a glass that ·stood on the table.

"That's my glass," he said quickly. "I've just been drinking out of it."

"Well, what of it? You haven't got syphilis, have you?"

"I hate drinking out of other people's glasses myself."

She was funny about cigarettes too. Once, when he hadn't been there very long, he had just lit one, when she passed and said:

"I want that."

She took it out of his mouth and began to smoke it. After two or three puffs, she said she did not want any more and handed it back to him. The end she had had in her mouth was red from the rouge on her lips, and he didn't want to go on smoking it at all. But he was afraid she would think it rude if he threw it away. It somewhat disgusted him. Often she would ask him for a cigarette and when he handed it to her, say:

"Oh, light it for me, will you?"

When he did so, and held it out to her, she opened her mouth so that he should put it in. He hadn't been able to help wetting the end a little. He wondered she could bear to put it in her mouth after it had been in his. The whole thing seemed to him awfully familiar. He was sure Munro wouldn't like it. She had even done this once **or twice at** the club. Neil had felt himself go

purple. He wished she hadn't got these rather unpleasant habits, but he supposed they were Russian, and
one couldn't deny that she was wonderfully good company. Her conversation was very stimulating. It was
like champagne (which Neil had tasted once and
thought wretched stuff) "metaphorically speaking."
There was nothing she couldn't talk about. She didn't
talk like a man; with a man you generally knew what
he would say next, but with her you never did; her intuition was quite remarkable. She gave you ideas. She
enlarged your mind and excited your imagination. Neil
felt alive as he had never felt alive before. He seemed to
walk on mountain peaks and the horizons of the spirit
were unbounded. Neil felt a certain complacency when
he stopped to reflect on what an exalted plane his mind
communed with hers. Such conversations made very
small beer of the vaunted pleasure of sense. She was in
many ways (he was of a cautious nature and seldom
made a statement even to himself that he did not
qualify) the most intelligent woman he had ever met.
And besides, she was Angus Munro's wife.

For, whatever Neil's reservations were about Darya,
he had none about Munro, and she would have had to
be a much less remarkable woman not to profit by the
enormous admiration he conceived for her husband.
With him Neil let himself go. He felt for him what he
had never felt for anyone before. He was so sane, so
balanced, so tolerant. This was the sort of man he
would himself like to be when he was older. He talked
little, but when he did, with good sense. He was wise.
He had a dry humour that Neil understood. It made the
hearty English fun of the men at the club seem inane.

He was kind and patient. He had a dignity that made it impossible to conceive of anyone taking a liberty with him, but he was neither pompous nor solemn. He was honest and absolutely truthful. But Neil admired him no less as a scientist than as a man. He had imagination. He was careful and painstaking. Though his interest was in research he did the routine work of the museum conscientiously. He was just then much interested in stick-insects and intended to write a paper on their powers of parthenogenetic reproduction. An incident occurred in connection with the experiments he was making that made a great impression on Neil. One day, a little captive gibbon escaped from its chain and ate up all the larvæ and so destroyed the whole of Munro's evidence. Neil nearly cried. Angus Munro took the gibbon in his arms and, smiling, stroked it.

"Diamond, Diamond," he said, quoting Sir Isaac Newton, "you little know the damage you have done."

He was also studying mimicry and instilled into Neil his absorbed interest in this controversial subject. They had interminable talks about it. Neil was astonished at the Curator's wonderful knowledge. It was encyclopædic, and he was abashed at his own ignorance. But it was when Munro spoke of the trips into the country to collect specimens that his enthusiasm was most contagious. That was the perfect life, a life of hardship, difficulty, often of privation and sometimes of danger, but rewarded by the thrill of finding a rare, or even a new species, by the beauty of the scenery and the intimate observation of nature, and above all by the sense of freedom from every tie. It was for this part of the work that Neil had been chiefly engaged. Munro was occupied in research work that made it difficult for him to be away from home for several weeks at a time, and Darya had always refused to accompany him. She had an unreasoning fear of the jungle. She was terrified of wild beasts, snakes and venomous insects. Though Munro had told her over and over again that no animal hurt you unless you molested or frightened it, she could not get over her instinctive horror. He did not like leaving her. She cared little for the local society and with him away he realised that life for her must be intolerably dull. But the Sultan was keenly interested in natural history and was anxious that the museum should be completely representative of the country's fauna. One expedition Munro and Neil were to make together, so that Neil should learn how to go to work, and the plans for this were discussed by them for months. Neil looked forward to it as he had never looked forward to anything in his life.

Meanwhile he learned Malay and acquired a smattering of the dialects that would be useful to him on future journeys. He played tennis and football. He soon knew everyone in the community. On the football field he threw off his absorption in science and his interest in Russian fiction and gave himself up to the pleasure of the game. He was strong, quick and active. After it was all over it was grand to have a sluice down and a long tonic with a slice of lemon and go over it all with the other fellows. It had never been intended that Neil should live permanently with the Munros. There was a roomy Rest House at Kuala Solor, but the rule was that no one should stay in it for more than a fortnight and such of the bachelors as had no official quarters clubbed together and took a house between them. When Neil arrived it so happened that there was no vacancy in any of these messes. One evening, however, when he had been about four months in the colony, two men, Waring and Jonson, when they were sitting together after a game of tennis, told him that one member of their mess was going home and if he would like to join them they would be glad to have him. They were young fellows of his own age, in the football team, and Neil liked them both. Waring was in the customs and Jonson in the police. He jumped at the suggestion. They told him how much it would cost and fixed a day, a fortnight later, when it would be convenient for him to move in.

At dinner he told the Munros.

"It's been awfully good of you to let me stay so long. It's made me very uncomfortable planting myself on you like this, I've been quite ashamed, but now there's no excuse for me."

"But we like having you here," said Darya. "You don't need an excuse."

"I can hardly go on staying here indefinitely?"

"Why not? Your salary's miserable, what's the use of wasting it on board and lodging? You'd be bored stiff with Jonson and Waring. Stupids. They haven't an idea in their heads outside playing the gramophone and knocking balls about."

It was true that it had been very convenient to live free of cost. He had saved the greater part of his salary. He had a thrifty soul and had never been used to spending money when it wasn't necessary, but he was proud. He could not go on living at other people's expense. Darya looked at him with her quiet, observant eyes.

"Angus and I have got used to you now. I think we'd miss you. If you like, you can pay us for your board. You don't cost anything, but if it'll make you easier I'll find out exactly what difference you make in cookie's book and you can pay that."

"It must be an awful nuisance having a stranger in the house," he answered uncertainly.

"It'll be miserable for you there. Good heavens, the filth they eat."

It was true also that at the Munros' you ate better than anywhere else at Kuala Solor. He had dined out now and then, and even at the Resident's you didn't get a very good dinner. Darya liked her food and kept the cook up to the mark. He made Russian dishes which were a fair treat. That cabbage soup of Darya's was worth walking five miles for. But Munro hadn't said anything.

"I'd be glad if you'd stay here," he said now. "It's very convenient to have you on the spot. If anything comes up we can talk it over there and then. Waring and Jonson are very good fellows, but I daresay you'd find them rather limited after a bit."

"Oh, well, then I'll be very pleased. Heaven knows, I couldn't want anything better than this. I was only afraid I was in the way."

Next day it was raining cats and dogs and it was impossible to play tennis or football, but towards six Neil put on a mackintosh and went to the club. It was empty, but for the Resident, who was sitting in an arm-

chair reading The Fortnightly. His name was Tre-
velyan, and he claimed to be related to the friend of
Byron. He was a tall fat man, with close-cropped
white hair and the large red face of a comic actor. He
was fond of amateur theatricals, and specialised in
cynical dukes and facetious butlers. He was a bachelor,
but generally supposed to be fond of the girls, and he
liked his gin pahit before dinner. He owed his position
to the Sultan's friendship. He was a slack, complacent
man, a great talker, not very fond of work, who wanted
everything to go smoothly and no one to give trouble.
Though not considered especially competent he was
popular in the community because he was easy-going
and hospitable, and he certainly made life more comfortable than if he had been energetic and efficient. He
nodded to Neil.

"Well, young fellow, how are bugs to-day?"

"Feeling the weather, sir," said Neil gravely.

"Hi-hi."

In a few minutes Waring, Jonson and another man,
called Bishop, came in. He was in the civil service. Neil
did not play bridge, so Bishop went up to the Resident.

"Would you care to make a fourth, sir?" he asked
him. "There's nobody much in the club to-day."

The Resident gave the others a glance.

"All right. I'll just finish this article and join you.
Cut for me and deal. I shall only be five minutes."

Neil went up to the three men.

"Oh, I say, Waring, thanks awfully, but I can't
move over to you after all. The Munros have asked
me to stay on with them for good."

A broad smile broke on Waring's face.

"Fancy that."

"It's awfully nice of them, isn't it? They made rather a point of it. I couldn't very well refuse."

"What did I tell you?" said Bishop.

"I don't blame the boy," said Waring.

There was something in their manner that Neil did not like. They seemed to be amused. He flushed.

"What the hell are you talking about?" he cried.

"Oh, come off it," said Bishop. "We know our Darya. You're not the first good-looking young fellow she's had a romp with, and you won't be the last."

The words were hardly out of his mouth before Neil's clenched fist shot out like a flash. He hit Bishop on the face and he fell heavily to the floor. Jonson sprang at Neil and seized him round the middle, for he was beside himself.

"Let me go," he shouted. "If he doesn't withdraw that I'll kill him."

The Resident, startled by the commotion, looked up and rose to his feet. He walked heavily towards them.

"What's this? What's this? What the hell are you boys playing at?"

They were taken aback. They had forgotten him. He was their master. Jonson let go of Neil and Bishop picked himself up. The Resident, a frown on his face, spoke to Neil sharply.

"What's the meaning of this? Did you hit Bishop?"

"Yes, sir."

"Why?"

"He made a foul suggestion reflecting on a woman's honour," said Neil, very haughtily, and still white with rage.

The Resident's eyes twinkled, but he kept a grave face.

"What woman?"

"I refuse to answer," said Neil, throwing back his head and drawing himself up to his full imposing height.

It would have been more effective if the Resident hadn't been a good two inches taller, and very much stouter.

"Don't be a damned young fool."

"Darya Munro," said Jonson.

"What did you say, Bishop?"

"I forget the exact words I used. I said she'd hopped into bed with a good many young chaps here, and I supposed she hadn't missed the chance of doing the same with MacAdam."

"It was a most offensive suggestion. Will you be so good as to apologise and shake hands. Both of you."

"I've had a hell of a biff, sir. My eye's going to look like the devil. I'm damned if I apologise for telling the truth."

"You're old enough to know that the fact that your statement is true only makes it more offensive, and as far as your eye is concerned I'm told that a raw beef-steak is very efficacious in these circumstances. Though I put my desire that you should apologise in the form of a request out of politeness, it is in point of fact an order."

There was a moment's silence. The Resident looked bland.

"I apologise for what I said, sir," Bishop said sulkily.

"Now then, MacAdam."

"I'm sorry I hit him, sir. I apologise, too."

"Shake hands."

The two young men solemnly did so.

"I shouldn't like this to go any further. It wouldn't be very nice for Munro, whom I think we all like. Can I count on you all holding your tongues?"

They nodded.

"Now be off with you. You stay, MacAdam, I want to have a few words with you."

When the two of them were left alone, the Resident sat down and lit himself a cheroot. He offered one to Neil, but he only smoked cigarettes.

"You're a very violent young man," said the Resident, with a smile. "I don't like my officers to make scenes in a public place like this."

"Mrs. Munro is a great friend of mine. She's been kindness itself to me. I won't hear a word said against her."

"Then I'm afraid you'll have your job cut out for you if you stay here much longer."

Neil was silent for a moment. He stood, tall and slim, before the Resident, and his grave young face was guileless. He flung back his head defiantly. His emotion made him speak in broader Scots even than usual.

"I've lived with the Munros for four months, and I give you my word of honour that so far as I am concerned there is not an iota of truth in what that beast said. Mrs. Munro has never treated me with anything that you could call undue familiarity. She's never by word or deed given me the smallest hint that she had an improper idea in her head. She's been like a mother to me or an elder sister."

The Resident watched him with ironical eyes.

"I'm very glad to hear it. That's the best thing I've heard about her for a long time."

"You believe me, sir, don't you?"

"Of course. Perhaps you've reformed her." He called out. "Boy. Bring me a gin pahit." And then to Neil. "That'll do. You can go now if you want to. But no more fighting, mind you, or you'll get the order of the boot."

When Neil walked back to the Munros' bungalow the rain had stopped and the velvet sky was bright with stars. In the garden the fire-flies were flitting here and there. From the earth rose a scented warmth and you felt that if you stopped you would hear the growth of that luxuriant vegetation. A white flower of the night gave forth an overwhelming perfume. In the verandah Munro was typing some notes and Darya, lying at full length on a long chair, was reading. The lamp behind her lit her smoky hair so that it shone like an aureole. She looked up at Neil and putting down her book, smiled. Her smile was very friendly.

"Where have you been, Neil?"

"At the club."

"Anybody there?"

The scene was so cosy and domestic, Darya's manner so peaceful and quietly assured, that it was impossible not to be touched. The two of them there, each occupied with his own concerns, seemed so united, their intimacy so natural, that no one could have conceived that they were not perfectly happy in one another. Neil did not believe a single word of what Bishop had said and the Resident had hinted. It was incredible. After all, he knew that what they had suspected of *him* was untrue, so what reason was there to think that the rest was any truer? They had dirty minds, all those people; because they were a lot of swine they thought everyone else as bad as they were. His knuckle hurt him a little. He was glad he had hit Bishop. He wished he knew who had started that filthy story. He'd wring his neck.

But now Munro fixed a date for the expedition that they had so much discussed, and in his careful way began to make preparations so that at the last moment nothing should be forgotten. The plan was to go as far up the river as possible and then make their way through the jungle and hunt for specimens on the little-known Mount Hitam. They expected to be away two months. As the day on which they were to start grew nearer Munro's spirits rose, and though he did not say very much, though he remained quiet and self-controlled, you could tell by the light in his eyes and the jauntiness of his step how much he looked forward to it. One morning, at the museum, he was almost sprightly.

"I've got some good news for you," he said suddenly to Neil, after they had been looking at some experiments they were making, "Darya's coming with us."

"Is she? That's grand."

Neil was delighted. That made it perfect.

"It's the first time I've ever been able to induce her to accompany me. I told her she'd enjoy it, but she would never listen to me. Queer cattle, women. I'd given it up and never thought of asking her to come this time, and suddenly, last night, out of a blue sky she said she'd like to."

"I'm awfully glad," said Neil.

"I didn't much like the idea of leaving her by herself

so long; now we can stay just as long as we want to."

They started early one morning in four prahus, manned by Malays, and besides themselves the party consisted of their servants and four Dyak hunters. The three of them lay on cushions side by side, under an awning; in the other boats were the Chinese servants and the Dyaks. They carried bags of rice for the whole party, provisions for themselves, clothes, books and all that was necessary for their work. It was heavenly to leave civilisation behind them and they were all excited. They talked. They smoked. They read. The motion of the river was exquisitely soothing. They lunched on a grassy bank. Dusk fell and they moored for the night. They slept at a long house and their Dyak hosts celebrated their visit with arak, eloquence and a fantastic dance. Next day the river, narrowing, gave them more definitely the feeling that they were adventuring into the unknown, and the exotic vegetation that crowded the banks to the water's edge, like an excited mob pushed from behind by a multitude, caused Neil a breathless ravishment. O wonder and delight! On the third day, because the water was shallower and the stream more rapid, they changed into lighter boats, and soon it grew so strong that the boatmen could paddle no longer, and they poled against the current with powerful and magnificent gestures. Now and then they came to rapids and had to disembark, unload and haul the boats through a rock-strewn passage. After five days they reached a point beyond which they could go no further. There was a government bungalow there, and they settled in for a couple of nights while Munro made arrangements for their excursion into the interior. He wanted bearers for their baggage, and men to build a house for them when they reached Mount Hitam. It was necessary for Munro to see the headman of a village in the vicinity and thinking it would save time if he went himself rather than let the headman come to him, the day after they arrived he set out at dawn with a guide and a couple of Dyaks. He expected to be back in a few hours. When he had seen him off Neil thought he would have a bathe. There was a pool a little way from the bungalow, and the water was so clear that you saw every grain of the sandy bottom. The river was so narrow there that the trees over-arched it. It was a lovely spot. It reminded Neil of the pools in Scotch streams he had bathed in as a boy, and yet it was strangely different. It had an air of romance, a feeling of virgin nature, that filled him with sensations that he found hard to analyse. He tried, of course, but older heads than his have found it difficult to anatomize happiness. A kingfisher was sitting on an overhanging branch and its vivid blue was reflected as bluely in the crystal stream. It flew away with a flashing glitter of jewelled wings when Neil, slipping off his sarong and baju, scrambled down into the water. It was fresh without being cold. He splashed and tumbled about. He enjoyed the movement of his strong limbs. He floated and looked at the blue sky peeping through the leaves and the sun that here and there gilded the water. Suddenly he heard a voice.

"How white your body is, Neil."

With a gasp he let himself sink and turning round saw Darya standing on the bank.

"I say, I haven't got any clothes on."

"So I saw. It's much nicer bathing without. Wait a minute, I'll come in, it looks lovely."

She also was wearing a sarong and a baju. He turned away his head quickly for he saw that she was taking them off. He heard her splash into the water. He gave two or three strokes in order that she should have room to swim about at a good distance from him, but she swam up to him.

"Isn't the feel of the water on one's body lovely?" she said.

She laughed and opening her hand splashed water in his face. He was so embarrassed he did not know which way to look. In that limpid water it was impossible not to see that she was stark naked. It was not so bad now, but he could not help thinking how difficult it would be to get out. She seemed to be having a grand time.

"I don't care if I do get my hair wet," she said.

She turned over on her back and with strong strokes swam round the pool. When she wanted to get out, he thought, the best thing would be if he turned his back, and when she was dressed she could go and he would get out later. She seemed quite unconscious of the awkwardness of the situation. He was vexed with her. It really was rather tactless to behave like that. She kept on talking to him just as if they were on dry land and properly dressed. She even called his attention to herself.

"Does my hair look awful? It's so fine it gets like rat tails when it's wet. Hold me under the shoulders a moment while I try to screw it up."

"Oh, it's all right," he said. "You'd better leave it now."

"I'm getting frightfully hungry," she said presently. "What about breakfast?"

"If you'll get out first and put on your things, I'll follow you in a minute."

"All right."

She swam the two strokes needed to bring her to the side, and he modestly looked away so that he should not see her get out nude from the water.

"I can't get up," she cried. "You'll have to help me."

It had been easy enough to get in, but the bank overhung the water and one had to lift oneself up by the branch of a tree.

"I can't. I haven't got a stitch of clothing on."

"I know that. Don't be so Scotch. Get up on the bank and give me a hand."

There was no help for it. Neil swung himself up and pulled her after him. She had left her sarong beside his. She took it up unconcernedly and began to dry herself with it. There was nothing for him but to do the same, but for decency's sake he turned his back on her.

"You really have a most lovely skin," she said. "It's as smooth and white as a woman's. It's funny on such a manly virile figure. And you haven't got a hair on your chest."

Neil wrapped the sarong round him and slipped his arms into the baju.

"Are you ready?"

She had porridge for breakfast, and eggs and bacon, cold meat and marmalade. Neil was a trifle sulky. She was really almost too Russian. It was stupid of her to behave like that; of course there was no harm in it, but it was just that sort of thing that made people think

the things they did about her. The worst of it was that
you couldn't give her a hint. She'd only laugh at you.
But the fact was that if any of those men at Kuala Solor
had seen them bathing like that together, stark naked,
nothing would have persuaded them that something
improper hadn't happened. In his judicious way Neil
admitted to himself that you could hardly blame them.
It was too bad of her. She had no right to put a fellow
in such a position. He had felt such a fool. And say what
you liked it was indecent.

Next morning, having seen their carriers on the way,
a long procession in single file, each man carrying his
load in a creel on his back, with their servants, guides
and hunters, they started to walk. The path ran over the
foothills of the mountain, through scrub and tall grass,
and now and then they came to narrow streams which
they crossed by rickety bridges of bamboo. The sun
beat on them fiercely. In the afternoon they reached the
shade of a bamboo forest, grateful after the glare, and
the bamboos in their slender elegance rose to incredible
heights, and the green light was like the light under the
sea. At last they reached the primeval forest, huge
trees swathed in luxuriant creepers, an inextricable
tangle, and awe descended upon them. They cut their
way through the undergrowth. They walked in twilight
and only now and then caught through the dense foliage
above them a glimpse of sunshine. They saw neither
man nor beast, for the denizens of the jungle are shy
and at the first sound of footsteps vanish from sight.
They heard birds up high in the tall trees, but saw none
save the twittering sunbirds that flew in the under-

woods and delicately coquetted with the wild flowers. They halted for the night. The carriers made a floor of branches and on this spread water-proof sheets. The Chinese cook made them their dinner and then they turned in.

It was the first night Neil had ever spent in the jungle and he could not sleep. The darkness was profound. The noise was deafening of innumerable insects, but like the roar of traffic in a great city it was so constant that in a little while it was like an impenetrable silence, and when on a sudden he heard the shriek of a monkey seized by a snake or the scream of a night-bird he nearly jumped out of his skin. He had a mysterious sensation that all around creatures were watching them. Over there, beyond the camp fires, savage warfare was waged and they three on their bed of branches were defenceless and alone in face of the horror of nature. By his side Munro was breathing quietly in his deep sleep.

"Are you awake, Neil?" Darya whispered.

"Yes. Is anything the matter?"

"I'm terrified."

"It's all right. There's nothing to be afraid of."

"The silence is so awful. I wish I hadn't come."

She lit a cigarette.

Neil, having at last dozed off, was awakened by the hammering of a woodpecker, and its complacent laugh as it flew from one tree to another seemed to mock the sluggards. A hurried breakfast and the caravan started. The gibbons swung from branch to branch, gathering in the dawn dew from the leaves, and their strange cry was like the call of a bird. The light had driven away

Darya's fears, and notwithstanding a sleepless night she was alert and gay. They continued to climb. In the afternoon they reached the spot that the guides had told them would be a good camping place, and here Munro decided to build a house. The men set to work. With their long knives they cut palm leaves and saplings and soon had erected a two-roomed hut raised on piles from the ground. It was neat and fresh and green. It smelt good.

The Munros, he from old habit, she because she had for years wandered about the world and had a catlike knack of making herself comfortable wherever she went, were at home anywhere. In a day they had arranged everything and settled down. Their routine was invariable. Every morning early Neil and Munro started out separately, collecting. The afternoon was devoted to pinning insects in boxes, placing butterflies between sheets of paper and skinning birds. When dusk came they caught moths. Darya busied herself with the hut and the servants, sewed and read and smoked innumerable cigarettes. The days passed very pleasantly, monotonous but eventful. Neil was enraptured. He explored the mountain in all directions. One day, to his pride, he found a new species of stick-insect. Munro named it Cuniculina MacAdami. This was fame. Neil (at twenty-two) realised that he had not lived in vain. But another day he only just escaped being bitten by a viper. Owing to its green colour he had not seen it and was only saved from lurching against it by the Dyak hunter who was with him. They killed it and brought it back to camp. Darya shuddered at the sight of it. She had a terror of the wild creatures of the jungle that was almost hysterical. She would never go more than a few yards from the camp for fear of being lost.

"Has Angus ever told you how he was lost?" she asked Neil one evening when they were sitting quietly together after dinner.

"It wasn't a very pleasant experience," he smiled.

"Tell him, Angus."

He hesitated a little. It was not a thing he liked to recall.

"It was some years ago, I'd gone out with my butter-fly net and I'd been very lucky, I'd got several rare specimens that I'd been looking for a long time. After a while I thought I was getting hungry so I turned back. I walked for some time and it struck me I'd come a good deal farther than I knew. Suddenly I caught sight of an empty match-box. I swore. I knew at once what had happened. I'd thrown it away when I started to come back, I'd been walking in a circle and was exactly where I was an hour before. I was not pleased. But I had a look round and set off again. It was fearfully hot, and I was simply dripping with sweat. I knew more or less the direction the camp was in and I looked about for traces of my passage to see if I had come that way. I thought I found one or two and went on hopefully. I was frightfully thirsty. I walked on and on, picking my way over snags and trailing plants, and suddenly I knew I was lost. I couldn't have gone so far in the right direction without hitting the camp. I can tell you I was startled. I knew I must keep my head, so I sat down and thought the situation over. I was tortured by thirst. It was long past midday and in three or four hours it would be dark. I didn't like the idea of spending a night in the jungle at all. The only thing I could think of was to try and find a stream; if I followed its course, it would eventually bring me to a larger stream and sooner or later to the river. But of course it might take a couple of days. I cursed myself for being such a fool, but there was nothing better to do and I began walking. At all events if I found a stream I should be able to get a drink. I couldn't find a trickle of water anywhere, not the smallest brook that might lead to something like a stream. I began to be alarmed. I saw myself wandering on till at last I fell exhausted. I knew there was a lot of game in the forest and if I came upon a rhino I was done for. The maddening thing was I knew I couldn't be more than ten miles from my camp. I forced myself to keep my head. The day was waning and in the depths of the jungle it was growing dark already. If I'd brought a gun I could have fired it. In the camp they must have realised I was lost and would be looking for me. The undergrowth was so thick that I couldn't see six feet into it and presently, I don't know if it was nerves or not, I had the sensation that some animal was walking stealthily beside me. I stopped and it stopped too. I went on and it went on. I couldn't see it. I could see no movement in the undergrowth. I didn't even hear the breaking of a twig or the brushing of a body through leaves, but I knew how silently those beasts could move, and I was positive something was stalking me. My heart beat so violently against my ribs that I thought it would break. I was scared out of my wits. It was only by the exercise of all the self-control I had that I prevented myself from breaking into a run. I knew if I did that I was lost. I should be tripped up before I had gone

twenty yards by a tangled root and when I was down it
would spring on me. And if I started to run God knew
where I should get to. And I had to husband my
strength. I felt very like crying. And that intolerable
thirst. I've never been so frightened in my life. Believe
me, if I'd had a revolver I think I'd have blown my
brains out. It was so awful I just wanted to finish with it.
I was so exhausted I could hardly stagger. If I had an
enemy who'd done me a deadly injury I wouldn't wish
him the agony I endured then. Suddenly I heard two
shots. My heart stood still. They were looking for me.
Then I did lose my head. I ran in the direction of the
sound, screaming at the top of my voice, I fell, I picked
myself up again, I ran on, I shouted till I thought my
lungs would burst, there was another shot, nearer, I
shouted again, I heard answering shouts; there was a
scramble of men in the undergrowth. In a minute I was
surrounded by Dyak hunters. They wrung and kissed
my hands. They laughed and cried. I very nearly
cried too. I was down and out, but they gave me a
drink. We were only three miles from the camp. It was
pitch dark when we got back. By God, it was a near
thing."

A convulsive shudder passed through Darya.

"Believe me, I don't want to be lost in the jungle
again."

"What would have happened if you hadn't been
found?"

"I can tell you. I should have gone mad. If I hadn't
been stung by a snake or attacked by a rhino I should
have gone on blindly till I fell exhausted. I should have
starved to death. I should have died of thirst. Wild

beasts would have eaten my body and ants cleaned my bones."

Silence fell upon them.

Then it happened, when they had spent nearly a month on Mount Hitam, that Neil, notwithstanding the quinine Munro had made him take regularly, was stricken with fever. It was not a bad attack, but he felt very sorry for himself and was obliged to stay in bed. Darya nursed him. He was ashamed to give her so much trouble, but she would not listen to his protests. She was certainly very capable. He resigned himself to letting her do things for him that one of the Chinese boys could have done just as well. He was touched. She waited on him hand and foot. But when the fever was at its height and she sponged him all over with cold water, though the comfort was indescribable, he was excessively embarrassed. She insisted on washing him night and morning.

"I wasn't in the British hospital at Yokohama for six months without learning at least the routine of nursing," she said, smiling.

She kissed him on the lips each time after she had finished. It was friendly and sweet of her. He rather liked it, but attached no importance to it; he even went so far, a rare thing for him, as to be facetious on the subject.

"Did you always kiss your patients at the hospital?" he asked her.

"Don't you like me to kiss you?" she smiled.

"It doesn't do me any harm."

"It may even hasten your recovery," she mocked.

One night he dreamt of her. He awoke with a start. He was sweating profusely. The relief was wonderful, and he knew that his temperature had fallen; he was well. He did not care. For what he had dreamt filled him with shame. He was horrified. That he should have such thoughts, even in his sleep, made him feel awful. He must be a monster of depravity. Day was breaking, and he heard Munro getting up in the room next door that he occupied with Darya. She slept late, and he took care not to disturb her. When he passed through Neil's room, Neil in a low voice called him.

"Hullo, are you awake?"

"Yes, I've had the crisis. I'm all right now."

"Good. You'd better stay in bed to-day. To-morrow you'll be as fit as a fiddle."

"Send Ah Tan to me when you've had your breakfast, will you?'

"Right-ho."

He heard Munro start out. The Chinese boy came and asked him what he wanted. An hour later Darya awoke. She came in to bid him good-morning. He could hardly look at her.

"I'll just have my breakfast and then I'll come in and wash you," she said.

"I'm washed. I got Ah Tan to do it."

"Why?"

"I wanted to spare you the trouble."

"It isn't a trouble. I like doing it."

She came over to the bed and bent down to kiss him, but he turned away his head.

"Oh, don't," he said.

"Why not?"

"It's silly."

She looked at him for a moment, surprised, and then

with a slight shrug of the shoulders left him. A little later she came back to see if there was anything he wanted. He pretended to be asleep. She very gently stroked his cheek.

"For God's sake don't do that," he cried.

"I thought you were sleeping. What's the matter with you to-day?"

"Nothing."

"Why are you being horrid to me? Have I done anything to offend you?"

"No."

"Tell me what it is."

She sat down on the bed and took his hand. He turned his face to the wall. He was so ashamed he could hardly speak.

"You seem to forget I'm a man. You treat me as if I was a boy of twelve."

"Oh?"

He was blushing furiously. He was angry with himself and vexed with her. She really should be more tactful. He plucked nervously at the sheet.

"I know it means nothing to you and it ought not to mean anything to me. It doesn't when I'm well and up and about. One can't help one's dreams, but they are an indication of what is going on in the subconscious."

"Have you been dreaming about me? Well, I don't think there's any harm in that."

He turned his head and looked at her. Her eyes were gleaming, but his were sombre with remorse.

"You don't know men," he said.

She gave a little burble of laughter. She bent down

and threw her arms round his neck. She had nothing on but her sarong and baju.

"You darling," she cried. "Tell me, what did you dream?"

He was startled out of his wits. He pushed her violently aside.

"What are you doing? You're crazy."

He jumped half out of bed.

"Don't you know that I'm madly in love with you?" she said.

"What *are* you talking about?"

He sat down on the side of the bed. He was frankly bewildered. She chuckled.

"Why do you suppose I came up to this horrible place? To be with you, ducky. Don't you know I'm scared stiff of the jungle? Even in here I'm frightened there'll be snakes or scorpions or something. I adore you."

"You have no right to speak to me like that," he said sternly.

"Oh, don't be so prim," she smiled.

"Let's get out of here."

He walked out on to the verandah and she followed him. He threw himself into a chair. She knelt by his side and tried to take his hands, but he withdrew them.

"I think you must be mad. I hope to God you don't mean what you say."

"I do. Every word of it," she smiled.

It exasperated him that she seemed unconscious of the frightfulness of her confession.

"Have you forgotten your husband?"

"Oh, what does he matter?"

"Darya."

"I can't be bothered about Angus now."

"I'm afraid you're a very wicked woman," he said slowly, a frown darkening his smooth brow.

She giggled.

"Because I've fallen in love with you? Darling, you shouldn't be so absurdly good-looking."

"For God's sake don't laugh."

"I can't help it; you're comic—but still adorable. I love your white skin and your shining curly hair. I love you because you're so prim and Scotch and humourless. I love your strength. I love your youth."

Her eyes glowed and her breath came quickly. She stooped and kissed his naked feet. He drew them away quickly, with a cry of protest, and in the agitation of his gesture nearly overthrew the rickety chair.

"Woman, you're insane. Have you no shame?"

"No."

"What do you want of me?" he asked fiercely.

"Love."

"What sort of a man do you take me for?"

"A man like any other," she replied calmly.

"Do you think after all that Angus Munro has done for me I could be such a damned beast as to play about with his wife? I admire him more than any man I've ever known. He's grand. He's worth a dozen of me and you put together. I'd sooner kill myself than betray him. I don't know how you can think me capable of such a dastardly act."

"Oh, my dear, don't talk such bilge. What harm is it going to do him? You mustn't take that sort of thing so tragically. After all life is very short; we're fools if we don't take what pleasure we can out of it."

"You can't make wrong right by talking about it."

"I don't know about that. I think that's a very controvertible statement."

He looked at her with amazement. She was sitting at his feet, cool to all appearance and collected, and she seemed to be enjoying the situation. She seemed quite unconscious of its seriousness.

"Do you know that I knocked a fellow down at the club because he made an insulting remark about you?"

"Who?"

"Bishop."

"Dirty dog. What did he say?"

"He said you'd had affairs with men."

"I don't know why people won't mind their own business. Anyhow, who cares what they say? I love you. I've never loved anyone like you. I'm absolutely sick with love for you."

"Be quiet. Be quiet."

"Listen, to-night when Angus is asleep, I'll slip into your room. He sleeps like a rock. There's no risk."

"You mustn't do that."

"Why not?"

"No, no, no."

He was frightened out of his wits. Suddenly she sprang to her feet and went into the house.

Munro came back at noon, and in the afternoon they busied themselves as usual. Darya, as she sometimes did, worked with them. She was in high spirits. She was so gay that Munro suggested that she was beginning to enjoy the life.

"It's not so bad," she admitted. "I'm feeling happy to-day."

She teased Neil. She seemed not to notice that he was silent and kept his eyes averted from her.

"Neil's very quiet," said Munro. "I suppose you're feeling a bit weak still."

"No, I just don't feel very talkative."

He was harassed. He was convinced that Darya was capable of anything. He remembered the hysterical frenzy of Nastasya Filipovna in The Idiot, and felt that she too could behave with that unfortunate lack of balance. He had seen her more than once fly into a temper with one of the Chinese servants and he knew how completely she could lose her self-control. Resistance only exasperated her. If she did not immediately get what she wanted she would go almost insane with rage. Fortunately she lost interest in a thing with the same suddenness with which she hankered for it, and if you could distract her attention for a minute she forgot all about it. It was in such situations that Neil had most admired Munro's tact. He had often been slyly amused to see with what a pawky and yet tender cunning he appeased her feminine tantrums. It was on Munro's account that Neil's indignation was so great. Munro was a saint, and from what a state of humiliation and penury and random shifts had he not taken her to make her his wife! She owed everything to him. His name protected her. She had respectability. The commonest gratitude should have made it impossible for her to harbour such thoughts as she had that morning expressed. It was all very well for men to make advances, that was what men did, but for women to do so was disgusting. His modesty was outraged. The passion he had seen in her face, and the indelicacy of her gestures, scandalised him.

He wondered whether she would really carry out her threat to come to his room. He didn't think she would dare. But when night came and they all went to bed, he was so terrified that he could not sleep. He lay there listening anxiously. The silence was broken only by the repeated and monotonous cry of an owl. Through the thin wall of woven palm leaves he heard Munro's steady breathing. Suddenly he was conscious that someone was stealthily creeping into his room. He had already made up his mind what to do.

"Is that you, Mr. Munro?" he called in a loud voice. Darya stopped suddenly. Munro awoke.

"There's someone in my room. I thought it was you."

"It's all right," said Darya. "It's only me. I couldn't sleep, so I thought I'd go and smoke a cigarette on the verandah."

"Oh, is that all?" said Munro. "Don't catch cold."

She walked through Neil's room and out. He saw her light a cigarette. Presently she went back and he heard her get into bed.

He did not see her next morning, for he started out collecting before she was up, and he took care not to get in till he was pretty sure Munro also would be back. He avoided being alone with her till it was dark and Munro went down for a few minutes to arrange the moth-traps.

"Why did you wake Angus last night?" she said in a low angry whisper.

He shrugged his shoulders and going on with his work did not answer.

"Were you frightened?"

"I have a certain sense of decency."

"Oh, don't be such a prig."

"I'd rather be a prig than a dirty swine."

"I hate you."

"Then leave me alone."

She did not answer, but with her open hand smartly slapped his face. He flushed, but did not speak. Munro returned and they pretended to be intent on whatever they were doing.

For the next few days Darya, except at meal-times and in the evenings, never spoke to Neil. Without pre-arrangement they exerted themselves to conceal from Munro that their relations were strained. But the effort with which Darya roused herself from a brooding silence would have been obvious to anyone more suspicious than Angus, and sometimes she could not help herself from being a trifle sharp with Neil. She chaffed him, but in her chaff was a sting. She knew how to wound and caught him on the raw, but he took care not to let her see it. He had an inkling that the good humour he affected infuriated her.

Then, one day when Neil came back from collecting, though he had delayed till the last possible minute before tiffin, he was surprised to find that Munro had not yet returned. Darya was lying on a mattress on the verandah, sipping a gin pahit and smoking. She did not speak to him when he passed through to wash. In a minute the Chinese boy came into his room and told him that tiffin was ready. He walked out.

"Where's Mr. Munro?" he asked.

"He's not coming," said Darya. "He sent a message

to say that the place he's at is so good he won't come down till night."

Munro had set out that morning for the summit of the mountain. The lower levels had yielded poor results in the way of mammals, and Munro's idea was, if he could find a good place higher up, with a supply of water, to transfer the camp. Neil and Darya ate their meal in silence. After they had finished he went into the house and came out again with his topi and his collecting gear. It was unusual for him to go out in the afternoon.

"Where are you going?" she asked abruptly.

"Out."

"Why?"

"I don't feel tired. I've got nothing much else to do this afternoon."

Suddenly she burst into tears.

"How can you be so unkind to me?" she sobbed. "Oh, it is cruel to treat me like this."

He looked down at her from his great height, his handsome, somewhat stolid face bearing a harassed look.

"What have *I* done?"

"You've been beastly to me. Bad as I am I haven't deserved to suffer like this. I've done everything in the world for you. Tell me one single little thing I could do that I haven't done gladly. I'm so terribly unhappy."

He moved on his feet uneasily. It was horrible to hear her say that. He loathed and feared her, but he had still the respect for her that he had always felt, not only because she was a woman, but because she was Angus Munro's wife. She wept uncontrollably. Fortunately the Dyak hunters had gone that morning with Munro. There was no one about the camp but the three Chinese servants and they, after tiffin, were asleep in their own quarters fifty yards away. They were alone.

"I don't want to make you unhappy. It's all so silly. It's absurd of a woman like you to fall in love with a fellow like me. It makes me look such a fool. Haven't you got any self-control?"

"Oh, God. Self-control!"

"I mean, if you really cared for me you couldn't want me to be such a cad. Doesn't it mean anything to you that your husband trusts us implicitly? The mere fact of his leaving us alone like this puts us on our honour. He's a man who would never hurt a fly. I should never respect myself again if I betrayed his confidence."

She looked up suddenly.

"What makes you think he would never hurt a fly? Why, all those bottles and cases are full of the harmless animals he's killed."

"In the interests of science. That's quite another thing."

"Oh, you fool, you fool."

"Well, if I am a fool I can't help it. Why do you bother about me?"

"Do you think I wanted to fall in love with you?"

"You ought to be ashamed of yourself."

"Ashamed? How stupid! My God, what have I done that I should eat my heart out for such a pretentious ass?"

"You talk about what you've done for me. What has Munro done for you?"

"Munro bores me to death. I'm sick of him. Sick to death of him."

"Then I'm not the first?"

Ever since her amazing avowal he had been tortured by the suspicion that what those men at Kuala Solor had said of her was true. He had refused to believe a word of it, and even now he could not bring himself to think that she could be such a monster of depravity. It was frightful to think that Angus Munro, so trusting and tender, should have lived in a fool's paradise. She could not be as bad as that. But she misunderstood him. She smiled through her tears.

"Of course not. How can you be so silly? Oh, darling, don't be so desperately serious. I love you."

Then it was true. He had sought to persuade himself that what she felt for him was exceptional, a madness that together they could contend with and vanquish. But she was simply promiscuous.

"Aren't you afraid Munro will find out?"

She was not crying any more. She adored talking about herself, and she had a feeling that she was inveigling Neil into a new interest in her.

"I sometimes wonder if he doesn't know, if not with his mind, then with his heart. He's got the intuition of a woman and a woman's sensitiveness. Sometimes I've been certain he suspected and in his anguish I've sensed a strange, spiritual exaltation. I've wondered if in his pain he didn't find an infinitely subtle pleasure. There are souls, you know, that feel a voluptuous joy in laceration."

"How horrible!" Neil had no patience with these conceits. "The only excuse for you is that you're insane."

She was now much more sure of herself. She gave him a bold look.

"Don't you think I'm attractive? A good many men

have. You must have had dozens of women in Scotland who weren't so well made as I am."

She looked down at her shapely, sensual figure with calm pride.

"I've never had a woman," he said gravely.

"Why not?"

She was so surprised that she sprang to her feet. He shrugged his shoulders. He could not bring himself to tell her how disgusting the idea of such a thing was to him, and how vile he had thought the haphazard amours of his fellow students at Edinburgh. He took a mystical joy in his purity. Love was sacred. The sexual act horrified him. Its excuse was the procreation of children and its sanctification marriage. But Darya, her whole body rigid, stared at him, panting; and suddenly, with a sobbing cry in which there was exultation and at the same time wild desire, she flung herself on her knees and seizing his hand passionately kissed it.

"Alyosha," she gasped. "Alyosha."

And then, crying and laughing, she crumpled up in a heap at his feet. Strange, hardly human sounds issued from her throat and convulsive tremors passed through her body so that you would have thought she was receiving one electric shock after another. Neil did not know if it was an attack of hysteria or an epileptic fit.

"Stop it," he cried. "Stop it."

He took her up in his strong arms and laid her in the chair. But when he tried to leave her she would not let him. She flung her arms round his neck and held him. She covered his face with kisses. He struggled. He turned his face away. He put his hand between her face

and his to protect himself. Suddenly she dug her teeth
into it. The pain was so great that, without thinking, he
gave her a great swinging blow.

"You devil," he cried.

His violent gesture had forced her to release him. He
held his hand and looked at it. She had caught him by
the fleshy part on the side and it was bleeding. Her eyes
blazed. She was feeling alert and active.

"I've had enough of this. I'm going out," he said.

She sprang to her feet.

"I'll come with you."

He put on his topi and, snatching up his collecting
gear, without a word turned on his heel. With one
stride he leaped down the three steps that led from the
floor of the house to the ground. She followed him.

"I'm going into the jungle," he said.

"I don't care."

In the ravening desire that possessed her she forgot
her morbid fear of the jungle. She recked nothing of
snakes and wild beasts. She did not mind the branches
that hit her face or the creepers that entangled her feet.
For a month Neil had explored all that part of the forest
and he knew every yard of it. He told himself grimly
that he'd teach her to come with him. He forced his
way through the undergrowth with rapid strides; she
followed him, stumbling but determined; he crashed on,
blind with rage, and she crashed after him. She talked;
he did not listen to what she said. She besought him to
have pity on her. She bemoaned her fate. She made
herself humble. She wept and wrung her hands. She
tried to cajole him. The words poured from her lips in

an unceasing stream. She was like a mad woman. At last in a little clearing he stopped suddenly and turning round faced her.

"This is impossible," he cried. "I'm fed up. When Angus comes back I must tell him I've got to go. I shall go back to Kuala Solor to-morrow morning and go home."

"He won't let you go, he wants you. He finds you invaluable."

"I don't care. I'll fake up something."

"What?"

He mistook her.

"Oh, you needn't be frightened, I shan't tell him the truth. You can break his heart if you want to; I'm not going to."

"You worship him, don't you? That dull, phlegmatic man."

"He's worth a hundred of you."

"It would be rather funny if I told him you'd gone because I wouldn't yield to your advances."

He gave a slight start and looked at her to see if she was serious.

"Don't be such a fool. You don't think he'd believe that, do you? He knows it would never occur to me."

"Don't be too sure."

She had spoken carelessly, with no particular intention other than to continue the argument, but she saw that he was frightened and some instinct of cruelty made her press the advantage.

"Do you expect mercy from me? You've humiliated me beyond endurance. You've treated me like dirt. I swear that if you make any suggestion of going I shall go straight to Angus and say that you took advantage of his absence to try and assault me."

"I can deny it. After all it's only your word against mine."

"Yes, but my word'll count. I can prove what I say."

"What do you mean?"

"I bruise easily. I can show him the bruise where you struck me. And look at your hand." He turned and gave it a sudden glance. "How did those teeth marks get there?"

He stared at her stupidly. He had gone quite pale. How could he explain that bruise and that scar? If he was forced to in self-defence he could tell the truth, but was it likely that Angus would believe it? He worshipped Darya. He would take her word against anyone's. What monstrous ingratitude it would seem for all Munro's kindness and what treachery in return for so much confidence! He would think him a filthy skunk and from his standpoint with justice. That was what shattered him, the thought that Munro, for whom he would willingly have laid down his life, should think ill of him. He was so unhappy that tears, unmanly tears that he hated, came to his eyes. Darya saw that he was broken. She exulted. She was paying him back for the misery he had made her suffer. She held him now. He was in her power. She savoured her triumph and in the midst of her anguish laughed in her heart because he was such a fool. At that moment she did not know whether she loved or despised him.

"Now will you be good?" she said.

He gave a sob and blindly, with a sudden instinct of escape from that abominable woman, took to his heels

and ran as hard as he could. He plunged through the
jungle, like a wounded animal, not looking where he
was going, till he was out of breath. Then, panting, he
stopped. He took out his handkerchief and wiped away
the sweat that was pouring into his eyes and blinding
him. He was exhausted and he sat down to rest.

"I must take care I don't get lost," he said to himself.

That was the least of his troubles, but all the same he
was glad that he had a pocket compass, and he knew in
which direction he must go. He heaved a deep sigh and
rose wearily to his feet. He started walking. He watched
his way and with another part of his mind miserably
asked himself what he should do. He was convinced
that Darya would do what she had threatened. They
were to be another three weeks in that accursed place.
He dared not go; he dared not stay. His mind was in a
whirl. The only thing was to get back to camp and
think it out quietly. In about a quarter of an hour he
came to a spot that he recognised. In an hour he was
back. He flung himself miserably into a chair. And it
was Angus who filled his thoughts. His heart bled for
him. Neil saw now all sorts of things that before had
been dark to him. They were revealed to him in a flash
of bitter insight. He knew why the women at Kuala
Solor were so hostile to Darya and why they looked at
Angus so strangely. They treated him with a sort of
affectionate levity. Neil thought it was because Angus
was a man of science and so in their foolish eyes somewhat absurd. He knew now it was because they were
sorry for him and at the same time found him ridiculous.
Darya had made him the laughing stock of the commun-

ity. If ever there was a man who hadn't deserved ill usage at a woman's hands it was he. Suddenly Neil gasped and began to tremble all over. It had suddenly occurred to him that Darya did not know her way through the jungle; in his anguish he had hardly been conscious of where they went. Supposing she could not find her way home? She would be terrified. He remembered the ghastly story Angus had told them of being lost in the forest. His first instinct was to go back and find her, and he sprang to his feet. Then a fierce anger seized him. No, let her shift for herself. She had gone of her own free will. Let her find her own way back. She was an abominable woman and deserved all that might come to her. Neil threw back his head defiantly, a frown of indignation on his smooth young brow, and clenched his hands. Courage. He made up his mind. It would be better for Angus if she never returned. He sat down and began trying to make a skin of a Mountain Trogon. But the Trogon has a skin like wet tissue paper and his hands trembled. He tried to apply his mind to the work he was doing, but his thoughts fluttered desperately, like moths in a trap, and he could not control them. What was happening over there in the jungle? What had she done when he suddenly bolted? Every now and then, against his will, he looked up. At any moment she might appear in the clearing and walk calmly up to the house. He was not to blame. It was the hand of God. He shuddered. Storm clouds were gathering in the sky and night fell quickly.

Just after dusk Munro arrived.

"Just in time," he said. "There's going to be a hell of a storm."

He was in great spirits. He had come upon a fine plateau, with lots of water, from which there was a magnificent view to the sea. He had found two or three rare butterflies and a flying squirrel. He was full of plans to move the camp to this new place. All about it he had seen abundant evidence of animal life. Presently he went into the house to take off his heavy walking boots. He came out at once.

"Where's Darya?"

Neil stiffened himself to behave with naturalness.

"Isn't she in her room?"

"No. Perhaps she's gone down to the servants' quarters for something."

He walked down the steps and strolled a few yards.

"Darya," he called. "Darya." There was no answer. "Boy."

A Chinese servant came running up and Angus asked him where his mistress was. He did not know. He had not seen her since tiffin.

"Where can she be?" asked Munro, coming back, puzzled.

He went to the back of the house and shouted.

"She can't have gone out. There's nowhere to go. When did you see her last, Neil?"

"I went out collecting after tiffin. I'd had a rather unsatisfactory morning and I thought I'd try my luck again."

"Strange."

They hunted everywhere round the camp. Munro thought she might have made herself comfortable somewhere and gone to sleep.

"It's too bad of her to frighten one like this."

The whole party joined in the search. Munro began to grow alarmed.

"It's not possible that she should have gone for a stroll in the jungle and lost her way. She's never moved more than a hundred yards from the house to the best of my knowledge since we've been here."

Neil saw the fear in Munro's eyes and looked down.

"We'd better get everyone along and start hunting. There's one thing, she can't be far. She knows that if you get lost the best thing is to stay where you are and wait for people to come and find you. She'll be scared out of her wits, poor thing."

He called out the Dyak hunters and told the Chinese servants to bring lanterns. He fired his gun as a signal. They separated into two parties, one under Munro, the other under Neil, and went down the two rough paths that in the course of the month they had made in their comings and goings. It was arranged that whoever found Darya should fire three shots in quick succession. Neil walked with his face stern and set. His conscience was clear. He seemed to bear in his hands the decree of imminent justice. He knew that Darya would never be found. The two parties met. It was not necessary to look at Munro's face. He was distracted. Neil felt like a surgeon who is forced to perform a dangerous operation without assistance or appliances to save the life of someone he loves. It behoved him to be firm.

"She could never have got so far as this," said Munro. "We must go back and beat the jungle within the radius of a mile from the house inch by inch. The only explanation is that she was frightened by something or fainted or was stung by a snake."

Neil did not answer. They started out again and, making lines, combed the undergrowth. They shouted. Every now and then they fired a gun and listened for a faint call in answer. Birds of the night flew with a whirring of wings, frightened, as they advanced with their lanterns; and now and then they half saw, half guessed at an animal, deer, boar or rhino, that fled at their approach. The storm broke suddenly. A great wind blew and then the lightning rent the darkness, like the scream of a woman in pain, and the tortured flashes, quick, quick, one on the heels of the other, like demon dancers in a frantic reel, wriggled down the night. The horror of the forest was revealed in an unearthly day. The thunder crashed down the sky in huge rollers, peal upon peal, like vast, primeval waves dashing against the shores of eternity. That fearful din hurtled through space as though sound had size and weight. The rain pelted in fierce torrents. Rocks and gigantic trees came tumbling down the mountain. The tumult was awful. The Dyak hunters cowered, gibbering in terror of the angry spirits who spoke in the storm, but Munro urged them on. The rain fell all night, with lightning and thunder, and did not cease till dawn. Wet through and shivering they returned to the camp. They were exhausted. When they had eaten Munro meant to resume the desperate search. But he knew that it was hopeless. They would never see her alive again. He flung himself down wearily. His face was tired and white and anguished.

"Poor child. Poor child."

THE END

THE WORKS OF
W. SOMERSET MAUGHAM

An Arno Press Collection

NOVELS

Ashenden: Or, The British Agent. 1941
The Bishop's Apron. 1906
Cakes and Ale. 1935
Catalina: A Romance. 1948
Christmas Holiday. 1939
The Explorer. With Four Illustrations by F. Graham Cootes. 1909
The Hero. 1901
The Hour Before the Dawn. 1942
Liza of Lambeth. 1936
The Magician: Together with a Fragment of Autobiography. 1957
The Making of a Saint: A Romance of Mediaeval Italy. 1966
The Moon and Sixpence. 1919
Mrs. Craddock. 1903
The Narrow Corner. 1932
Of Human Bondage. 1915
The Painted Veil. 1925
The Razor's Edge. 1943
Then and Now. 1946
Theatre. 1937
Up at the Villa. 1941

ESSAYS

The Art of Fiction: An Introduction to Ten Novels and Their
    Authors. 1955
Books and You. 1940
Points of View: Five Essays. 1959
Selected Prefaces and Introductions. 1963
Strictly Personal. 1941
The Summing Up. 1938
The Vagrant Mood: Six Essays. 1953
A Writer's Notebook. 1949

TRAVEL

Andalusia: The Land of the Blessed Virgin. 1935
Don Fernando: Or Variations on Some Spanish Themes. 1935
France at War. 1940
The Gentleman in the Parlour: A Record of a Journey from
    Rangoon to Haiphong. 1930
On a Chinese Screen. 1942

PLAYS

East of Suez: A Play in Seven Scenes. 1922
For Services Rendered: A Play in Three Acts. 1933
The Letter: A Play in Three Acts. 1925
The Sacred Flame: A Play in Three Acts. 1928
Sheppey: A Play in Three Acts. 1933
Six Comedies. 1939

SHORT STORIES

Ah King. 1933
Casuarina Tree. 1926
Cosmopolitans. 1938
Creatures of Circumstance. 1947
First Person Singular. 1931
The Mixture as Before. 1940
The Trembling of a Leaf. 1934
Seventeen Lost Stories. Compiled and with an Introduction by
    Craig V. Showalter. 1969